COMING HOME

M.J. O'Shea

Published by
Dreamspinner Press
382 NE 191st Street #88329
Miami, FL 33179-3899, USA
http://www.dreamspinnerpress.com/

This is a work of fiction. Names, characters, places, and incidents either are the product of the author's imagination or are used fictitiously, and any resemblance to actual persons, living or dead, business establishments, events, or locales is entirely coincidental.

Coming Home
Copyright © 2012 by M.J. O'Shea

Cover Art by Anne Cain   annecain.art@gmail.com
Cover Design by Mara McKennen

All rights reserved. No part of this book may be reproduced or transmitted in any form or by any means, electronic or mechanical, including photocopying, recording, or by any information storage and retrieval system without the written permission of the Publisher, except where permitted by law. To request permission and all other inquiries, contact Dreamspinner Press, 382 NE 191st Street #88329, Miami, FL 33179-3899, USA
http://www.dreamspinnerpress.com/

ISBN: 978-1-61372-442-2

Printed in the United States of America
First Edition
April 2012

eBook edition available
eBook ISBN: 978-1-61372-443-9

A big thank you to all my AWA friends who read this book in stages and encouraged me to finish it when I'd set it aside. Without you guys, it would still be sitting half-complete on my computer. Couldn't have done it without you!

PROLOGUE

"HEY, Butters, you dropped your books again!"

Lex looked up from the floor where he'd been hastily gathering his books and papers, hopefully before anyone noticed. Damn, shit, hell. Too late. It was Tallis Carrington and his dick squad.

"Aren't you guys missing remedial math or something?" Lex knew he was getting himself in more trouble, but he'd never had much luck keeping his mouth shut.

"What'd you say, fat ass?"

He wasn't sure what that particular goon's name was. Bradley, maybe. He looked like an undergrown gorilla. Probably not quite that smart, though. Wouldn't want to insult the gorilla.

"Nothing," he muttered.

"I think our well-fed, little freshman friend called us stupid," Carrington said, his aristocratic voice ringing out in the nearly empty hallway. "Not such a good plan, junior."

Why did he have to be so damn beautiful? Lex looked at the floor, hating himself for even thinking it. The last thing he needed was something else for the self-proclaimed king of Rock Bay High School and his loyal sycophants to torture him for. It wasn't like he asked to have daydreams about making out with the biggest asshole on the face of the planet.

"Just leave me the hell alone. You don't even know me." Lex held onto his books as hard as he could, trying not to slip on the newly waxed floor. His cheeks heated.

"Awww, is little butterball James going to cry?"

"My name's not James."

"*How come it says that on your ID card?*" Carrington brandished Lex's brand new freshman ID. "*James A. Barry,*" he read in a singsong voice.

Great. His parents would kill him if they had to pay to replace that thing. "Give it back, please. My family doesn't have a lot of money like yours does."

Tallis Carrington laughed. "Oh, poor, Jamie. Is that why you're wearing the same thing you had on Monday?"

Lex gritted his teeth. He hated being called Jamie. "You might want to ask yourself why you know what I was wearing on Monday."

Lex knew that wasn't the smartest accusation for him to make—at least not to a big jock who was a half second away from wiping the linoleum floor with his ass. It just slipped out.

The look of stunned anger on Carrington's face was even worse than he thought it would be. He used the momentary silence to reach up and snatch his ID card from stunned fingers and was about to make his escape when he found himself slammed, cheek first, against the air grate of the closest locker with Tallis Carrington's hot breath against his neck.

Aw, shit, shit, shit. Trouble.

The teasing laughter was gone, and in its place there was anger—seething anger—that frightened the crap out of Lex.

"Listen, you little fucker. You're lucky my dad's the damn mayor or I'd pound you to the ground right here. I'm not a fag, you got that?" His words came in angry heated whispers tinged with something wild and afraid, like he didn't even want the possibility of that accusation to be... released into the atmosphere or something. What was his problem? Insinuating that a guy was gay was like, the oldest insult in the book. Practically generic.

Lex nodded against the chill of the locker, hopefully saved by the fact that Tallis didn't want the word "fag" associated with him—oh, and because the asshole's father was a damn public hero. Whole town loved him. He'd probably threatened his jerk of a son within an inch of his life the last time he'd caused trouble, which from what Lex heard was fairly regularly.

"Just get the fuck outta here, Butters. I don't want to hear another word from you this year."

Lex squirmed out from under the big jock and escaped, making it to the front entrance of the school where he turned and gave Tallis Carrington and his friends a silent salute with his free middle finger. Before they could come after him, he scrambled out the front doors and into his older sister's car. While it had felt great at the moment, he realized that final little bit of retaliation would most likely mean he hadn't seen the last of Carrington and his friends. He'd have to watch his back for the rest of the school year.

Great. Assholes.

CHAPTER One

IT WAS raining. Again. The kind of rain that fell in large wet drops and splashed noisily on the windshield. Rain that seemed to seep all the way through the glass to drown Tallis Carrington's skin until even his bones were cold. It had been raining like that the whole damn four-hour drive from Seattle back to the last place he ever wanted to go again. Home.

He cursed and turned the windshield wipers to their highest speed. Any more of that bone chilling, godforsaken rain and he'd have to pull over. He was already nearly blinded by the downpour.

"Why didn't I ever move to California?" he grumbled to the silence of his car. The only thing he had to talk to was a few beat up duffle bags that held every last possession he had to his name. "Why am I talking to myself is a better question. I'm already going freaking nuts, and I'm not even there yet."

His car chose that moment to make a scary choking noise and shudder violently. It wobbled for a few minutes between life and death before finally settling itself in the world of the living… at least for the moment. He petted the steering wheel like it was the neck of some skittish prized horse.

Please don't die, baby girl. I promise to take good care of you from now on if you just get me there.

Walking the last fifteen miles to town at midnight in the middle of a storm appealed to Tally about as much as sleeping in his car on the side of the road (and most likely getting arrested for it if his usual luck held out). Tally's usual luck was nothing but bad, and that bad had taken a turn for complete and total shit in the past few weeks.

"HEY, Tally, I'm moving tables fifty-nine and sixty into your section starting tonight. Shelley's having a hard time keeping up." His manager's voice was smug. The bastard didn't like Tally much, and Tally knew it. He didn't like that Tally was gay, liked it even less when Tally refused to give him head for a four-dollar-an-hour raise.

"Craig, that's not fair. Shelley already has four less tables than me."

His manager smirked at him. "Well, then I guess this will be an opportunity for you to make that extra money you were in my office whining about last week."

Tally gritted his teeth together. He couldn't afford to lose his job because his manager was a prick.

"Fine. Tables fifty-nine and sixty."

Craig's smirk grew more pronounced. "Table fifty-nine is a birthday party. Ten plates."

Aw, fuck you, Craig. Tally bit his lip to keep it from coming out.

The gig at Cutter's, a ridiculously expensive seafood place on the pier, had been his longest so far. He hated coming home every night smelling like beer batter and tartar sauce, but the tips were great. He didn't want to lose it like he had all the rest of them.

Tally peered around the corner of the servers' station to take a look at the party at table fifty-nine. Women. All women. He sighed. Hopefully they'd be drunk enough to leave a decent tip.

"Hey, ladies, can I get you started with some drinks tonight?"

"I'll take a drink of him," one of them stage whispered. Tally pretended not to hear. He took their drink orders and promised them he'd be back.

When Tally returned to pass out the drinks, the brunette in the corner with the loud whisper leaned back and looked up at him. "Hey, handsome, do you recommend the steak? I want something juicy."

Tally gritted his teeth. "The steak is great paired with our Australian lobster tail." He tried to ignore the hand curled around his hamstring.

"I'll take that. I love a nice… lobster tail." Her hand crept higher. Tally backed away quickly and moved on to the next woman at the table.

By the time he returned with their salads, the ladies had each had another round of drinks. He started on the opposite end of the table, dreading going near the groper again. At last, though, all of the other salads were served. He had no choice. As he was leaning over to place her salad on the table, he felt a hand grab onto his ass and squeeze. Hard. There was no way he could pretend he didn't feel it. The other women twittered behind their hands, but Tally had had enough. Not okay. He'd been groped, pinched, propositioned, and just about everything else, more times than he could count. Apparently for him, it was one time too many.

The plate in his hand started tipping. He couldn't seem to help it. Oh well, it was just too bad. The woman let out a bloodcurdling scream when her lap was all of a sudden filled with Caesar salad.

"Sorry," Tally muttered with a small smile. It was hard to hold in the laugh. Craig was rushing toward him, face beet red. Tally could almost see the steam coming off of him.

Less than ten minutes later, he was sitting on the pier with the contents of his locker in a plastic bag.

AFTER that, he'd tried to find another job, really he had, but apparently, the market for guys with few real skills who'd spent the last fourteen years relying on their looks had finally dried up.

And then there was the eviction notice.

Tally wanted to groan just thinking about it. It had been exactly one week, five hours, and twenty-three minutes since he'd gotten fired that he came home to the last in a long line of shitty apartments, only to find his stuff piled out in the hallway and a glaring final eviction notice tacked to his door. Like he had the damn money to pay his rent. That notice had landed him broke, newly homeless, and with the exception of his mother, who refused to speak to him, and one grandmother who he hadn't seen in nearly fifteen years, he was completely and utterly alone. So he'd made an extremely humiliating call to the long-lost grandmother, the kind of call that no thirty-two-year-old man should ever have to make, and he hit the road—back to the town where he'd once been a god but was now something like the sludge that was collecting in the ditch on the side of the road. If he'd had a different choice, other than perhaps a park bench and a tarp or selling his ass for dinner, he'd never have chosen to go back to a place where his family's name was practically a cussword.

But that's where he was going. Back to Rock Bay, Washington, small town USA, south and west of Seattle—almost in Oregon, almost on the ocean, almost quaint and picturesque, but missing the mark every single time. Home sweet home.

He'd ruled the town once, a bit less than benevolently, but left under a cloud of shame years before, vowing to never return. Didn't quite work out that way, did it? Well, they were going to have to put up with his presence again. At least until he got his shit together enough to leave—and this time for good.

Tally slowed when he noticed the faint lights of town gleaming wetly through the rain. He unconsciously let up on the gas a little more every time one of the distant landmarks grew clearer. And then he was there, pulling onto Old Main, the street that ran through the center of Rock Bay. *The prodigal son returns.* He felt like he was on the walk of shame to beat all walks of shame. Even though there was no one out, the wet streets gleamed bare in the late night storm, Tally felt people's eyes on him, boring under his skin. He could feel them judging him for his past and the sins of his family. He wanted to turn back, run like blazing hell—he would have if he'd had any other choice. He didn't.

Welcome back to Rock Bay—home of everyone who doesn't have any other goddamned choice.

"YOU seriously need to get laid."

Lex sputtered, droplets of chocolate-flavored merlot decorating his once-pale-blue polo. He'd been lounging in his best friend Amy's living room after their usual Saturday night dinner and video game standoff. She'd lit a fire to warm the still crisp early spring evening. The flames smelled green, like new cedar and apple wood, and they gleamed off her rich burgundy leather furniture and the shiny white molding she'd installed the spring before.

The whole night had been peaceful and relaxing. Almost. Lex had wondered how much longer it would be before she started bugging him about finding a guy. Amy usually didn't last more than a week or two. Apparently those two weeks had passed. Lex poked her in the side, causing her to flinch and nearly spill her own wine.

"Like you can talk, Ames. I can't even remember your last girlfriend." Amy made a bratty face at him from under her mane of sandy brown streaked waves, and he snorted into his wine again. "Better be careful. You know what your mom always said about making faces."

"Yeah, yeah, it'll stay like that forever. Besides, I don't need a girlfriend. I have you."

Lex rolled his eyes. "I am *not* your girlfriend."

"Can you be my gay boyfriend?"

"I only think that works if you have a straight boyfriend too." He grinned, anticipating her reaction.

"Eww. Gross."

"Exactly. Which is why I said you needed a girlfriend."

Amy cocked her head to the side. "Wait, you didn't say I needed a girlfriend. *I* said *you* needed to get laid. Nice attempt at misdirection, *Alexis*."

"Bite me, *Amelia*." The insult was tempered with a grin. Lex loved their little spats. It was the most entertainment a guy like him could hope for on a Saturday night in Rock Bay. "How 'bout this. You find me one decent gay guy within a fifty-mile radius, which I think is impossible because I've already met all three of them, and I will do my very best to get laid."

She snickered. "Okay, then you find me a decent lesbian, and I'll do my very best to make her my girlfriend."

Lex sighed. "We need to get the hell out of here."

"You're never going to leave. You love this place."

"I know." Lex looked at his watch. "Hey, I'd better go. Gotta be up to get the shop open for the before church caffeine injection."

"Yeah," Amy mocked with a grin. "Wouldn't want them to have to gossip without their fix." It was well-known that the main purpose of church for most of the townspeople was rampant and unapologetic rumormongering. "Tiki, come say goodnight to your uncle."

An adorable and over-loved little French bulldog came waddling around the corner from her bed, nails clicking on the pale birch floor. She grunted and nudged at Lex's hand, ready for attention.

"Goodnight, princess," Lex crooned, pulling her into his lap and nuzzling kisses into her furry neck before sending her back off to bed with a pat on her rump. Then he stood and gave Amy a hug before heading for the door.

TALLY pulled up to his grandmother's house, surprised that his memory of it was so clear after fourteen years of trying to forget. The miniature gingerbread Victorian was everything he'd remembered. Painted in shades of mint green, white, and dusky rose, it was delicate and dainty, exactly what his survivor of a grandma was not. The yard was surrounded by a meandering white picket fence, and, even in the dark, Tally saw a riot of early spring flowers popping around the white boards.

As soon as he turned the car off, the front door of the house was opened, and his grandmother, still standing tall and straight, waited ready to greet him.

"Come inside, Tallis, my boy. It's raining horses!"

Tally hid his first smile in weeks and reached into the back seat to grab his few bags.

His grandmother settled him in her sunny yellow kitchen with a mug of tea and a chicken salad sandwich, muttering about how skinny and pale he was. It was true. He had gotten skinny, and his skin hadn't had the glow of pampered youth in years—but his dark brown hair was cut as expensively as he could afford, and he'd tried to keep his few well-made and carefully chosen clothes from falling apart for as long as possible.

His grandma had gotten noticeably older. Her hair, once tied constantly in a thick salt and pepper ponytail, had grown mostly white and been cut into a practical shag. The weirdest part was seeing that she'd gotten smaller—and he knew she had since he was the same height he'd been at eighteen. Tally realized that it was a fact of life, people grew up, got old, changed, but it was still a bit of a shock to see someone who'd remained unaltered in his memories for so many years showing the wear and tear of time.

"Eat your sandwich, boy, then I'll take you to your old room, and you can get some sleep."

"Grandma, I'm not a boy."

She rolled her eyes, looking for a second like the sassy rebellious teenager he knew she'd once been. "This is my house, Tallis Carrington. I'm glad you're here, but while you are, I'll call you anything I damn well please. Now finish your sandwich so I can put you to bed. You look like the ass end of a horse. You need sleep."

"Yes, ma'am," Tally forced out, nearly choking on his sandwich.

He'd nearly forgotten about his grandmother's mouth, even if he had inherited it. Honestly, most people around Rock Bay would probably be surprised to hear Tally call anyone ma'am, but he'd never be able to manage the level of disrespect with his grandmother that he'd shown most everyone else. He took another bite of his sandwich and a long, appreciative swallow of his tea, which she always mixed with honey and a generous dollop of whole milk.

It felt good to sit in that old kitchen, full of warmth and cheer even on a cold, wet night. And, as much as Tally might protest, it felt even better to be tutted over and treated like a boy for five minutes. He'd been in charge of every miserable little part of his life for so long that it was nice to be taken care of for a change.

He finished his tea and sandwich, then placed the cup on a plate that only contained crumbs. It was hard to stand, warmed inside and full, but there was no way he was spending the night on one of his grandmother's spindly wooden kitchen chairs, so Tally rinsed his dishes and put them in the sink. Then he followed his grandma, dragging his bags lethargically, up to the room he'd slept over in as a kid. He kissed her on the cheek and shut the door before sinking gratefully onto the twin bed that had been in the room since the dawn of time. He stared unseeingly at his bags for a minute or two, then, fully dressed, fell backward on the bed and passed out.

CHAPTER TWO

TALLY looked at the folded paper in his hand. The day so far had been yet another among the recent multitude of object lessons in humility. The grocery store with a line of people ten deep would rather say they weren't hiring than even consider talking to him. The man at the hardware store had simply removed his "help wanted" sign before Tally could even ask for an application. It seemed like all they did was look at his face and decide that he was the same worthless asshole he'd been back in high school—not to mention the son of the town's dead pariah. He wished he could say "fuck them all," but the time of his life when he had the luxury of doing whatever he felt like was long gone. He had no choice but to suck it up and face rejection yet another time in hopes that someone, *anyone*, wouldn't remember him.

What was left? He looked at his newspaper, which listed the meager job offerings for the small town of Rock Bay. The city was hiring street crews and grounds maintenance for town hall—his father's old office building. Shit. Even if they would hire him, he couldn't imagine mowing the lawn and planting shrubs in front of the building he'd once teepeed just to piss off his parents. The grocery store was obviously out and the hardware store too. The florist was hiring, but Tally knew the owners were the parents of a girl he'd once dated. She'd always wondered why he wasn't very interested in her. It wasn't like he could tell her he was gay. The whole thing ended badly with her crying and her parents hating him, and he wasn't about to relive that experience. Once had been more than enough.

The only place left on the list that hadn't rejected him or been crossed out due to sheer humiliation potential was called The Rock Bay Coffee and Sandwich Company. Great, like he knew a damn thing about coffee, other than how to drink it. Tally shook his head. Not much of a choice, was there? At least the coffee shop hadn't been there back when he was a kid. If there was one bright side it was that he had a fighting chance of not being recognized. He checked the ad again and flinched at the listed hourly pay. With tips, he'd made easily three times that in Seattle. But Seattle was no longer on his menu. Hopefully the Rock Bay Coffee and Sandwich Company would be. Tally took a deep breath and headed to the corner of Old Main and Marshall Streets, where he prayed to find some small form of redemption.

The coffee shop was in one of those turn-of-the-century brick buildings that seemed to line the streets of small towns all over Washington. From the outside, the place looked cheery and inviting, nestled among the renovated lofts at the far end of Old Main. A good sign, Tally hoped. The door was flanked by two potted Italian cypresses and inlaid with stained glass. There was a quaint hand-painted "open" sign dangling from a hook near the top. The hinges squeaked when Tally pushed it open, but even the squeak was oddly homey.

Inside the shop was even better. Warm and fragrant, the air drew him in and enveloped him. The walls had been painted spring green and decorated with framed black and white photographs of the surrounding beaches. Miles of old woodwork and wainscoting gleamed glossy white, and the floors were stained a warm cherry color. He longed to sink into one of the soft, cushy armchairs and close his eyes for about a week. But he couldn't. He had work to do—and at that moment, his work was convincing one damn business in his wretched hometown that he wasn't the big loser they all seemed to think he was.

Tally heard a shuffling sound coming from behind the granite-topped counter.

"Hello?" he called tentatively. "I'm here to fill out an application."

There was a small crash and a muffled "*shit.*"

Tally leaned over the counter to see what all the fuss was. There was a man kneeling on the floor trying to hold a halfway slit bag of coffee beans together while at the same time balancing a stack of white plates with his knee so they didn't crash to the floor and break. Tally fought laughter as he leaned over to right the stack of plates.

"Thank you so much!" came a relieved voice... a relieved voice that made Tally's heart pound in his chest, throbbing and trying to be noticed as if it were saying "pay attention to this one." The rest of his body responded in that one short moment, hardening, quickening, coming to life. Tally gave himself a mental slap on the wrist. *Really. Not the best time for that.*

The man started to stand, turning slowly with the slit coffee bag still balanced on his thigh.

"Hey, not a problem. My name is—" Tally's voice stuck in his throat, like he was some little kid with his first crush. The other guy's name must have been *gorgeous*—sandy hair somewhere between brown and blond, a little shaggy and curling at the ends, big hazel eyes with long curly lashes and a mouth that Tally could have spent hours kissing. Tally wanted to drool. He stuck out his hand and tried to repeat himself. "My name is—"

After one look at Tally, the stranger's beautiful face had gone from friendly to scathingly irritated in a matter of nanoseconds. "Yeah, I know who you are. I don't really think I need the help after all."

Not another one. Tally started to panic.

"Listen...." He paused, hoping for a name.

"Lex," the man supplied grudgingly.

"Listen, Lex," Tally repeated. "I know everyone in this town hates me. Obviously even people I've never met. But I really need a job, and you wouldn't have had an ad in the paper if you didn't need someone to help you. Couldn't it maybe be possible that you might put aside whatever it is that you've been told about me and my father and just take a chance that maybe I'll be a good employee?"

Lex cocked his head to the side, regarding Tally silently. Talk about nerve-wracking.

"Everything I know about you tells me you won't."

Tally backed away toward the door. "It was a long time ago," he mumbled. "People change. Even me." *Or maybe people were never really what they seemed.*

Lex gave him one more long pensive stare, completing Tally's humiliation. Everyone who remembered him hated him, and it seemed that his reputation had spread to gorgeous strangers as well. He wanted to crawl back to his grandmother's house and hide in his room to lick his wounds. *Was I really that bad?* He reached for the handle on the paned- glass door.

"You know what?" Lex's voice surprised him. He froze. "Fine. I'll give it a try. Not like I've had any other takers." The last part was mumbled, but Tally heard it just the same. "I start early. Five on weekdays, six on Saturday and Sunday."

"That's okay," Tally said quickly, ready to agree with nearly anything.

"Do you know how to make coffee?"

"No, but I worked in restaurants for years." *Please let that be enough.*

"I'm not going to want to tell you how to do things twice."

"I learn quickly." Tally hated to feel hope welling in his chest, but it was there—faint yet insistent. As grudging as beautiful Lex seemed to be, there was finally someone willing to give him half a chance.

"Then I'll see you in the morning. Five. Not even a minute late."

"I'll be here," Tally answered. "But don't you need me to fill out an application—or at least a tax form?"

Lex looked at Tally for a long moment, confused and unblinking, then it seemed to dawn on him what Tally was talking about, and he turned, flustered, to rifle through a drawer. "Just bring this with you tomorrow," he muttered, thrusting a thin sheaf of papers at Tally.

"I will," Tally assured Lex with a tentative smile. *That wasn't so bad*, he told himself. *Now I just have to get through tomorrow.*

"YOU did *what?*" Amy's face was incredulous and halfway between laughter and horror. She was perched on one of the leather barstools near the counter in Lex's shop. He'd tried to butter her up with a raspberry jelly donut so she wouldn't freak out. Should've known it was useless.

"I hired Tallis Carrington to work at my shop?" It came out more like a question than a statement.

"Yeah, that's what I thought I heard. I hoped I'd been hallucinating."

"I need the help, Ames. I haven't exactly had applicants pounding on the door."

"So that's what it is? It's about the shop and not at all about you and your past with him?"

"What past? I was some kid that he harassed in high school. He doesn't even know who I am."

Amy nearly spit her coffee out. "What are you talking about? You were that asshole's personal punching bag! He was awful to you for like three quarters of freshman year—well, until he left, anyway. How could anyone forget that?"

"I sure as hell haven't. That's not what I mean, though. He thought I was a newcomer. He said 'forget what you've *been told* about me and my father.' The guy doesn't have a clue why I know him."

"Are you going to tell him?"

Lex reacted immediately. "Hell no!"

"You're just going to relive your ancient masochistic crush on him every day."

Lex almost told Amy he'd never had a crush on Carrington, but he figured she'd know he was lying. He still hated himself for that.

"Give me some credit for growing up, huh? Besides. Maybe I'll make him do all the crappy jobs like taking out the trash and stuff. It would be kind of fun paying him back for all the times he slammed my face against the lockers."

Amy chuckled. "As long as you're clear about what's really going on here."

"All clear. I promise it's just about work. I'll ignore the bastard otherwise, okay?"

"Okay." It was obvious she didn't believe it for a second. "I just don't want to see you get hurt, hon. You know that."

Lex laughed out loud at that one. "Jesus, Amy. I hired the guy to make coffee. I didn't ask him to be my date for the homecoming dance. Besides, he's straight, remember? Last time I checked that meant no touching."

Amy raised her eyebrows. "So you admit that you want to touch him."

"Well, sure, he's still hot, but I—" Lex stopped when he realized there was no way in hell he could say anything without her taking it to mean that he still had that ridiculous, no, *masochistic*, crush he'd tried to hide all those years back. "I'm not saying another word. I know how you operate. You'll twist everything that comes out of my mouth into some lascivious double entendre."

"Argh. Nice word choice. English minor rears its ugly head. Anyway, you know I gotta practice if I want to be one of the churchyard newscasters once my hair starts turning gray."

Lex rolled his eyes. *She'd have to go to church for once first.* "You'll be a natural."

"Hey, I should head out, but I'll stop by the shop on my way to the hospital tomorrow." Amy was an ER nurse at Columbia Memorial Hospital across the river in Astoria. She usually left her house early so she'd have time to hang out with Lex and drink a coffee before driving the twenty minutes or so to work.

"Ames, I'm not sure that's the best idea."

"Why not?"

He sighed. "I know you. Can I at least get him trained before you butt your well-meaning head in?"

"I'm not going to *do* anything to him. I'm just curious."

Lex grunted skeptically. "Let's just say that things have a tendency to come flying out of your mouth before you've thought them over. I need to figure him out on my own before I have you in here poking around, okay?"

"Okay. You know, there *is* a lovely Starbucks down the road from the hospital. I could always stop there and get a nice, big, expensive latte—and maybe I'll buy treats for all the other nurses too."

Lex winced. "Fine. I'll see you tomorrow."

CHAPTER
Three

IT WAS pitch black outside when Lex's alarm started blaring the next morning. Except in the height of summer, it usually was. He reached over groggily with a slow-moving hand and slapped ineffectually at the snooze button on his alarm until the god-awful thing was finally silenced. Groaning, he flipped his legs over the side of the bed until his feet were resting on the small Persian replica he had there for chilly mornings just like that one. Sometimes, Lex wondered what on earth had made him choose a business that required him to be up *before* the crack of dawn. He'd never been a huge fan of early mornings, and most of the time when he got up, it still felt like night. *Too late to rethink that now.*

Too late to rethink hiring Tallis Carrington as well. Lex halfway thought that perhaps Amy was right. Maybe it was a bad idea to hire his old nemesis and misguided crush. He shrugged it off and stepped into the shower, hoping that the steam would wake him up. He really *had* needed the help. It didn't mean he had to like the person who was helping him.

His back hurt like hell from the heavy box of new cups he'd put down the wrong way the day before. *Damn, I'm getting old.* He could almost feel his mother smacking him on the arm with a rolled up newspaper and saying "If you're old, what on earth does that make me?" Lex grinned to himself. Twenty-eight wasn't so bad, anyway. It would be nicer if he wasn't alone, he imagined, but there was no way he was going to give Amy the satisfaction of knowing that thought had even crossed his mind.

Lex got out of the shower and ran a towel cursorily over his skin, missing a few drops here and there but in too much of a rush to care. As usual, he'd lain in bed till the last possible moment, and there was so much to do in the mornings before he could open. He pulled a pair of jeans from his dresser and shoved his legs into them before grabbing a shirt from the closet.

Dressed and as awake as he could possibly be, Lex closed and locked the door to his upstairs apartment and walked down the staircase that ended in the hallway behind the coffee shop where his office and the storage room were. Some days he wished his home were more removed from work, but usually in the morning, when he could barely drag himself out of bed, he loved the fact that he was already where he needed to go.

He was almost surprised to see Tallis waiting for him outside the glass door of the shop. Almost. There had been a desperation in Carrington's eyes the day before that Lex definitely didn't remember. It seemed that things hadn't been so easy for him after… well, everything that had happened. So perhaps life had changed Tallis Carrington just a touch. Didn't mean Lex could trust him.

"Carrington. You're on time," he said as he opened the door. Snapped was more like it. He was annoyed with himself for thinking that the guy looked amazing in his well-worn designer jeans. "You need some new jeans. Work on that." *God, why did I say that? What a jerk.*

"Well, yeah, you told me not to be late. Here's my paperwork."

Lex grunted noncommittally as he took the stack of papers with a less than gentle swipe.

"Um, Lex?"

"Yeah?"

"Could you please not call me Carrington? I'm not a huge fan of my last name anymore. Tally is fine."

"Yeah. Whatever."

"And I'll get some new jeans after a paycheck or two. It hasn't been an easy few months."

Lex wanted to tell Tally not to worry about it, but he stopped himself. *This guy isn't unassuming Tally. He's still Tallis Carrington, no matter how far he's fallen. Give him one rung to pull himself up on and he'll squash you on his way back to the top.* Instead, Lex opened a bottom shelf and got out an extra apron.

"Here. Put this on. Today is little stuff: cleaning, garbage, we'll see how it goes from there."

Cleaning? Garbage? I'm not fifteen. Tally bit his lip. Gorgeous Lex's expression couldn't have said asshole any more clearly than it did. Too bad, because it kind of ruined that perfect face. Tally plastered a smile on his own face, ready to take whatever was dealt out. He needed the job too much to be picky. He started by Windexing the counters and the glass in front of the display shelves. He could only imagine that's what Lex Luthor had in mind when he'd thrust the cleaner and a towel into his hands with a taciturn grunt. Tally had to stop himself from chuckling at the spontaneous nickname. Lex Luthor it was. Gorgeous and a dick—but his employer just the same.

"Hey, I'm done with counters and the glass. Hit all of the tables too. What's next?"

He watched his boss look around the nearly pristine shop. There was nothing left to clean, and they both knew it. Tally could almost see the mental wheels spinning.

"The store's going to open in about fifteen minutes. You know how to work a cash register?"

What happened to cleaning and garbage? If nothing else, maybe cash register experience would save him from a day of busboy duties.

"Yeah, I've been using them for years."

"And I'm assuming you are pretty good with taking orders down, restaurant history and all."

Tally flinched. Somehow, Lex had made the words "restaurant history" sound like "rap sheet."

"Yes. I'm good at taking orders down."

"Good. Here's the menu. The food's pretty self-explanatory as far as pricing, but the coffee is a bit more involved. The prices listed here are for one flavor twelve, sixteen, and twenty-four ounce drinks. It's another fifty cents per flavor and another dollar on top of that for anything special like *breve* or specialty milks like soy or rice. If they want the powdered white chocolate flavor, it's seventy-five cents extra because it's more expensive than the syrup to buy. Oh, and our special this week is the butter pecan. That's two dollars flat if it's a sixteen, regular price for any other size. Every week it'll be a different flavor, but the same rules apply."

Is he fucking kidding? Tally knew what Lex was doing could only be new-employee homicide. Tally wanted to call him on it, but he was fairly sure that Lex knew exactly what he was up to and would never even consider doing it to anyone else. *The jerk wants me to quit. Screw that.* The little surge of his old competitive spirit felt better than anything had in years. He used to hate losing, but he'd spent so long doing nothing but losing that it'd become second nature. Not this time. He was sure this whole town would delight in seeing him fail, new guy obviously included. Hell if he'd give them the pleasure.

"You got a pen and a blank piece of paper? I'll need to have a cheat sheet for a few days until I get the coffee pricing down."

"I said I didn't want to tell you anything twice."

Tally took a deep breath. "I'm not asking you to tell me again, I just want to write it down. Is that okay?" *Patience. You need this job.*

Lex seemed to relax a little, like he'd caught himself being a prick and didn't know quite how to get out of it. "Yeah, that's fine. I'll get you a sheet out of my printer."

It was going to be a trial by fire for sure. More like a trial by hot steaming espresso… and a possible tarring and feathering by his old fellow townspeople. Honestly, that worried Tally a whole hell of a lot more than any complicated price list. Lex wordlessly handed him a blank sheet of printer paper. Writing the pricing rules helped him to start memorizing them. It also helped him to relax a little, in what he supposed was the calm before the coming tempest. Lex waited, in an unexpected show of patience, for him to finish writing his list before speaking again.

"So you take orders, call the drinks and sandwiches to me, and ring them through. If you have extra time, you can also bag any pastries that are ordered. You think you can handle that?" Lex's face said that he assumed the answer was no.

"I think so," Tally answered. He didn't want to be too cocky, but he wanted to show confidence, despite the general non-existence of any form of training. It was a balancing act, trying not to piss the new boss off.

Lex only nodded, then walked to the front of the shop to unlock the front door.

"It's showtime."

Jesus, what is my effing problem? Lex couldn't believe how much of a dick he was being. He hadn't come down the stairs that morning with any intention of acting like the biggest asshole in the western hemisphere, but for some reason, every time he opened his mouth it just got worse. *Guess I'm still angrier with him than I thought I was.* He'd honestly thought he'd let go of his old humiliations years before. But apparently, the name calling, toilet dunking, pantsing, egging, and the shit bomb in his locker....

"*Awww, poor Butters. Don't cry, little baby. Mom's not here now, is she?*"

Lex wanted to cry, but he blinked the tears from his eyes. Why had he told his mother? Shit. She'd promised him she wouldn't go to the principal. Clearly, she'd decided to anyway.

"*Leave me alone, Carrington. I haven't done anything to you.*"

Tallis grinned gleefully and smashed Lex's face against the bathroom stall. "*But it's so much fun to mess with you.*" His friends laughed and gave each other high fives.

Lex was desperate. "*You left me alone last week when we were in—*"

His face was wiped down the stall until he was kissing the toilet. Tallis had *left him alone the week before when it had just been them in the room. Clearly he didn't want his friends to know about it.*

"*Ready, Butters?*"

"*No!*"

Carrington didn't listen. He dunked Lex's head in the toilet and flushed, laughing the whole time. Then the pressure holding Lex down was gone, and he was alone in the restroom, accompanied only by the slam of the metal door.

Yeah, the hurt was obviously still lurking and ready to lash out and bite him in the ass. The last thing Lex needed was to freak out on his new employee—the one he was still trying to decide what his motivation was for hiring. He honestly needed the guy to stay. It was probably a little too late for first impressions, though. If looking either nuts or like a huge jerk was what he wanted, then he was off to a bang of a start. *It's all about the business. Try to remember that....*

THE first few customers were a bit tense. Tally was scared that they'd come, raw eggs in hand, ready to chase him back to the big city where he belonged. He sure as hell didn't feel like he belonged in Rock Bay any longer. But Lex's early morning customers were mostly kids, desperate for a big caffeine high before morning band rehearsal or zero hour study hall. Tally didn't envy their teachers—probably the same poor souls who'd had to put up with him. He was glad they didn't seem to know who he was, or else they were so involved in their own self-centered teenage angst that they didn't even notice him. Tally didn't much care, as long as he could avoid the spotlight. He was also glad he wasn't doing too horribly at his job. He'd take orders and pass them to Lex; he only got one or two wrong and fixed his mistakes really fast. He was actually kind of proud of how easily he slipped into the position, and weirdly enough, he found himself caring—caring that the people of Rock Bay and his cranky boss didn't see him fuck up. By seven thirty, an hour into the morning coffee rush, he was starting to feel pretty damn good.

Then came the adults on the way to work or out for an early morning walk and gossip session. That's when the looks started rolling in—from the "don't I know you?" questioning stares to the same kind of downright hostility he'd encountered the day before. Tally started to wonder if that was what the animals felt like in a zoo. The looks flustered him; they'd do it to anyone. He tried not to let it get to him too badly. *Take their orders, smile, pretend you don't know why they're all looking at you.* It was surprisingly not all that bad after he got used to the bug-under-a-microscope feeling. Well, not until lunchtime, anyway.

Tally had actually started to feel slightly comfortable with his new position, easily ringing people through, stares and all, and barely checking the complicated price cheat sheet. He'd marveled at Lex's public persona as well, the sweet smiles and bashful chuckles he dished out along with coffee and snacks. One kinda had to wonder where the hell it came from. Public Lex was so different than the irritable grunts and half answers Tally got whenever the bustling little shop had a silent moment or two. Grumpy boss aside, though, the morning hadn't been horrible. Tally was starting to think he was going to survive.

Then *she* came in.

The woman was middle-aged, with a long, silver-threaded ponytail and surprisingly chic clothes. She looked at him like something distasteful her cat may have left on the kitchen floor. He thought she may have worked at the high school before; she looked vaguely familiar. He couldn't be sure. It was quite apparent that she knew him, however.

"May I help you?" Tally put on his best kiss-ass face. He even tried to affect the shy, unassuming charm that Lex pulled off so magnificently.

The woman acted like she hadn't heard him speak. She turned and regarded Lex. "I refuse to deal with trash. Lex, darling, I'd love a tall vanilla mocha and one of those delicious orange chocolate chip muffins."

This is it. Tally knew the woman had drawn a line. He'd gotten his share of silent stares, from mocking and hateful to borderline sympathetic, but she was the first person to actually pull out an egg and aim for his face.

"Ms. Franklin, Tally will take your order and ring you up. I'll be glad to make your coffee when I'm done with my current order here. And please treat my employee with the same amount of respect that I gave him by hiring him."

Tally nearly lost his cool; his hands were trembling from the adrenaline confrontation always caused. But he remained silent—possibly because of shock alone.

He couldn't believe Lex was publicly going to bat for him. Why? He understood that Lex had to stand by his business decisions, but it felt so personal. Like a victory. Lex flashed him a small but genuine smile and continued on with the order he'd started. The poor girl waiting for her coffee, who'd told Tally she was from out of town and just driving through, stood and watched the whole exchange in stunned silence. She even sent Tally a sympathetic smile before she turned and walked out the door.

Tally could tell that Ms. Franklin, whoever she was, was trying to decide if she wanted to walk out herself or pretend that the earlier conversation hadn't happened and just get her coffee. She must have decided on the latter.

"I'll have a tall vanilla mocha and an orange chocolate chip muffin." She said the words grudgingly, refusing to look Tally in the face.

He took Ms. Franklin's order with resolutely steady hands and passed it on to Lex, just like he'd been doing all morning. Then he rung up her order as efficiently as possible and willed Lex to make her damn drink already so she'd get the hell out of the shop. In an effort to speed her departure, he removed an orange chocolate chip muffin from the glass cabinet with tongs and placed it in a small paper bag with the coffee shop logo on it. The woman snatched it out of his hand without so much as a thank you, pulled it out of the bag, and nibbled on it nervously as she waited for her coffee. As soon as it was in her hand, she turned with no comment and walked out the door. He'd never been so glad to see anyone leave a room in his life. He could only hope that she wasn't a daily customer.

"Thank you for sticking up for me," Tally said to Lex once the place was blissfully empty.

Lex shrugged, his narrow shoulders quietly eloquent under a thin long-sleeved T-shirt. "I can't have customers disrespecting my business decisions. And you, Tally, were a business decision. I needed an employee, and I decided you were right for the job."

Thanks for the reminder. I was hoping you hired me because you want to strip me naked and fuck my brains out.

Which was on some level true, or at least it had been the day before when he was drooling over Lex's gorgeous, um, assets. But it was also not the best thought avenue to meander down if he planned on keeping his job.

"Well, thanks all the same. I appreciate it after the reception I've gotten in this town."

Lex looked honestly perplexed. "Did you expect anything different after the way you treated people?"

"Please don't take this the wrong way, but what's *your* problem with me? I don't even know you! Besides, I figured most of it was about my father."

Lex appeared to consider that for a few seconds. "No. I think what happened with your father was an excuse. People never liked how you treated them, but they were scared to turn away from you. You were the mayor's son: rich, super popular, and athletic, but not very well-liked—at least outside your little crew of stooges. After your dad's... thing, they didn't have to like you anymore, so they didn't. And then you just disappeared—never did a thing to redeem yourself."

Harsh. But probably true. And weirdly accurate. "Who *are* you?" Tally was all of a sudden not so sure that Lex was a well-informed newcomer.

"Doesn't matter. I'm just saying, you're going to have a long, steep road ahead of you convincing people around here that you've changed. Me included."

Tally sighed. Hearing out loud what he already knew didn't make the situation any more pleasant. "I'm not trying to be the prom queen. Just want to get my life together so I can leave again. Get away from the damn stares."

"Understandable. Why did you come back here anyway? You had to have known how it would be."

"Didn't really have much choice. Ran out of money and have never been a big fan of either homelessness or prostitution, you know? Listen, I'd rather not talk about it. Would you mind?"

THE words could've come out rude, or like a joke, but instead, to Lex, they sounded tentative and worn down. Like Tally couldn't stand to even think about his mess of a life. Lex found himself feeling a little bad for the guy. *Hey, remember this is the asshole who stuck your head in a toilet!* The memory of running out of the school in the middle of passing period, humiliated, with toilet water dripping down the back of his shirt, was enough to make Lex's spine stiffen—like he could still feel the cold, wet slide of the water running down his skin and into the waistband of his pants.

"Yeah, whatever," Lex replied and turned to go to his office in the back. "Let me know when a customer comes. I'm going to do some bookkeeping."

Lex was glad to escape into the blissful solitude of his office. It had been one hell of a morning. He had no idea why he'd pushed Tally so hard, but the man had risen quickly and gracefully to the challenge, working so well with Lex that it felt like he'd been there for weeks rather than a few hectic hours. And that first part wasn't true. He did know why he'd pushed Tally, why he'd piled tons of information on him and basically ordered him to run with it or walk out the door. Lex would've thought he was over high school enough, grown up enough, that he wouldn't have to kick a guy who was obviously so down that he was nearly lying in the street. Apparently, he wasn't. Perhaps it would be best to let Carrington go if he couldn't act more professional around him, but that would be even worse—act like a big asshole and then fire him. Nice.

He took a deep breath and stood, ready to go out to his shop and act like the mature business owner he was instead of some vengeful kid. He would've done it too, if Tally's head hadn't popped into his doorway.

"Uh, Lex, there's someone here to see you. I tried to ring up her coffee before I came back here, and she nearly bit my nuts off."

Oh Lord. Amy.

"Sorry. I forgot to warn you about her." He gave Tally a genuinely regretful smile. He could easily see Tally relax.

"Evil bitch or something?"

"Close." Lex rolled his eyes and smiled so Tally would know he wasn't serious. Then he came out from behind his desk and led the way out into the hallway. He looked over his shoulder. "Oh, and I don't charge her for anything. Next time she's here, come get me right away. She can be a little scary."

"No kidding," Tally muttered and followed Lex meekly, like a little whipped puppy.

"Hey, sweetie," the woman chirped as soon as he and Lex rounded the corner. Tally couldn't believe how nice she looked once she smiled. She gave Lex a familiar peck on the lips and brushed his bangs out of his eyes. *His girlfriend. Of course, he's straight.* Tally was surprised by the lighting quick flash of disappointment, as unreasonable as it was. Even if Lex was the gayest man in Washington, he obviously hated Tally's guts. *I would have gone for an anger fuck too*, Tally mused, smiling to himself. But not a straight-guy fuck. The last one of those he'd tried had ended with him in the ER paying for stitches he couldn't afford.

"Are you going to introduce me to your employee?" The woman batted her eyelashes at Lex. Tally nearly chuckled at the obvious insincerity of her flirting. From Lex's annoyed face he assumed she was there to meddle.

Lex sighed. "Tally, this is my best friend Amy. She's a little intense sometimes."

"Best friend? You mean she's not your girlfriend?"

Amy laughed out loud. "In his dreams."

"In your dreams is more like it," Lex teased back. "You know you're not my type."

"True. I guess I'd be more of your dream girl if I looked like Zac Efron."

Lex groaned. "*One time*. One time I say he might be slightly cute, and you will never let me forget it."

"I can't help that you're a total cougar." Amy was still giggling.

They continued to tease each other, the teasing turning into poking and pinching just like they were brother and sister and about ten years old. Tally barely noticed the hilarity. *He's gay?* It was the only fact that seemed to make it into Tally's brain, rustling around in there until it finally started to sink in. He couldn't help the momentary thrill the thought sent chasing through his body.

"You're gay?" he blurted out before he had a chance to think about how it would sound coming from him… or at least the "him" he used to be.

Lex's face instantly turned standoffish. Amy stood, orienting herself in front of Lex, expression hostile and protective.

"Yeah, I am. Is that going to be a problem, Carrington?"

Tally sputtered. "Oh, no—" He tried to hold in a smile. "Not a problem at all, I just—" *Want you to throw me on the floor and take me now.* "Can I go on my break?" He needed to get out of there before he opened his mouth and shoved his whole leg down his throat.

"Yeah, go ahead. Fifteen minutes," Lex warned him.

"I know. I'll be back in fifteen. And please. Tally or Tallis, not Carrington."

Tally escaped through the back door with what little was left of his tattered dignity.

"He's not what I expected at all!" Amy whispered heatedly as soon as Tally left the room. Lex nodded, agreeing. He still wasn't sure what to think of that last strange exchange, but it was starting to seem like Amy was right. Tally wasn't what anybody in town had expected him to be. At least not so far.

"Yeah. He's been really *good* all morning. I was acting like a total asshole, Ames, and piled all of this info on him, but he took it and did the job well. Better than anyone else I could've hired. I hate to say it, but—"

"Maybe he's changed," Amy finished. Lex scrunched up his face. "But you still look at him and see that guy who tied you to the flag pole."

"Shit. I'd forgotten about that one."

Amy chuckled, and Lex glared at her. "Oh, come on, it's funny now! That was fourteen years ago! It did take me almost two hours to untie you, though."

Lex groaned. "Wasn't that the day that we decided to start dating?"

Amy laughed. "Yeah. Partners in deception. We were probably the longest lasting couple in that whole school. Too bad the straight kids couldn't figure out how to make it work like we did."

"It's easy if there's no hormones involved. No fighting, no crying, no breaking up. I might have to break up with you now, though, if you keep telling people I'm in love with Zac Efron."

Amy looked thoughtful for a second. "Don't you think Tally looks a little bit like Zac Efron?"

"Not at all! He's way taller, and his hair's dark brown, and his eyes are brown instead of blue, and… oh you're a wench."

"I knew you were still looking. Gotta go to work." She gave him a self-satisfied smirk and slid off her stool. "Love ya."

"Love you too." As annoyed as Lex was with the trick that he fell for so easily, he did still love her. She was practically his sister, after all. Amy trotted off toward the front entrance of the shop.

"See you tomorrow," she called as she swung the glass door open and sailed through it.

"See you tomorrow," Lex echoed quietly, considering what he'd learned so far about the new Tallis Carrington.

TALLY collapsed on his bed that afternoon, feet tired, body aching, but unable to keep the smile from his face. There had been a few hiccups, but all in all it had been a pretty good day. He honestly liked his new job. He wished he could say he liked Lex, or even that he disliked him, for that matter. He wished he could say *anything* concrete about Lex. The guy confused the hell out of him. He was the definition of hot and cold. Well, lukewarm and cold at least.

Tally realized he had obviously done something to wrong the guy, but for some reason he just couldn't place Lex anywhere in his past. He would have thought he had everyone he used to torture burned into his subconscious. He sure as hell felt awful about the ones he did remember, like that cute little pudgy James kid who'd made the mistake of suggesting he might be looking at guys. He'd been so terrified that one of his friends might notice the same thing that he'd tormented the kid for a good part of the year just to make sure he knew that Tally was no one to mess with.

Maybe on my day off I'll look him up and apologize. Tally cringed at the idea of facing that kid down. *Not that he'd accept it. He'd probably punch the crap out of me.* Didn't matter. He didn't remember what the kid's last name was—only remembered taunting him with the nickname Jamie, since he'd obviously hated it.

Tally closed his eyes, thinking he'd just lay there for a minute more then get up and find some way to help his grandmother around the house, but when he woke, the daylight had turned to a misty twilight that darkened his room to a near pitch black. He could smell something lovely and fattening wafting up from the kitchen.

"Hey, Grams, whatchya makin'?" He'd wandered down the narrow stairs, yawning and pulling on a hooded sweatshirt. The nights were much colder out on the coast than they'd been in Seattle. Gram's kitchen was as sunny and happy as it had been the night before, filled with the scents of Italy and the oldies that she had pumping from her small countertop radio. There was a pan cooling on the top of the oven.

"I made baked ziti with lots of extra cheese—just like you used to like it when you were little."

Tally's mouth watered. The fantastic smell mingled with his memory of tomatoey cheesy perfection. "That's really nice of you. Hey, do you want me to get some groceries after work tomorrow?" He didn't have money for much, but he already felt bad for freeloading.

"If you had money for groceries I doubt you'd be here, now would you? Just keep your job, and I'll be happy. You couldn't have picked a nicer boy to work for."

"So everybody says," Tally murmured.

He pulled plates out from the cabinet and put them on the table with silverware and water glasses. His grandmother puttered around the kitchen, chopping vegetables and mixing salad dressing in a bowl. That was another thing about her he loved. Tally had never seen a bottle of store bought salad dressing, pasta sauce, any cake mixes—nothing. She made everything from scratch. Her food was the only thing left that still seemed like home to Tally.

"Did you have a good first day?"

"Huh?" Tally said, snapping his head up. "Oh, yeah, it was pretty good. A little tense at first, you know, but whatever. It's not like they don't have a reason to stare."

"You think people are still worried about what your father did? That was so long ago."

"It could be me too. You remember how I used to be. Going to try my best to change their minds, though."

"And working with Lex? How was that?"

"Not sure yet. He doesn't like me much, that's for sure. But I'm going to do a good job for him."

"I'm glad. That's the best you can do, after all. Sit down, Tally. Let's have some dinner."

TALLY went to his room after the dinner dishes were done, stripped off his work clothes, and put them into a basket by his door. Then he gathered up a towel and slipped on a pair of sweatpants before he headed to the bathroom at the end of the narrow Victorian hallway. He nearly had to duck under the doorframe of the bathroom, and it felt like his shoulders barely fit through. *These old houses weren't made for guys like me.* Then he hung his towel on the old brass hook and went back to dig through his duffels for the bag of shower supplies he remembered seeing on the hallway floor at his old apartment building.

As soon as he walked back into his room, he noticed the smell of coffee, most likely emanating from the pile of clothes he had in the hamper. He hadn't smelled it before, probably because he'd been around it all day. *Guess everything I own will smell like French Roast soon enough.* Could be worse. It smelled pretty great on Lex, for damn sure. Every time Lex had brushed by him in close proximity, Tally had inhaled, loving the odd blend of coffee, vanilla, cedar, and warm sexy man. Of course, as soon as Lex was gone he'd silently berate himself for drooling over any part of his hot as hell but prickly boss. As much as his personal history would beg to differ, Tally wasn't a huge fan of trouble, and a crush on his boss? Trouble times ten.

The shower was hot and delightfully intense. Obviously nobody had ever talked his grandmother into buying environmental showerheads. Tally was grateful. The pounding pressure of the water on his neck felt amazing, and it was easy to tilt his head back and close his eyes. It wasn't as easy to dissolve the tensions of the day. He was both excited and apprehensive to see what the next one held in store for him. The day had ended earlier fairly well, with a barely less-than-hostile Lex bidding him good afternoon after he'd cleaned up as much as he could. Tally could only hope they weren't back to ice water come morning.

Very early morning.

Tally groaned. *How does Lex do this open to close every day?* He understood why the guy would want to have a helper or, *gulp*, someone to take over for him part of the time. Tally imagined that eventually he'd be in the store by himself running the till and making drinks while Lex took a much needed break. He tried not to freak out at the thought of facing those people without Lex at his back. Lex on his own was a bit nerve-wracking, but in a group of slightly hostile Rock Bay residents there wasn't anyone Tally wanted standing next to him more. They liked Lex and respected him, and oddly enough, Tally already trusted him as well. At least in a public setting.

He stepped out of the shower and dried off with one of his grandmother's fluffy cream-colored towels that were covered with bouquets of pink garden flowers. Then Tally pulled his sweats and a tank top back on before leaving the bathroom.

"Night, Grams. I'm going to go to bed," he called from the landing. He could hear sirens and gunshots coming from the television. When he'd come upstairs earlier she'd just been starting Law and Order. He smiled to himself. *Gotta love Grams.*

"Goodnight, Tally," she called distractedly. "I'll see you tomorrow, dear."

CHAPTER Four

ANOTHER day with Tallis Carrington. Lex sighed. He hadn't slept well, even though he'd been more tired last night than he could remember being in a long, long time. The day before had been a strange sort of emotional purgatory. Not quite hell, but way too uncomfortable to be anything close to contentment. He'd wavered for hours between remembered hatred, strong attraction, and the odd new feeling that perhaps Tallis Carrington was gone and the Tally that had taken his place was actually a decent human being who'd come upon harder times than he wanted to admit.

Don't be a moron, Lex Barry. The saying "a wolf in sheep's clothing" didn't come out of nowhere. Even so, Tally was probably the saddest wolf Lex had ever seen. He sighed as he pulled on a freshly washed pair of jeans and a soft black T-shirt that was worn and comfortable against his skin. He didn't want to go downstairs and deal with his conflicting feelings. He didn't want to be having feelings at all. He didn't mind acknowledging Tally's good looks. It was a fact; the guy was gorgeous. It was the rest of it that bothered Lex—the butterflies, the wavering between anger and admiration, the odd, annoying impulse to pull Tally into his arms and tell him that everything would be okay.

Jesus! Moron city! Lex knew he needed to teach Tally the ropes, and quickly, so he could leave Tally alone in the shop and not torture himself constantly with Tally's proximity. His original intention in hiring an employee, which was to finally have a few minutes in the day where he wasn't working, seemed secondary. He just needed to escape.

Lex locked his apartment door and trotted quickly down the stairs to the hallway below. He knew Tally would be waiting for him, and, as he'd said yesterday, it was showtime.

THE day had gone well. Better than Lex could've imagined. He'd expected hiring someone would be more work than doing the work himself—at least for a few weeks. But Tally was smart, and he picked things up faster than Lex could've hoped. Lex was confident that he'd be able to leave Tally alone in the shop soon. And he needed to be able to. Being near the guy was driving him nuts. It was nearly impossible to keep up the cold facade around him when Lex was genuinely curious. He wanted to know what'd happened to change Tally so much, where he'd been, why he seemed so sad and worn down. That prostitution or homelessness comment stuck in Lex's head. He couldn't forget the total lack of hope on Tally's face when he'd said that.

Jesus. Knock it off. His problems are not yours to solve. Nor are they any of your business.

Lex locked the door to his shop and grabbed the can of trim paint that was sitting at his feet. His mother had said their baseboards were getting chipped, and Lex knew it hurt his father's knees to bend down like that. He thought he'd at least do the dining room and the living room that night and maybe look at the other rooms after he had Tally trained and could take some more time off. He set the can of paint on the floor under his glove compartment and started his car, ready to drive the short distance to the house he'd grown up in.

His parents' house looked a lot better than it had in years past. Lex's shop had been successful enough that he'd been able to help them with painting and paid for a few renovations and landscaping in the front yard. It meant a lot to Lex that he could help them. They'd never had enough money to pay for much, but he'd always been certain they loved him and Emily. Not every kid could say that. He worked hard to make sure he had enough to cover his own bills and do some things for them now and again. Of course, he had to talk them into accepting. He rolled his eyes and glanced at the can of paint on the floor. His father wasn't going to let him do the work without putting up a decent fight.

His dad had been fully retired for five years. He'd spent the previous thirty doing janitorial work and maintenance in the town hall building. Their family had always been invited to the city's holiday parties and the Carrington's Fourth of July barbecue—which was always full of the country club elite and their designer-clad children. Lex hated them. He hated how they flourished on the backs of people like his father, who made sure their expensive little world was clean and sparkling. It had prodded both him and his sister to be successful, though. Neither one of them wanted to have to smile at the rich assholes of the town while they were looked at like servants.

He hauled the can of paint from the floor of his car and grabbed a few other supplies he'd bought from the trunk before struggling it all to the front door and banging lightly with his toe so they'd let him in.

"Lex, darling, what are you doing here?" His mother had on her kitchen apron and was carrying a dripping pot.

"You said the baseboards were looking chipped. I was going to take care of the dining room and living room tonight. I'll get to the rest as soon as I can. I've been pretty busy."

"Oh, yes, dear. That's very sweet of you." She backed away from the door to let him walk through with his supplies. "Are you still having a hard time finding someone to help you? I swear, the people in this town. What do they think you're going to do with their children? Convert them?"

"Mom, I'm sure it's not that."

Actually, he was pretty sure it was. He'd been looking for an employee for months, and while no one had a problem eating at his cafe, every time he'd found someone interested in working there the kid would come back with a disappointed face, saying their parents wanted them to concentrate on schoolwork or that a job would disrupt the football season. It was frustrating as hell.

Lex didn't know why he didn't correct his mother's assumption that he hadn't hired anyone yet. Well, that wasn't true. He knew exactly why he was hiding that volatile little piece of info. Telling his mother that he'd hired Tally, no, *Tallis Carrington*, wasn't going to be fun. She'd witnessed a few of his private breakdowns after he'd been tortured to the point of near tears back in high school. She hated the memory of Tally and the years of damage he'd done to her son's self-esteem. Lex didn't blame her. It had taken him a long time to get over what'd happened to him back then. He wasn't sure if he *was* over it yet, to tell the truth. But the past two days had been eye opening for sure. Even if he wasn't quite done with the past, it was hard to keep blaming the guy who it seemed Tally had turned into.

Lex's mother had gone back to the kitchen to finish up with the dishes she was in the middle of doing, but his father wandered in from the family room with a bowl of ice cream. Lex smiled. He knew exactly where the whole exchange was headed.

"Let me change, son, and I'll help you with the painting."

He'd been putting down his drop cloth and getting the wall taped off so white trim paint wouldn't get all over the blue.

"Dad. I got it this time. You can help me when I come back and do the crown molding." He pointed at the ceiling, where the molding looked faded, although not chipped like the baseboards.

"I'm not an invalid."

He'd been ready for it. "I know, and you'd probably make a straighter paint line than me, too, but I'm here now, so what's the point of you doing it? Plus, isn't there a Mariners game on? You know I think baseball is boring."

"It's just the beginning of the season. I don't have to watch."

"Dad…."

"Okay, but let me know if you get to the crown molding. Your cut lines are wavy."

Lex chuckled. His dad always had to have the last word. But it didn't bother Lex. His dad was opinionated and stubborn, but he was loving, and he'd accepted Lex when most other men in the area would've been disgusted. It couldn't have been easy getting older for him, either. He'd always been the competent type. But he'd been forty when Lex was born, and as much as he didn't want to admit it, his body didn't work quite like it had when he was younger. Lex didn't want to be annoying about it, but he wanted to help.

He made quick work of the baseboards in the dining room. It wasn't a very big room, and he hadn't had to move any furniture. The living room was going to be a different case. His parents had long since moved the TV and big, comfy, overstuffed chairs into the family room off the kitchen, but the living room had his mother's old, out-of-tune upright piano and the furniture set she'd inherited from her parents, which in Lex's opinion was ugly and overly formal for their little craftsman house. He did his best to keep his mouth shut about it, though. His mother loved the old junk.

He was in the middle of moving the ugly, and heavy, furniture away from the walls when his mother stopped in. Her hair was curling wildly away from a pink-cheeked face, a sign that she'd been standing over the steamy sink finishing the dishes.

"You're moving fast, darling. Do you need help with the furniture?"

"It's okay, Mom. I brought some furniture movers." He held up one of the smooth plastic discs. "They make everything really easy to move."

"Interesting. Hey, listen, what ever panned out with that pharmacist gentleman that Amy told me about at Easter dinner?"

Oh, Jesus. Did that woman ever keep her mouth shut?

"What pharmacist?" He decided to play dumb until his mother lost interest… hopefully. He'd already ignored Amy's not-so-subtle hints that he should give the guy a call—if you could even call a sticky note with a phone number slapped to his chest a hint at all.

"Lex, why won't you give him a try? You've been single for so long."

Because it's easier than getting hurt. "I'm too busy. Don't really have time for a relationship right now, and it wouldn't be fair to the other person."

His mother shrugged. "You're such a handsome man, honey. I hate to see you alone."

Lex didn't want to be alone. Not really. But it seemed like what he did want was impossible. Respect, love, companionship… nobody cheating on him with his supposedly straight college roommate. The best part about that last one was they thought it was harmless since they asked him to join in when he walked in on them. *I knew there was a reason I didn't date.*

"I'm fine, Ma. I promise. Let me just get this baseboard done so I can go home and hit the sack. If I leave the furniture movers on, can you guys push this stuff back when it's dry?"

"Of course." She smiled and ruffled his hair.

Lex finished the baseboard, cleaned his supplies up, and gave both of his parents a hug before bundling everything into his trunk to head home. He was tired, but it felt nice to have taken care of at least one thing so his dad wouldn't have to deal with it. It was hard to keep his eyes open on the way home, but it wasn't hard to worry. He knew his mother wasn't going to love the idea of Tally working for him, and she was going to love the fact that Lex had kept it from her even less.

He supposed that keeping it hidden from his family meant it was probably a bad idea—or maybe he just didn't want to get nagged.

Lex only wished he knew.

IT HAD been nearly a week that Tally worked for Lex, and he was determined to make his new boss like him. It was important to him; who knew why. Maybe because he had to work for the guy every day, or because he was so damn gorgeous, and Tally hated the idea of someone that pretty not liking him. Or maybe, just maybe, it was because there was something in Lex's smile that he wanted more of.

Every day he learned more about the business, the people of Rock Bay who he'd always considered beneath his notice before, and Lex— him most of all. Tally learned that Lex was nothing like the asshole he'd thought at first, at least not with most people. He smiled at people's long-winded stories and remembered what they liked. He laughed with his best friend every day and fed her free coffee and treats and talked about her dog like it was a real person. He had a smile and a wave for everyone who came in and seemed to know them all by first name. Tally had never seen a friendlier person.

But when they were alone and there was no more business to talk about, Lex was completely different. It grew awkward and quiet, almost like Lex was trying *not* to get to know him, trying not to let him in like he so obviously did for everyone else. Tally understood, at least to a point. He'd been a jerk. His dad was the town scandal. But that was all so long ago. It didn't make sense for Lex to still hate him, but it made Tally even more determined to win the guy over.

When Lex had let him in that morning, he'd looked cautious, guarded, not a whole lot more friendly than he'd been the morning before, or the other three before that, for that matter. He'd quietly greeted Tally and then gone to work setting up the pastries, which had been delivered soon after Lex had unlocked the door. They'd worked through the morning customers, exchanging only the words necessary for the job, never anything personal. Tally had spent the time making sure he was comfortable with the ordering and pricing, while observing Lex so that when it came time for him to learn the coffee machines he would already have a basic idea of how everything worked. Tally tried not to notice Lex's ass or the way his scent made Tally's nose and chest and stomach tingle every time he got close enough.

It didn't matter how much Tally wanted to strip him naked and lick him up and down, though. Project "Win Lex Over" wasn't exactly going swimmingly. Every time Tally thought he was getting somewhere, everything went right back to the uncomfortable silence that was, right at that moment, lying heavy on the shop.

Tally was busily wiping the crumbs and coffee dribbles off of the bistro tables and surreptitiously watching Lex as he continuously reorganized the offerings in his glass shelves until they looked perfect. Lex had a soft little smile on his face, the genuine kind that already made Tally's stomach weak, but Tally knew that as soon as Lex looked up and caught him watching, the smile would disappear like it had never been there in the first place. It surprised the hell out of him when, instead, Lex looked up and continued smiling, hesitant.

"So, Tally, I know you've got a day off coming up the day after tomorrow, right?"

Tally nodded. "Yeah, is that still okay? I mean, I can work if you want. Honestly, I could use the hours."

"It's fine. I was just hoping you could stay a little late tomorrow. I host a local open mic once a month. It gets a little hectic. I can pay you overtime."

"Really?" Tally tried to control his grin. "I mean, yeah, that's no problem."

"Good. You won't have to stay until it closes down, just until the main crowd gets settled in with their orders."

"I'll help as long as you need, Lex. Really, I'd be happy to."

Lex nodded and went back to arranging the pastries on his shelves.

TALLY was shocked by how many people flooded the little coffee shop come seven o'clock on a Friday night. He wouldn't have even guessed that there were that many people in Rock Bay, let alone people who wanted to watch nervous teenagers and wannabe singer/songwriters sit on a stool and attempt to entertain. The shop was warm and filled with the smells of coffee and warmed muffins and a mix of perfumes and colognes. It was almost too much, but still somehow pleasant.

"Here you go, Lex." Tally handed his most recent order slip, an orange mocha, to Lex who put it in his queue. He bagged the sugar cookie the woman had ordered with it and handed it to her with a smile. "Your drink will be right up."

He and Lex were kept ridiculously busy taking orders and making hot drinks. It was a good thing that he'd had a few days to learn the contents of the pastry shelves, because there was no way that Lex would've been able to keep up with the drink making if he had to dish out muffins and cookies as well. Tally only hoped that no one ordered a sandwich because he would probably have to make it, and he was so rushed that he'd most likely do it all wrong.

They worked well together, busy as they were. It was a kind of well-timed counterpoint dance behind the counter: Tally working the register, dishing up desserts, and giving Lex drink orders while Lex made the drinks and lined them up neatly on the counter with handwritten stickers that described the contents.

The customers seemed to be used to Lex's methods, and went very smoothly, even with the hectic pace. Tally liked working there with Lex, watching how organized and relaxed he was. Tally hoped things were going to keep getting better. He'd already figured out a few days before that he really enjoyed the job, and Lex finally seemed to be warming up to him—not exactly tropical, but not the deep freeze they'd had the first few days, either. He could only hope that he was finally getting somewhere with his mystery of a boss. Lex brushed by Tally and gave him a half smile that sent Tally's stomach spinning. *Professional. Friendly. That's it. Knock it off, dumbass.* He figured if he just kept giving himself that lecture, eventually it would sink in.

IT WAS an unavoidable fact. Tallis Carrington was going to drive Lex insane. Every day it got harder not to touch—the kind of touching that he'd told Amy was off limits. He wanted to test Tally's hair and see if it was as soft as it looked, run the pad of his thumb across too prominent cheekbones, brush his lips against Tally's pulse, and inhale that mind-numbing scent he'd been trying to ignore. Lex couldn't believe how stupid he was. Tally knew he was gay and seemed to have no issue with it, but that didn't mean he'd want Lex pawing him—and pawing was exactly what Lex wanted to do. It didn't seem to matter that he couldn't bring himself to trust the guy's motivations. His body didn't notice his mind's ambivalence. Hell, his body hadn't noticed all those years ago when Tally was an outright asshole. Of course it was responding now that, at least on the surface, he seemed to be genuinely nice.

Lex knew it had been a mistake to ask for his help at the open mic night. He should've just had Amy do it like he always had before. The whole night had been torture, worse than the past five days combined. Smelling Tally in the heat of the crowded shop, bumping up against him constantly as they worked together in the cramped space that had only seemed to shrink in the crush of the crowd—it was testing his willpower like nothing before. Lex wasn't sure if he was going to make it much longer before he did something he'd regret forever, like maybe throwing Tallis Carrington on the ground and taking every drop of his frustration out in a punishing kiss.

He was foaming a latte, the fourth pumpkin spice of the night, when he felt Tally's presence behind him, close and warm and looming. Tally brushed up against him and reached around Lex's shoulder to grab the big cinnamon shaker that was sitting on the counter right in front of Lex.

"Sorry," he muttered quietly, right up against Lex's ear. "Molly wants cinnamon sprinkled on her muffin."

Shivers burst across Lex's skin. "It's okay," he tried to mumble back. His voice came out in a squeak.

He felt the warmth of Tally's breath on his neck, and when he inhaled he could smell him, spicy and sexy and lingering in the air. Tally hadn't moved. The moment stretched, excruciating and hot. Lex felt every single one of his crashing heartbeats. *Why doesn't he move? He has to know what he's doing to me!* And then Tally did move, but closer, just a small little movement, the difference barely perceptible other than from the wash of warmth that Lex felt deep in his belly. There were fingers brushing lightly at his hip, a touch that could be interpreted in so many ways, and then he was gone—back to chatting with Molly Bates, the girl who always wanted cinnamon sprinkled on her chocolate muffin.

Lex clenched his jaw. *Get a grip, Barry!* But he couldn't. His pulse thundered, turning his face red, making his groin throb painfully. He had to stare at the counter and do multiplication tables in his head for long moments before he could even consider turning to place the drink on the counter without making a public spectacle of himself.

"You okay, Lex?" There it was again—that light touch, on his shoulder this time, and Tally's voice so concerned against his ear. Lex's stomach quivered and clenched in on itself.

"Yeah, just hungry I guess," he lied. "Got a little lightheaded."

"You want me to make you a bagel with cream cheese? You probably need to get some carbs in you."

No, I need you in me. Or maybe me in you. I don't care as long as I can fill my mouth with your skin.

"Sure," Lex answered weakly. He'd have to choke the bagel down. Bread wasn't even close to what he wanted to swallow.

Moron. That's Tallis Carrington. Tallis jerk-of-the-century Carrington. Straight, asshole... well, reformed asshole. Maybe. Point is, hands off!

In the self-lecture department, Lex knew he'd get an A for effort. It was the follow-through where he failed. Couldn't seem to talk his body into listening... or his mind, for that matter. They both kept screaming "I want him!"

"Here, eat this, Lex. You'll feel better."

A toasted bagel with cream cheese was placed in front of him, accompanied by another hand on the shoulder. Lex stood at the counter, breathing slowly and trying to slow his racecar libido down before it crashed all over the place.

"I'm good. Thanks."

Lex was surprised by the sharpness of his voice. His lust and self-annoyance had come out of his mouth aimed at the undeserving Tally. He turned to apologize, but by the time he'd turned, Tally was on the other side of their space, taking an order from two giggly teenage girls who made no secret of the fact that they were checking him out. Lex thought he might look a bit hurt, but he hid it with an open smile and flirtatious banter. The two girls ate it up, flipping their hair and applying lip gloss. Tally silently handed Lex the girls' drink order, then turned to wipe off the counter.

"Hey, Tally. I'm sorry. It's been a long week. I don't want you to think I'm a big asshole, I'm just—"

"Really, don't worry about it. I understand. No hard feelings." Tally gave Lex a shy smile. "You better make those two girls their drinks before they eat me alive," he whispered. "I think one of them tried to slip me her phone number."

Lex returned the smile, glad that he could breathe again. "You should escape while you have the chance," he whispered back. "I think I can take it from here if you want to get home."

"You sure?" Did Tally look disappointed? *No, more like you're projecting your own shit onto him.*

"Yeah, I'm sure. Go get some rest. I'll see you Sunday morning."

Tally untied his apron and gave Lex another one of those killer shy smiles. "Night, Lex. I'll see you Sunday."

TALLY couldn't keep from smiling. The entire morning as he did his laundry, straightened up his grandma's kitchen, and started a pot of soup for dinner, he'd break into these silly smiles when he was least expecting them. He understood. He finally got why Lex had been acting so squirrelly all week, holding Tally at arm's length and being what could only be called a jerk.

He's attracted to me. There it was again. That grin Tally couldn't control. The only problem was that it was pretty obvious Lex didn't want to be attracted to him. Maybe because of what he'd heard, maybe because Tally worked for him… maybe because he thought Tally was straight. Tally stopped still in his chopping and tried to remember any single moment where he may have told Lex that he was gay too. There wasn't one. Tally knew he couldn't rule that out as Lex's reason for not wanting to like him unless it was eliminated.

Hmmmm… now to come up with the perfect way to tell him. Tally went back to chopping potatoes for the soup, trying to decide how he was going to let it slip to Lex that he'd been dreaming of sex with boys since the day he figured out he wanted sex at all… and how more than anything he wanted it with Lex. His boss. And from what he could tell, Lex wanted him too. Tally made a face into the pile of potatoes on the cutting board. Only problem was going to be getting him to admit it.

Tally had a pleasant and peaceful dinner with his grandmother, potato soup and rolls with butter. Dessert was some store-bought cheesecake served with tea. She'd been surprised that he could cook, but he'd been taking care of himself since he was eighteen and hadn't been able to afford daily takeout for nearly that long. Cooking had come to him slowly but was a necessary skill.

After dinner, things got a bit hairy—in only the way they can when one is living with an opinionated and nosey grandmother.

"Tallis, have you spoken with your mother lately?"

He sighed and stood, preferring to wash the dinner dishes rather than be grilled about the woman who deserted him.

"No, Grandma. You know she'd rather pretend that I don't exist."

"Because you're gay?"

Tally shrugged. He'd been avoiding this conversation for nearly fifteen years. "Yes. I guess it was just one too many scandals for her… not that my sexuality was one, but the potential was there. Plus, I think she sees too much of dad in me. She calls him the 'nineteen year long mistake' that she wants to forget."

His grandmother looked annoyed. "If I hadn't pushed her out myself, I'd wonder if that woman was really my child. To turn on her own son—"

"I wasn't the greatest kid back then, Grandma. And Troy didn't want a sullen, gay eighteen-year-old around to interfere with his new relationship."

Troy was his mother's second husband. He was money with a capital "M" and had joined Tally's mother in the ardent wish that Tally wouldn't stay and ruin their perfect Pottery-Barn-catalog life. Grandma rolled her eyes at the mention of his name. Tally had the feeling that she didn't have anything positive to say about him. He couldn't agree more. Probably best not to say anything at all.

"And your father? Are we going to talk about him?"

Tally groaned. "Do we have to?"

"I think so. He hurt you."

"Grandma, he's dead. The man made some huge mistakes, but he's gone. Can't we leave it alone?"

Tally's grandma took a long drink from her tea, then nodded. "Yes, for now. But I think you need to talk about it. Have you ever?"

Tally shook his head. "I never knew anyone well enough to lay the whole sordid tale on them."

His grandmother gave him a rare gentle look and reached over to cup his chin in her palm. "I'm sorry for that, boy."

"It's okay, Grandma. I'm fine. Do you want to watch a movie? I rented a few at the store."

"Action?"

Tally chuckled. After all the missing years, it turned out he still knew his grandmother pretty well. "Yeah. I got a spy thriller and one of those big bloody historical epics."

"Either one of them would be excellent. I'll make popcorn."

It was somehow both funny and a bit scary to watch his lovely grandmother get all bloodthirsty over the hundreds of longsword eviscerations that littered the screen for the next few hours. Those kinds of movies had honestly always turned his stomach a bit. He didn't mind watching the hero, though. Tight, skimpy leather and sweat? Mmmm.

TALLY wasn't sure what he'd expected to meet with Sunday morning, but a Lex only slightly less surly and taciturn than the one he'd met on his first day for sure wasn't it. Tally watched in a bit of shock while Lex organized his pastries and sandwich supplies into neat little displays. He'd barely even looked up when Tally walked in.

"Um, morning, Lex," Tally mumbled. He couldn't believe how unsure of himself he felt. Even on his worst day back in Seattle, no one had been able to turn him inside out like Lex could.

"Morning, Tally." His tone wasn't exactly unfriendly, but it wasn't Friday night, either. "I want to start teaching you how to make the coffee drinks today. We'll have some work to do before you'll be able to be left on your own."

Tally knew that was the eventual point of his employment, but the idea of being in the shop, not to mention dealing with the natives, without Lex, made his stomach twist.

"Okay," he answered. His voice came out hoarse and half-squeaky. *Great. Nothing like showing such a lack of confidence in front of your employer... and the guy you want like it's nobody's business. Even better that they're one and the same.*

"You'll be fine. Once you get the basics down, building the drinks is no problem."

I only wish it was the coffee I was worried about.

After that Lex warmed up a bit. There wasn't any flirting or nervous-looking glances, but he was professional and a good teacher. At least they weren't back to piling a million directions on at once, like the first day. By the time the shop opened for the before-church crowd, Tally felt that he'd be able to confidently make a few of the drinks... during the slump after church started. He didn't think he was quite ready to do any concocting under pressure. As it was he was kept very busy running the register, passing out cinnamon rolls and blueberry muffins, and grilling the odd breakfast sandwich when someone ordered one. By the time the church crowd was out of the shop, he was sweaty and ready for a break.

Lex handed him a huge steaming latte. "Here, take your fifteen and drink this, then we'll start round two of espresso 101."

"Thanks, Lex."

"Sure," Lex answered, but his attention was drawn to the front door, where the overhead bell had just rung. His face broke into a huge grin, and he dodged around Tally, running toward the open door.

Tally turned to see… a familiar face. Emily Barry. She'd been in his class, and he'd always had a secret respect for her—smart, had her shit together, knew that good grades were her ticket out of their little temperate swamp of a town.

"Hey, fancy lawyer lady, when did you get into town?" Lex was hugging her tight, and they were spinning around in circles together.

"Last night. Mom said you needed some help at the shop and were having a hard time finding an employee. I'm between cases and had some vacation time, so I figured I'd lend a hand."

Emily Barry was Lex's sister? Aw, Jesus, he is *a local.* Tally felt a little niggling feeling in the back of his neck, like there was something he should know about the two forcefully whispering siblings, but for the life of him he couldn't come up with anything. He didn't remember Emily having a brother; other than his respect for her work ethic, he hadn't really noticed her much at all. She'd been far below his social level but not the kind of girl any guy who had a good relationship with his nuts would dare mess with.

"Emmy, it's fine. I swear. Jesus. This is why I haven't told mom yet."

"And what happens when she stops by?"

"You know, I'm not deaf," Tally interjected with a wry smile. "You didn't tell your family you hired me, huh?"

Lex reddened. "I'm an adult with my own business. I don't have to tell them certain details that I don't find necessary to share."

"Which means you were afraid you'd get in trouble. Am I really that bad?"

He shrugged. "Not now. Before…." Lex trailed off.

"Great." Tally couldn't help but sound defeated. "I'm done with my coffee if you want to get back into training, or I could clean if you want to talk to your sister."

"No, it's fine." He turned to Emily. "I'll see ya at dinner, Sis. I'm assuming mom wants me to come over."

"Assumed correctly. Six o'clock—and don't worry. I won't tell. I'll let you do that."

"*Bitch*," Lex muttered.

Tally chuckled under his breath. He'd always wanted a sister, or any sibling, for that matter.

"So, espresso 101 part two? And then you can spend the rest of the afternoon thinking about how you're going to tell your mom you hired the biggest asshole in town." He grinned at Lex to offset the bitter words.

Lex looked like he might want to say something, but instead, he handed Tally an empty cup. "Part two—mochas."

LEX was trying not to sweat. He pulled his car in front of his parents' house and turned off the radio. It was probably too much to hope that his sister had managed to keep her mouth shut. The gossip really was just too good—but then again so was the prospect of watching Lex stammer and stumble over the news that he'd kept from them for over a week.

His parents' house was loud and cheerful as usual, filled with the smells of dinner cooking on the stove and burning cedar from the fireplace, where a crackling fire was warding off the early spring's evening chill.

"Ma, Dad, I'm here."

"Lex, sweetheart, we're in the kitchen. Emmy tells me you have some news."

Shit.

Lex walked in on a typical scene; his mother was chopping tomatoes for a salad while his sister transferred sugar cookies to a paper towel. They had the radio on and were shaking their hips in time with the music while they talked a mile a minute. It was no wonder where Lex's sometimes unfortunately vocal nature had come from. Only his father was the quiet type.

"Hi, guys. Need any help?"

"You mind getting out the salad dressing?" his mom asked after she kissed him on the cheek. "And tell me about your new employee."

Lex glared at Emily. She tossed him a saucy grin and started sprinkling cinnamon and sugar on top of the cookies.

"He's working out really well. Learning fast. Pretty soon I'll be able to take an hour or two off here and there."

"That's good. What's his name? Is it one of the high school kids?"

Here we go. "His name is Tally, and no, he's actually a little older than me."

"Tally? That's an odd name."

"So is Alexis," Lex said in a wry voice. "At least for a guy."

"It's your middle name and it's traditional. You know that."

He did. He was the fourth James Alexis Barry in the family. At least they hadn't done that whole number thing at the end of his name. He liked it much better without. Anyway, after a James, a Jamie, and his father, Jimmy, they'd decided to call him Lex. It would have been too confusing. The few times he'd been called James felt really strange.

"I know, Ma. Hey, you have ranch and honey mustard. Which one do you want?"

His mother said "ranch" at the same time as his sister said "honey mustard." Then they both poked each other and broke out into giggles.

Lex rolled his eyes and smiled. "Why don't I put both of them on the table?"

"Wanna cookie?" Emmy asked when he'd come in from the dining room.

"No, thanks." He'd lost all of his chubbiness junior year when he shot up six inches in a semester, but he still had the memory of how it felt to be teased for it.

"You look skinny," his sister told him encouragingly and pinched his side.

"All work, no time for eating," he joked.

"Lex, you know that's not good for you," his mother called from the kitchen.

"Mom, I'm kidding. I eat all the time. I just run around the shop constantly and burn it off."

"Speaking of the shop, tell me about this Tally."

"You mean Tallis Carrington," Emmy singsonged.

"I'm going to get you," Lex whispered and waited for his mother's guaranteed tirade. He wasn't disappointed.

"You hired Tallis Carrington?" she screeched. "Lex, don't you remember what that awful boy did to you? I'd heard he was back in town and, oh, the nerve! To ask *you* for a job, of all people. I can't believe he even considered it; I can't believe you did, either, for that matter!"

"He doesn't know who I am, Mom, and really, you should see him." Lex paused, then spoke almost to himself. "He's so different."

Emmy whipped her head around. "Oh, Lexie," she whispered. "Not again."

Shit. Sometimes it sucked having a sister who knew him so well.

"What do you mean he doesn't know who you are? He spent months terrorizing you, and he doesn't have the decency to remember it?" His mother's face had turned an odd shade of hot pink.

"No. I mean, well, I don't know if he remembers that, but he seriously doesn't know who I am. The first day he asked what I'd heard about him, like I was a newcomer. Besides, he called me James in high school, because that's what it said on my ID card, or sometimes Jamie because he could tell it pissed me off. He'd have never known that I went by Lex—never bothered to ask. And you have to admit, I couldn't be recognized by looks. I look nothing like I did back then."

"You don't. Your face is so thin now."

Lex rolled his eyes. His mother was always on her own personal crusade to feed the world.

"Emmy, can you go get dad? I better eat before I waste away to nothing."

Lex's mom swatted him with a towel. "Bring the lasagna in, and I'll grab the garlic bread. Then we can eat."

They thankfully dropped the subject of Tallis Carrington for the rest of the meal. Lex could tell it was on his mother's mind, though. Her face showed it. He was grateful that she'd let it rest but knew that a shop visit wasn't far off. If there was one thing his mother was, it was protective, and she had a very clear memory of Lex's year as Tally's number one victim. He shook his head a bit at that thought. No, he was never *Tally's* victim.

Tally was a different person than the dick who'd ruled the school with his gang of apes in lettermen's jackets. Tally was... *real* and hardworking and interested in learning new things. Lex couldn't believe how much the new Tally had superimposed itself in his mind over the old snarling image that had been imprinted there. Now all Lex could see was the way he smiled or how he went out of his way to help as much as he could... *oh Jesus. It's too late.*

Lex excused himself soon after dinner was over, claiming early mornings and breakfast rushes as he backed hastily toward the door before another well-meaning intervention could start. In the peace and quiet of his car he admitted what he'd been avoiding all week, especially during the tenseness of Friday night.

"I want him," he muttered, testing out the words to see how they felt in his mouth. "I want my straight employee who also happens to be the same guy everyone in town hates. Except me."

Oh, God.

CHAPTER Five

THEY'D done it. Tally had spent his first afternoon alone at the shop, and everybody had survived. Lex had gone in the back to do some bookwork in the office, and Tally knew it was really hard for him to leave and not come popping back in every five minutes, but after a week of practicing with the coffee drinks and nearly three weeks at the register, they'd both decided that Tally was as ready as he was ever going to be. The afternoon had passed with little incident. Tally still got a few glares from the older locals, but the after-school crowd was cool, and he'd gotten used to the uncomfortable stares from those who remembered him not so fondly. His basic strategy was to respond as if they were smiling, and that usually threw them off enough that they just ordered their drink and went away. Even with the relative success of the afternoon, it was still a relief to flip the sign to "closed," clean up, and walk into the back so he could stick his head in Lex's office and tell him he was done for the day.

Tally found Lex bent over his desk, a pair of wire rims perched on his nose, angrily tapping the keys of an oversized calculator.

"Hey, uh, Lex? I'm done cleaning, and I was going to clock out."

Lex looked up, startled. "It's already six?"

"Yeah, actually it's six fifteen."

"Aw, shit! I'm supposed to be at Amy's in twenty minutes. We changed it to Friday this week. If you're done, I'll see you Monday. You've got the whole weekend off."

Tally smiled. He'd been thinking of going to sit at the beach the next day, maybe relax and read a book or something. "Yeah, I'll see you Monday. Have fun with Amy."

"I will—and great job today. I did spy a few times, and it seemed like you were doing really well. Hopefully, if this damn drive-through window permit ever goes through, I'll be able to hire another employee and really get things going."

"The city giving you grief?"

"Yeah. I've applied at least four times, and I keep getting railroaded."

"Is it a problem with blocking alley traffic?"

"No, I have plenty of room to put a drive-through on the north side of the building, which is part of my property, it's just the asshole who does permits—you know what? I'm sorry to dump all this on you. It's really not your problem. Have a nice weekend."

"Thanks, Lex. You too."

It was blindingly obvious that there was something more to the permit story, and Tally was determined to see if he could do something to help—he'd have to see who it was downtown. A few of the people in that office would remember him fondly. Jerk that Tally may have been when he was with his friends, he'd known who to suck up to. He hadn't brought out his ass-kissing skills in a while. Perhaps it was time for them to get a nice polishing.

But it would have to be on Monday. He was bushed, Lex was late for his dinner, and more than anything, Tally was looking forward to hitting the grocery store for some ice cream and going home to a long night of lounging. It was kind of a relief not to have much of a social life anymore—no social life at all, honestly. The gay scene in Seattle had always seemed like so much *work*. Looking good, having the right (rich) date, hiding his sub-par apartment from the obnoxious stuck-up queens who ruled the social universe; none of it had been easy. A night of the Food Network and some well-earned dessert was exactly what he wanted, and since there was nothing else going on in Butt Crack, Washington, he didn't have to feel like a loser for wanting it.

But the universe, as usual, was fucking with him. This time, fate came out to play on the side of a muddy road at least two miles from his grandmother's place. Just when a blissful night of Disney cake challenges and ice cream gluttony was so close he could taste it, smell it, and feel it melting on his tongue, his dumb car decided it had a different idea of the perfect Friday night, one that included dying when he was still nowhere close to home and a spring storm was pouring down in sheeting, splashing gushes that would soak him in seconds. Fan-fucking-tastic.

No help for it.

In an attempt to avoid explaining his circumstances to a bevy of half friends, he'd deliberately canceled his cell service the day he'd moved back to town. Of course that meant there wasn't even a way for him to call his grandmother. Rolling his eyes, Tally grabbed the bag that contained two different kinds of ice cream, pocketed his keys, and pulled the hood that he was luckily wearing over his head. He only had about fifteen minutes of daylight left, and the last stretch of road to his grandmother's was along the coast, heavy with trees and lacking in any sort of streetlights.

Tally trudged along, trying not to let the chilly ice cream bag rest against his leg too much. He scooted far onto the shoulder every time he heard a car coming and picked up the pace, knowing his grandmother was going to panic if he was more than a few minutes late. When he was a little more than halfway there, Tally heard a car coming and veered off into the gravelly ditch along the road once again. He saw the shadows looming ominously, like they always did when headlights curved along the densely wooded road, and shivered, trying not to creep himself out. It didn't help when the headlights slowed down. Tally picked up his pace, trying to remain casual.

"Tally?"

To hear a familiar voice coming from the car, now idling on the side of the road, wasn't what he was expecting. He stopped and turned, walking with relief toward the blinding headlights.

"Hey, Lex."

LEX had been running even later than usual, speeding down a back road to Amy's, when he saw the car parked by the side of the road. *Tally.* Nobody else in town had a car that looked even similar to Tally's old red Triumph. The thing had shuddered to a stop outside the shop nearly every morning for three weeks, each time sounding like it was heaving its last breath. That last breath must have finally come. Lex pulled up behind the car slowly, pulling his parking brake and getting out to see if Tally needed any help. The doors were locked, and Tally was nowhere in sight.

Would he have started walking? Lex guessed so, if he had no other choice. He'd never remembered Tally getting out a cell phone of any kind. Maybe he was one of the last people in the universe who didn't have one. Lex jogged back to his car, through the downpour, which had gone from normal to gale force in a matter of minutes. Instead of turning onto Amy's road, he took a right onto twisty Shorecrest Drive. He knew Tally's grandmother lived at least a mile down that dangerous, dark stretch. He didn't want his one employee turned into road kill.

When he saw Tally trudging, hood over his head, looking dejected and worn, something pulled painfully in Lex's chest. He felt it, plucking at his heart, every weary step that Tally took pounding into him again and again the fact that Tally really wasn't the jerk he'd once been. That person would've never been walking in the rain, grocery bag in hand, because his sad old car couldn't make one last trip home, and he didn't even have a phone to call anyone. The whole scene made Lex's throat tighten.

Pulling over slowly so he didn't spin out on the wet gravel, he rolled down his window and called out to Tally.

"Come get in the car," he said when he'd gotten Tally's attention. "I'll give you a ride to your grandmother's."

"Are you sure?" Tally looked questioningly at the expensive leather seats. "I'm soaked."

"Do you honestly think I'm going to let you walk the rest of the way home in this? You'd be out sick for a week. C'mon."

The ride was quiet, but not uncomfortably so. Lex turned his heater up, and Tally sighed, sinking against the supple leather of his car seat. Lex found himself smiling at him, against his better judgment. The next thing out of his mouth surprised even him.

"Hey, do you want to come to Amy's with me, after you get out of those wet clothes, of course. She always makes a ton of food."

Tally's glance was surprised and pleased. "Um, yeah. That sounds nice?" It came out like a question. "Are you sure?"

Lex chuckled to cover the fact that his insides were churning. *No turning back now.* "Yeah. I asked you, didn't I?"

They were pulling up to Grace Loman's driveway. Lex had forgotten at first that she was Tally's grandmother—she'd always been one of his favorite customers. Lex hadn't seen her in a few days. He hoped she was doing well.

"Let me go change and put this ice cream in the freezer. I'll be out in five minutes. Is that okay?"

"Yeah. Take your time. I'm going to call Amy and tell her to expect one more."

Amy took the news of their third dining partner with a giggle and a naughty innuendo that Lex stifled before she could run away with it.

"He's just a friend, Ames. He had a rough night; I think it'll be good for him to hang out."

"Oh, he's a friend now, is he? Last week he was just your *employee*."

"Shut it. Here he comes. I'll be there in a few minutes."

Tally looked disturbingly edible with his hastily dried hair and those perfectly worn-out designer jeans that hugged his hips and ass so lovingly.

"Ready?"

"Yeah. Grandma says she's locking the door at midnight, though, and I better be back." Tally rolled his eyes. "It's like I'm in junior high again."

Lex chuckled. "At least you got midnight. Junior high was like a permanent lockdown for me."

"Maybe if my parents had been stricter I'd have turned out more like you." Tally said it with a smile but cringed at the word "parents." Lex was sure the last thing he wanted to do was bring up the taboo subject of his father.

"I think you turned out pretty good, all things considered. Not what I would've expected, for sure."

They were pulling into Amy's driveway. Tally looked pensively at Lex.

"You really went to my high school. And you're Emily's brother. I wish I could remember…."

Lex panicked for a second but tried to look nonchalant. "Oh, I was quiet. You'd have never even seen me." Not a word of that was true, but Lex got a huge pit in his stomach every time he thought of Tally figuring out who he was. "We're here!" he added, probably a little too brightly. "Let's head in."

Amy greeted Lex with a hug and Tally with a friendly smile. She raised her eyebrows at Lex as Tally walked by, but he gave her a significant look. *Please keep your mouth shut.* He tried to send quiet vibes her way. *This was probably a huge mistake, bringing Tally here.* Too late.

"So, dinner's ready. It has been for a while, since you were almost a half an hour late." She glared at Lex jokingly.

"You know me. If it's not for the shop...."

"Yeah. Then you're not on time. It's a good thing that you had Emily and then me to get you to school. Other than that, you'd have failed first period four years in a row."

Lex choked a little. "Yeah, good thing I had my faithful girlfriend to keep me in line," he joked, trying to cover up his discomfort.

"Too bad you broke up with me for Zac Efron."

He punched her shoulder lightly. "Let's go eat. I'm starving."

Lex and Amy kept up their usual banter through dinner, with Tally leaning back and smiling. Lex hoped Tally wasn't bored out of his mind, but he did chuckle at Amy's jabs and add comments when he had a clue what they were talking about. Lex couldn't help the giddiness in his stomach. Tally's warmth radiated next to him at the small table, and when he smiled, God, if it wasn't like the sun rising on that sad face. He was tired of telling himself not to be attracted to Tally, of reminding himself what a complete train wreck it would be if he started having serious feelings for the guy. He wanted him, plain and simple. *Train wreck, Lex.* Too bad the words didn't have anywhere near the effect they'd had at the beginning.

The meal passed without much incident, at least until the end when Amy brought up the damn drive-through window again. Lex still got all heated up every time he thought of that homophobic old asshole MacAuliffe down at the city building. The man had made no secret of the fact that he thought Rock Bay was no place for homos like Lex and that Lex should go off in search of greener pastures in some place like San Francisco, where most folks didn't have a problem with his kind. If MacAuliffe's signature weren't necessary for the drive-through that would bring more money into his shop, then Lex would have told him to shove it months before.

"So what is the deal with the permit?" Amy asked. She'd been hounding him to go over MacAuliffe's head for weeks. Tally, who'd been relaxed and halfway listening to their bullshit, suddenly perked up.

"Yeah, what is the deal? I wanted to ask you earlier, but you seemed like you were in a hurry."

"Nothing new, especially not in a small town like this one. I'm sure you know Gerald MacAuliffe?" Lex shot a pointed look at Tally, who flushed. He'd been good friends with Gerald's son Drew, so he had to have some familiarity with the old goat. "He's being his usual homophobic self."

"He won't give you the permit because you're gay?" Lex had to give Tally credit for looking appalled.

"He hasn't said it in so many words, but I know that's it. He's always been very clear about his dislike for me and 'my kind', and he keeps throwing out these ridiculous reasons for rejecting my permit. The most recent rejection said he didn't want to bring any drive-through food places into town when he just approved Cheeky Coffee, that bikini stand down on Dock Street." Lex rolled his eyes. Even the existence of that stupid place still annoyed him to no end.

Tally chuckled. "Did those make it all the way out here? We have them in Seattle too. I call it stripper coffee. The coffee is usually awful."

Amy made a grunting noise and rolled her eyes. "That's not what you're paying for."

"Thanks for being loyal, babe." Lex leaned over and gave her a kiss on the cheek.

"But seriously, you think he's not approving it because he has some personal thing against you?"

Lex nodded. "Yep." He couldn't help making a disgusted face.

"I'll go talk to him on Monday, if you want. As you said, I do know him… and he loved me. I was a total suck-up to him because I thought he could get me into Stanford."

"You went to Stanford?" Lex tried not to sound shocked.

Tally snorted. "I didn't go anywhere. Except to the Spaghetti Factory to wait tables. After everything that happened, college wasn't even close to my list of possibilities."

"What exactly did happen?" Lex couldn't believe that had come out of his mouth.

"As far as I knew, that was very public record."

"Not with your dad—I meant what happened to you? You disappeared."

Tally stood and started gathering the dishes. "You have any idea what time it is, Lex? You're going to be in a world of hurt if you've gotta open without me." He spoke fast, looking uncomfortable. Lex let it slide. He'd been the one to ask the probing question in the first place. Tally escaped to the kitchen with a stack of dishes and promptly started washing them.

Amy shot him a glare. "What the hell did you bring that up for?" she hissed as quietly as she could, glancing out toward the kitchen where the water had just flipped on.

Lex shrugged, not even knowing the answer himself. The question had slipped out before he could think too carefully about it. "Sorry. I don't know. I guess I'm just tired. I'd better go get him before he cleans your whole kitchen."

Amy winked. "If that's the case, then please leave him in there! I've got two double shifts at the hospital this week."

Lex pinched her and turned to walk into the kitchen.

DINNER had been hard. Literally. Tally couldn't remember the last time he'd had to sit in a semi-public place and try to control his body's response to a guy—probably high school. But Lex's laugh, that brilliant smile, the way his tongue darted out to lick a drop of wine from the side of his glass.... *God*, what Tally wished that tongue would do to him. He'd do it right back, run his own tongue down the center of Lex's spine and lower, until it nudged into the warmth of Lex's body.

A shot of heat whipped through Tally and centered in his groin at the thought of licking into Lex, making him painfully hard and even more turned on than before, if that was possible. It had been so long since he'd been touched at all, and before that it had never been anything other than the impersonal efficiency of a one-night hookup. He didn't want that with Lex. What he imagined between them would be very, very personal—for the first time in years his fantasies involved kissing and touching, even talking and cuddling. *Jesus.*

They'd been alone together for hours in the past few weeks, but Tally couldn't remember being so aware of it. In the darkness of Lex's car it was the only thing he could think of. Lex chuckled at something the radio DJ said, and that rich sound made the hairs up and down Tally's back rise in the most pleasant shiver possible. He crossed his legs and tried to dig his short fingernails into the side of his thigh—hoping the pain would calm his rampaging lust. Tally couldn't remember ever wanting anyone as bad as the lanky man sitting in the driver's seat right next to him.

They were pulling into his grandmother's driveway, turning slowly onto the crunching gravel. The night had been so nice, and Tally didn't know if he could stand it if things went back to the way they were. All of a sudden he wanted to tell Lex everything, all the stuff he couldn't say when it came up at dinner—his whole past, his messy present, hell, he even wanted to tell him every little thing he'd like to do to him in bed, including the cuddling and the talking, but he figured that part was going to have to wait. Tally took a long, slow breath.

"Nothing happened really, we just... left."

His voice echoed in the car, easily carrying above the quiet chatter of the radio. He cringed at the loudness.

Lex looked at him sharply. "What?" He reached over and turned the radio off.

"You asked after dinner what happened to me. I'm telling you. My mom couldn't take it anymore, all the people staring at her, pitying her for what my father had done. The day after the funeral she packed us up and moved us to Seattle, where hopefully no one knew who we were. Then the will came out and with it all the bank statements; turned out that high school girls weren't my dad's only closet pleasure. He'd cleaned out the savings accounts gambling—at the casinos, playing poker online. The lawyers' fees took the last little bit of money in the checking account. We didn't have a damn thing. God. He was such a cliché. Couldn't even come up with a unique vice. Girls and gambling." Tally made a disgusted noise.

He remembered the day when the news had broken, spreading over town like some infectious disease. *Jack Carrington was caught in his office with his seventeen-year-old intern. Other girls have come forward alleging affairs. We trusted him, we liked him! How could he be so disgusting?* The gossip had gone from truth to wildly speculative rumors about young boys and drugs and skimming money from the town's budget for tequila-soaked vacations south of the border. And then the final blow. Jack Carrington had been found, shot by his own hand in the study of the Carringtons' mansion up by the golf course. Even thinking about it made Tally want to curl up—he'd had nobody in those long couple of weeks. His friends had disappeared, either on their own or at the insistence of their parents; his mother had been okay, well, until that one afternoon….

"So you just finished school in Seattle and got a job?"

Tally shook his head. "Never graduated." He squeezed his eyes shut for a second, like perhaps there was something even worse than what everyone already knew.

"How come? Didn't you enroll in Seattle?"

"Yeah, and I was there for a month or so, but around that time my mother found a new rich boyfriend and decided she'd rather not be burdened by my presence in her apartment any longer."

"What do you mean?"

"She kicked me out. I got a job and lived in some, um, interesting places for a while before I got my feet under me. Well, sort of under me, anyway."

"Interesting places?"

Tally shuddered. "You really don't want to know. Anyway, I wasn't going to come back here. Everything was such a big mess with my dad, and well… let's just say after everything happened, I found out who my real friends were, and the answer to that was pretty much nobody. A few of them may have been willing to help, but their parents told them not to see me."

"I can't believe your mother would just kick you out with nowhere to go. Why?"

Tally felt his face explode in an agonized blush. He was glad for the car's darkness. "She didn't want me there anyway, but her excuse?" Tally chuckled mirthlessly. "She came home to the apartment on a day when she was supposed to be out. She found me with Jeremy, my boyfriend. He'd come up to Seattle to see if I was okay."

Lex made a choking noise and turned off the car. "You're going to have to repeat that one for me."

Tally couldn't help but chuckle. He'd been trying to find a way to tell him, anyway. "Um, in high school, I wasn't out, but I was dating a guy who lived in Astoria. Sometimes it seemed like he was the only person who actually knew me. He came to Seattle after the whole thing with my dad. I broke down when I saw the first friendly face in what seemed like forever. He was hugging me and kissing me when my mom walked in. I was out on the street two hours later."

Lex looked like he was reeling in shock. "Wait, so you're… gay?"

Tally chuckled again. "Last time I checked. Always have been."

"And you had a *boyfriend* in high school?"

"Yes," he answered patiently.

"And your mom…."

"Didn't want to deal with a gay eighteen-year-old that she'd never really liked anyway."

"You're really gay?"

Tally took Lex by the shoulders and turned him so they were facing each other.

"Lex. I'm really gay."

Lex took a deep shuddering breath, then started to slowly smile.

"Well, that explains some things about high school," he muttered.

Tally'd had enough. "I just spilled my guts all over this car. Don't you think it's time to tell me how the hell you know me?"

Lex didn't say anything. He closed his eyes for a second, then silently reached for his wallet and pulled out his driver's license. Reluctantly, he handed the card over to a confused Tally. Tally didn't understand until he looked closer and saw the name on the card. James A. Barry. At that second, every memory he had of a small, pudgy, brown-haired freshman came crashing into his consciousness. Suddenly it was hard to breathe.

"Oh my God. I had no idea...." He stared at Lex, bewildered and in shock, trying to find some similarity between the man in the car and that big-eyed kid with too much to say.

"I know you didn't, Tally."

"I can't believe you didn't say anything!"

"I didn't know what to say. Still don't, honestly."

"How can you even look at me without wanting to kick my ass?"

Lex chuckled. "You've still got a few inches on me. Plus, you're not that guy anymore. It didn't take me very long to realize that."

"I've never been that guy. At least I didn't want to be. When I was with Jeremy, I was like this. He wouldn't have even spoken to the person you knew at school." Tally wanted Lex to know that even then there had been some redeeming qualities—even if he'd never been the recipient of them.

"Then why act like asshole of the century?"

Tally shrugged. "It's the way my friends were, and I guess I was afraid that if I wasn't the king then they'd see me for who I really was."

"Which was gay?"

Tally nodded. "That, and the fact that I'm basically a big nerd." Lex chuckled and poked Tally in the side. "No, seriously. Even back then I'd have rather spent the weekend at Jeremy's house reading comic books and playing video games than going to parties and getting wasted. I hated all that shit."

"So you hid your real personality from your friends at school and you hid your school personality from your boyfriend. Wasn't it exhausting?"

"It was exhausting when I was here. Not when I was with Jeremy, though—that was such a relief."

"Until your mother found you two."

"Yep. That was the last time I saw him."

"I'm sorry, Tally. That... isn't what I expected."

Tally chuckled tiredly. "Why are you apologizing to me? I'm just grateful that you gave me a chance. No one else would."

Then Lex did something that shocked Tally. He reached up and cupped his face in a comforting gesture, rubbing his thumb across Tally's cheekbone.

"I'm glad I did," he murmured.

Before Tally could open his mouth to ask another question, his lips were covered with Lex's: soft, wine-flavored, everything Tally had wanted so desperately for the past too many weeks. He reached up tentatively and curled his hand around Lex's neck, testing the softness of his skin. Tally felt a small nibble, and he opened his lips, needing everything that little bite had offered. Lex's tongue slipped into his mouth, wet and delicious, making Tally moan.

His senses were reeling; he couldn't believe it was really happening. He'd have never guessed that his night would end up where it was—in the dark warmth of Lex's car with Lex's tongue twined around his and loving every second of it. He wanted to pull Lex over the stick shift and into his lap, wanted to strip every stitch of clothing off of him and taste all of his dark, secret places. He wanted to feel Lex come, hot and wet all over him, until they were both shivering piles of worn-out happiness. Tally's fingers tightened reflexively in Lex's hair, and he bit gently at the softness of that plump lower lip. He never wanted the kiss to end.

Apparently, he was the only one who felt that way. Lex pulled back and hung his head.

"God, I'm sorry."

"What for? Didn't you notice me kissing you back?" Tally went to pull him in for another kiss, but Lex resisted.

"But you work for me, and you just found out about me, *before*—and I didn't ask, and this is such a bad idea." He was stammering and tripping over his tongue.

"It was pretty amazing for being so bad." Tally couldn't help but smile, even though his hands were starting to shake.

"Bad ideas tend to be that way." Lex gave him a nervous glance. "I really am sorry. Just 'cause you're the one gay guy in town doesn't mean I should hit on you, right? Listen, I'd better go. I'll see you on Monday, okay?"

That last part stung. Tally *wanted* Lex to hit on him. So bad. He wanted Lex to want him period, but not because he was an available body. He'd spent years being just that. For perhaps the first time since Jeremy back in high school, he craved the connection. He wanted to be liked for him.

"I'll see you Monday," he mumbled and felt for the car handle, humiliated. What else was he supposed to say?

"Tally, I didn't mean—I just think it's a bad idea. We work together. It could get so awkward."

"Like now?"

Lex smiled ironically. "Yeah, like now. Can we just go back to being like it was? I mean like earlier tonight, not like at the beginning."

"Yeah… and Lex?"

"Yes?"

"No matter what, thank you for forgiving me. I've felt awful about what I did to you for years."

Lex nodded, and Tally stepped out of the car. "See you Monday," he said one more time before he closed the door.

TALLY ducked out of the rain and into Gianelli's Pizza. The shop hadn't been there when he'd left town, but pizza on a cold and boring Saturday night had sounded great. His grandma was out at her monthly poker game, and Tally had nothing but time on his hands. He wished more than anything that he could be at work with Lex. He'd spent the entire day reliving that kiss from the night before. Didn't matter how many times he told himself it was just a dumb kiss, nothing big at all. It *felt* big—and it was still replaying in his memory over and over, little flashes: the sensation of Lex's tongue sliding against his, the slight tug of fingers in his hair. It was even better than he'd imagined in his many fantasies. Tally wanted that kiss again and again. He wanted those lips everywhere. *Damn. Doing it again.* He walked up to the counter, hoping that perhaps his favorite pizza might distract him from those random waves of punishing lust for at least a few minutes.

"Hey, I called in an order for Carrington."

The man at the counter nodded and started ringing in the ticket he had waiting for Tally.

"Did I hear the name Carrington?" Tally turned at the sound of his name from the other side of the restaurant. *Oh, shit. Should've recognized that voice.* "Ho-lee fuck. Now that's a face I never thought I'd see again."

I was kind of hoping for the exact same thing. "Hey, Brock."

Brock-the-Rock. Tally's old second in command and the biggest asshole in the western hemisphere… after himself, of course. Tally had thought, hoped, that Brock would've been long gone from Rock Bay. Seemed he was wrong. The guy looked nearly the same, but puffed out, a bit like rising bread. His hair was still strawberry blond, and he clearly went tanning on a regular basis. Tally wanted to groan.

"I didn't expect to see you around here." He hoped his voice sounded casual. He sure as hell didn't feel casual. Things were starting to go so *well*, random Lex lust aside. He didn't need more ghosts from his past screwing things up.

"I heard you were back in town. Why didn't you look me up?"

I thought you made it pretty clear what our friendship meant to you a long time ago. "Just busy, I guess. I've been helping my grandma out a lot."

Brock whipped a card out of his pocket. "Well, I can't stay and talk, gotta get dinner back for the ol' ball and chain." He rolled his eyes. "But call me sometime. We'll get a beer."

Never in a million years. "Sure. I'll give you a call. We'll hang out."

"Right on! Hey, thanks, sweet cheeks," Brock said to the girl who'd handed him his pizza. He chucked her gently on the chin, then winked at Tally and chuckled low in his throat. "Nice," he whispered as he turned toward the door.

Tally thought he might gag. The girl might have been sixteen… if he was being generous. Tally knew she was part of his morning high school crowd. She was fresh-faced and sweet, totally not interested. Plus, Brock was *married*. Tally hoped that could at least mean fidelity in the short time it took to pick up a pizza.

Brock waved enthusiastically from the door, hot cardboard boxes balanced on one hip. *What an asshole.* Tally waved back, willing Brock to get the hell out.

"You're friends with him, Tally?" He hadn't expected the girl, *Lacey*, he remembered now, to talk. They'd smiled at each other but never had any real conversations.

He shook his head vehemently. "No. Sorry if he came on a little strong."

She made a disgusted face. "That guy comes in for pizza every Saturday, and let's just say tonight was nothing compared to what I usually get. He's a total horndog."

Tally had to laugh. She'd never been so vocal in the coffee shop. "Listen, I know I'm just the coffee guy, but if you want me to talk to your manager, I will."

"Nah. He knows. He said if the jerk ever really touches me he'll get rid of him, but until then he doesn't want to make waves. That guy has a lot of clout with the country club crowd. I usually stay in the back if I know he's in the restaurant."

Tally cringed. *Fucking small towns.* "Sorry, hon."

She gave him a shy smile. "It's okay. I'll see you Monday?"

"Actually, no. I'm not working early mornings anymore."

"I'll stop by after school to say hi."

Tally was a bit worried. "Uh, listen, Lacey—"

She giggled softly. "Give me a break, Tally. I just never had a sibling. You're cool, protective, kind of like having an older brother to laugh with—nothing like octopus fingers out there." She gestured at the parking lot where Brock's car had been.

He smiled, relieved. "Well, then, I'll see you Monday after school."

Lacey handed him his newly boxed pizza. "It's a date!"

CHAPTER
Six

AWKWARD. God. Shit. Why did I kiss him? Because you wanted to. Now you get to deal with the fallout. Maybe there wouldn't be any. Maybe he and Tally were both mature enough that one little *amazing, sexy, totally full-on delicious* kiss wouldn't mean days of feeling weird working together. Or maybe he was full of shit.

Tally was due to be at the shop in minutes. Lex had opened on his own for a few hours, and as soon as Tally got there, they'd finish the morning rush together. Then Lex would thankfully get to retreat to his office and get his battle plan for the permit office ready, or at least valiantly try to work and not spend all of his time thinking about the flavor of Tally's lips. He'd been able to push thoughts of the kiss out of his mind that weekend—for a few minutes at a time, at least. Then, without warning, it would come back, flashes of Tally's tongue slipping into his mouth, those warm fingers curling around the back of his neck. Lex shivered, then squeezed his eyes shut in frustration. He wanted to pound his fist against the wall until it bled but was grown up enough to know that would mean hours of work fixing the dent in the drywall and touching up the paint.

I can do this. It won't be weird.

The overhead bell rang, and Lex's stomach flip-flopped before taking a nosedive to his toes. Tally. Shit.

"Morning, boss, how were things over the weekend?"

Long. I missed you. He stared at a chip in the old wood flooring. "It was okay. Saturday was quiet, but there was a big line before church yesterday since it was so cold and rainy."

"You could've called me if you needed me to come in. I wasn't doing anything, really."

Lex finally looked up. His cheeks turned pink at the sight of Tally's long-lashed brown eyes, eyes that were currently looking at him appraisingly, like he was wondering what was wrong. Not too surprising, since Lex was acting like a sixth grader with an awkward crush.

"Lex, is this about Friday night?" He seemed concerned and sweet, and Lex wanted so bad to close the foot and a half between them and sink his tongue back into Tally's mouth so it could be happy again.

"No. I'm fine. What do you mean?"

"Fine?" Tally chuckled. "Okay. Just remember that I really liked kissing you, that I'd kiss you again in a heartbeat if you would let me. There's no bad anything on my side, okay?"

Lex nodded, his heart skipping at just the thought of that kiss. "I need to use the bathroom. Can you watch the shop for a few minutes?"

Tally chuckled, and Lex knew why. They both knew Tally was perfectly capable of watching the shop for more than a few minutes, and he *also* probably knew Lex was asking because he was nervous. About the kiss. *Moron.*

The rest of the morning was painful, in a comfortable sort of way. They slid into their respective jobs with ease. Tally had conquered the high school kids days before, smiling and flirting with the giggling girls as they dropped their dollars in the tip jar while they batted their eyelashes at him. The older crowd, which began to trickle in just as Tally was tying his apron, had started to warm up to him too. Women in tracksuits with strollers and friends smiled at him, tentative but genuine, as he took their orders and chatted. Lex noticed that Tally had learned names, asked about their gardens or the dinner they'd made over the weekend. Made them feel like he cared. They guy was a natural. Lex supposed it was from all the years of waiting tables. It was fun to watch, all the same—all those prickly people turning slowly toward him. He knew from experience working at a similar shop in college, that it was hard enough to win over people who knew nothing about you. Tally was managing it with people who would've been happy to kick him in the knees a few short weeks before. Impressive.

But it was still hard to be in the shop with Tally. *He* was hard. Almost constantly. And that one little fact made Lex want to curl up and die. Every time they bumped up against each other, every time he heard Tally's low flirtatious chuckle or smelled him or thought of how perfect it felt when Tally's tongue slid up against his, up he went again. *Jesus.*

"Hey, Lex?" It took him a moment to realize Tally was talking to him.

"Oh, sorry, I was spacing." There it was, that sexy chuckle that made his stomach all weak.

"Sherri wants a peppermint mocha, and I just noticed the peppermint syrup is empty."

"Oh, I'm sure I have another one of those in the storeroom. I'll be right back."

Breathe, moron. He stood in the storeroom, peppermint syrup bottle squeezed tightly in his hand, willing his body to get over the reaction it always had to Tally. Why did he even bother? No matter how hard he concentrated, it just got stronger.

Lex was grateful when it was time for him to hit his office and do paperwork. Entering information into his accounting program had never been Lex's idea of entertainment, but he was exhausted. Hours wanting to kiss Tally, wishing he could get right up against him and inhale as long as possible, had worn Lex out. Mind-numbing repetitive tasks were all he had the brain energy for.

He forced himself to concentrate on the work that honestly did need to get done. There was usually a stack of papers and invoices the size of a football field to be entered into his computer. It had gotten better since he had Tally to take over in the afternoon, but paper organization had never been Lex's strong suit, and it was still something that would constantly need work. Lex started with the invoices, entering them methodically and making sure they were allocated to the correct accounts. When he'd just pulled out his stack of cash register receipts from the previous week, he was startled by a shout from the front room.

"Hey, Lex, Amy's here. Should I send her back, or are you coming out?" Tally's friendly call startled Lex out of the quiet trance he'd been in. As much as he hated doing the picky little accounting shit, it was probably the only thing that occupied his mind enough to push Tally out of it.

"Yeah, send her back," he called and dropped the pile of papers he still needed to deal with back in their basket. *Later*....

"Hey, sweetie," Amy chirped as she dropped into the only other chair in his office.

"Hey, Ames. What's up today?"

"First of all, this latte is divine. Either you're a master at training, or he's just naturally gifted."

"Lemme taste." Lex held out his hand. What he'd already had of Tally's was good but—*ohhh*. Heaven in a cup. "What *is* this?"

"I don't know. He asked if I'd be the guinea pig for something he'd been working on."

Lex had to know. "Tally, can you come back here?" he called.

A few seconds later a startled looking Tally stuck his head around the doorjamb. "Yeah?"

"What on earth did you put in here? It's amazing."

"Hold on."

He came back after a minute or so holding a syrup bottle with a piece of masking tape that had "T-special" written on it. "It's a special mix I've been working on. It's based on this cake they serve at Le Gateau, one of the restaurants I used to work at in Seattle."

"Le Gateau?" Amy asked.

"Yeah, it's a dessert cafe right outside of Pacific Place. Next time you're in Seattle, you should go there. I can't even begin to tell you how good it is. Anyway, there was this cake with cherries and almonds and apricots and a bunch of other stuff. I used to get it with coffee after work sometimes. The combination of the two was perfect. I thought it might work as a drink."

"You were right. Amazing job. Do you mind if I make it the special next week? Maybe we can advertise it to go with one of the pastries."

Tally grinned, his face so open and beautiful. It was the first time Lex had seen him looking completely happy since they'd met. Even before, in high school, he'd never had such a genuine grin on his face. Not that Lex remembered, anyway. It made his palms itch to slip around Tally's face, and his lips wanted to.... Damn. Not again. He focused on Tally's excitement instead of his mouth.

"You really want to make it the special? That's great! I thought it would go maybe with that plum crumble, or if that's too much fruit it might be good as a contrast to the bittersweet brownies, you know, sweeter to balance out the dark?"

Lex smiled in return and started to wonder if, awkward after-kiss feelings or not, hiring Tally might have been the best thing he'd ever done. The guy had great instincts.

"Let's run it with the brownie. They're popular anyway. But write down the proportions in that syrup. We don't want to run out in case it's a huge hit."

"Already did!" Tally slipped a note card from his back pocket and handed it to Lex. He knew Lex kept a recipe file for all the special mixes he'd concocted over the past few years.

"Thanks—" Just then the shop bell rang, and Tally froze before tossing them a rueful smile and jogging back to the front to wait on the new customer.

"You do know you just made his entire week, right?"

"Mine too. Give me another sip of that." He drank appreciatively. "You know what, go out and have Tally make you another one. This is mine."

"Hey!" Amy laughed. "Oh, I almost forgot. Perfect coffee addled my brains. That new nurse, Mason, in my ER that I was telling you about a few weeks ago?"

Lex groaned. He'd forgotten their conversation about the nurse in the wake of everything that had happened lately. It had been one of the times that Amy tried to set him up with someone she knew from Astoria. He routinely blew her efforts off.

"I was trying to forget. I'm really not into blind dating, Ames."

"I know, but he's cute, Lexie, and he's asked me about you a few times."

"How old is he again?"

"Twenty. But he's really mature."

Lex shook his head. He didn't want some twenty-year-old nurse, he wanted Tal—Lex caught himself thinking about exactly how much he did want Tally for what had to be the hundredth time that day and cringed. What was it going to take to get over one kiss?

"You know what? Give the kid my number. I'll ask him to dinner."

"Really?" Amy looked ridiculously pleased with herself.

"Yes, really. Dinner only, though."

"Yeah, yeah. Dinner only."

After Amy left, humming to herself and happy that she'd finally gotten Lex a date, or at least the potential of a date, Lex slipped out into the hallway to watch Tally. He'd done it a few times a day since Tally had started taking the afternoons. Lex told himself that it was just good business to keep tabs on his employee, and he was right. It was. But it was also pure joy to watch Tally work, wiping the counter, taking orders, leaning over to get something from the shelf under the espresso machine. Lex groaned. It was not in his best interest to watch Tally bend over. Those artfully faded jeans and that *uh-maaaz-ing* butt had a way of making Lex lose the ability to breathe.

Lex was in the middle of staring at Tally when his cell rang. Tally jumped a little at the ringer.

"You scared me. I didn't know you were in here." He smiled nervously.

"Just watching my shop. I miss it in the afternoons, sometimes."

Tally chuckled as Lex hit talk on his phone and stepped back into the office.

IT HAD been a hell of a day. Tally had managed to psych himself up so he didn't act like a complete fool the second he saw Lex again. He managed to make it work, at least he thought so. He smiled, calm and friendly like he practiced Sunday night, and even kept himself from throwing Lex over the counter and kissing him like he wanted to so desperately. That part was nearly impossible. Those awkward little smiles, nervous chuckles, and the way Lex held his breath for a second every time Tally brushed by him; it was *killing* him. Even the sight of Lex enjoying the drink Tally had made in hopes of impressing him was enough to warm the insides of his stomach. He wasn't ready to give up.

They had so much chemistry; he didn't think Lex could pretend to ignore it forever. Lex Barry was going to be in his bed, damn it. Well, *a bed somewhere*, he amended, thinking of his little cramped twin. All Tally needed was time to wear him down....

LEX drummed his fingers on the steering wheel of his BMW. *I shouldn't have said yes.* The pit in his stomach was telling him that it had been a horrible idea to accept a date with someone else when all he could think about, the only person he was even aware of in his world, was Tally. Tally, who'd said he would happily kiss Lex again and again if only he had the chance. Lex's stomach tightened the same way it did every time he thought of Tally saying that. It was unfair to the poor kid… Mason, right? His phone beeped with a message.

> I just got here but I'll have the host seat me. The reservation's under Anderson.

Lex swore, typed back a quick "ok," and gunned the gas on his car. He needed to get to the restaurant quickly, or else he'd end up turning around and heading straight for Tally. He wanted to. Hell, he wanted to. It was too late, though. If he ditched his poor blind date, he'd be the biggest bastard in the universe. He already felt like a bastard for going on the date in the first place when there was someone else he wanted to be with. Lex knew he had to smile at the guy and seem pleasant and interested, and, even harder, he had to keep his mind off the way Tally tasted—which was amazing. Lex gritted his teeth together. *What a mistake.* The only thing he wasn't sure of was which part was the bigger mistake.

The restaurant was nice, wood paneled, dark, and candlelit, perfect for a date. Booths surrounded a thickly carpeted main dining area, and lush acoustic guitar was subtly piped in through hidden speakers. *Laying it on a bit thick, weren't they?* The place practically screamed romance.

Lex squashed the picture his brain made of him and Tally sitting in the intimate darkness, sharing wine and trading bites of a dinner roll, kissing sauce from each other's lips. Lex ground his nails into his palm.

Shit. He knew he needed to stop making everything about Tally but, God, lately everything *was* about Tally. The way he felt when Tally was near, the way Tally's voice sounded in the morning, all gravelly and low.

The hostess led him to a table where an undeniably cute but very young-looking man sat waiting. He cringed inside, knowing it wasn't right for him to be there, but he was determined to at least have a nice dinner and hopefully make a new friend.

"Hi, Mason. Lex." He stuck out his hand as he was sitting down.

"Hey, Lex. Amy's told me a lot about you."

Lex smiled his nicest smile and reached for the wine menu.

TALLY ground the heels of his hands into the counter and tried not to scream. Lex had come, only a few minutes earlier, with a brand new copied key to the shop and told Tally he'd have to lock up on his own that evening. Tally was proud of Lex for taking a night off, *finally*, and doing something on his own, and happy that Lex trusted him enough to close up his precious shop all alone… until Tally found out why Lex was leaving early. *That* news had him grinding his teeth and wishing he could kick something. He had a blind date with some kid from the hospital that Amy had hooked him up with. A date? Fuck.

Tally's mind went wild, picturing them at some intimate, expensive, candlelit table, the kind he used to serve fifty-dollar steaks at. They'd talk, they'd laugh, share funny anecdotes about Amy, bond over their love of French film or something. Maybe Lex would give the kid a kiss goodnight with those soft amazing lips. He pictured Lex's hand coming up to cup the guy's jaw, thumb running across a cheekbone before his lips settled in.

He made a retching sound in his throat. Tally didn't want Lex kissing anyone else. *Kiss me instead! I'll make us dinner, and then we can spend the night naked and touching and… and that kid can't have you, you're mine!* Tally did scream then, but quietly in his throat. It didn't feel as good as letting a real one out, and he sure as hell knew he couldn't kick anything, as much as he wanted to.

Why was Lex torturing them?

His rationale made sense, he supposed. But it was just *dumb*. They worked together, yeah—Tally worked for Lex—but they were both adults and so completely hot for each other. Like "take my clothes off now" hot for each other. Tally felt it, and he knew damn well that Lex did too. It was so frustrating! Lex didn't have any higher boss to answer to; he could make his own choices. Tally couldn't believe he was choosing to go on a date with someone else, a damn kid for shit's sake, when they could be eating dinner, kissing, taking every last stitch of their clothing off and fucking each other for hours, *days*, until neither one of them could breathe.

Lex had seemed hesitant to tell Tally about the date. He'd probably known it would sting. He was right. It did. And Tally hated it. If he'd known what that phone call was about on Monday, he'd have come up with some excuse to make Lex hang up. But he hadn't, and because of that, Lex was out on a Friday-night date with someone else while he seethed in silence.

It was seven thirty. Tally had locked up the shop, cleaned all the machines, and was technically allowed to go home. He had no idea how he would stand it, though, sitting in his room or on his grandmother's couch and pretending he wasn't going insane. Pretending he wasn't jealous as fucking hell. He picked up the shop's phone and dialed his grandmother's house.

"Hey, Grams, Lex needs some help organizing the stock room. I'm going to get in late tonight, okay? Don't wait up."

She said something about how it was nice that he was getting overtime, and he agreed, not really listening, before he hung up the phone. Tally had no idea what he was going to do; he just knew he couldn't stand to be sitting, making polite small talk with his grandmother.

So this is what jealousy feels like?

Tally had never felt it before, and he sure as shit didn't like it. He'd felt *envy*, of someone's nice apartment or swanky job, but never this possessive need to roar "He's mine!" at whatever unassuming little boy had dared to try and take Lex away from him. And it seemed to come out of nowhere—yeah, he thought Lex was hot, and he wanted to get him naked like there was no tomorrow, but what the hell?

Tally stomped back to the stockroom, hoping that it was as big of a jumble as it usually was so he could spend some energy cleaning it and hopefully make himself feel the tiniest bit better. He wasn't disappointed. Lex may have been a genius with the customers, but he was lucky the shop was small. His mess of a storeroom would never fly in a bigger restaurant. The flavored syrups were packed haphazardly onto shelves, neither organized alphabetically or by type. There were cups and plates and napkins shoved in every available nook, and sealed bags of beans were stacked in a tower that would only take a whisper of a breeze to tumble over.

Perfect, something to do.

Tally pushed his sleeves up and started to pull everything off the shelves. He knew he'd have to make a big mess before any organization could come out of it. He piled the stuff in the hallway in somewhat of an order so that he'd have a bit of a head start when he went to put it back.

At least two hours later, he'd gotten all of the syrups organized in alphabetical order, bottles lined up perfectly, jewel bright and shiny along two shelves. He was about to tackle the awkwardly shaped bags of cups and lids when he heard the back door squeak open. It was right about then that he started feeling nervous. It wasn't as if he'd asked Lex if he wanted his entire stockroom rearranged.

"Tally?" Lex's voice sounded perplexed but not angry. "What on earth are you doing?"

Tally stuck his head out of the stockroom into the hallway and tried his best to look sheepish.

"The stockroom needed to be organized. I needed to blow off some steam. Is that okay?"

Lex cocked his head and gave Tally an odd look. "Yeah, I guess. Is everything all right?"

"It's fine," Tally lied. "I can just finish up down here if you want to go to bed. It's a late night for you."

Lex rolled his eyes. "It's nine. I'm not quite ready for the early-bird special yet."

"How was your—" Tally couldn't even say the word, although he was dying to find out.

"Fine. I'm going to the movies with him next weeken—"

That was it. Tally couldn't hear another word.

"No!" He stalked over to Lex, grabbed him by the shoulders, and shoved him up against the wall. "No more dates with twenty-year-old kids. No more movies, no more dinners. *I* want you. And you want me too." With that, he slammed his mouth against Lex's, delving with his insistent tongue until Lex opened up and let him in.

Tally knew he was pushing it, that Lex could fire him, never talk to him again, pull an arm back and punch the shit out of him—but at that moment, he didn't care. He was kissing Lex again, and it was *glorious*.

LEX was drowning in bliss. He was finally getting to do what he'd wanted to do for five long and torturous days. Days? Who was he kidding? It had been weeks since he started dreaming about Tally's lips, years, if he were completely honest with himself. Even making that date on Monday hadn't changed a thing. Fuck, *going* on the date hadn't changed a thing. Every moment of the time he was with Tally, all he could think about was last Friday's kiss. Most of the time when he wasn't with Tally, it felt like his body was counting the minutes until it could be near Tally again. It was driving Lex out of his ever-loving mind.

He wrapped his arms around Tally's neck and moaned his approval. Mistake or not, he'd never had anything in his entire life that lit him on fire the way Tallis Carrington could. He couldn't make himself end it before it even had a chance to begin.

Fuck the consequences.

Lex slid his tongue along Tally's, shivering at the silky wetness. Tally tugged at his shirt, and Lex reached down to help him, all of a sudden needing those big blunt fingers all over his skin.

"Upstairs," he murmured and sighed when a finger trailed gently up his spine.

"What about the storeroom?"

Lex chuckled and nipped at Tally's damp lower lip. "Screw the storeroom. You can fix it tomorrow. I want you."

"You sure? I mean, we can forget that I just kissed you again."

"Kiss? Is that what that was?" Lex huffed out a soft laugh. "Can you forget? I haven't been able to."

Tally shook his head. "No. I've thought about kissing you just about every second since last weekend."

He grabbed Tally's hand and pulled. "You want to come with me, then? Put ourselves out of our misery?"

Tally nodded and gripped his hand tightly. They tripped and ran up the stairs, Lex's impatience and Tally's excitement making their steps awkward and fumbling. Lex threw his door open and yanked Tally inside before slamming it shut again. Tally pulled him close, winding big strong arms around him. *Yes. That's what I want.*

"Nice place," Tally murmured, his chin resting on Lex's hair.

"Thanks. Bedroom's that way." He gestured behind him with his head.

Tally grinned. "No wine? No candlelight dinner? You're gonna think I'm easy."

Lex groaned into a laugh and started to walk them backward down the hallway.

"I sure as shit hope you're easy. I'm going nuts here. You're not allowed to throw a guy against the wall and ravish him if you're not planning to put out."

It was Tally's turn to chuckle. He pulled off Lex's shirt and tossed it on the floor of the hallway before crossing the threshold into Lex's bedroom.

"Not a rule I was aware of, but I'll be happy to follow it."

He leaned over and kissed Lex, then trailed his lips downward, making short sucking stops at his neck, his nipples, his stomach. Lex squeezed his eyes shut and threw his head back.

When Lex opened his eyes and realized that Tally was on the floor and had Lex's slacks unzipped and halfway down his thighs, he nearly choked on the lust that raged through him. He impatiently kicked out of his pants and kneeled down next to Tally, worming his hands under Tally's soft black T-shirt. He peeled it up and off, then held the warm fabric to his face and inhaled.

"Smells like you," he mumbled before dropping the shirt and leaning forward to suck on Tally's bottom lip.

Tally's hands were all over, running across the heated skin of Lex's back, through his hair, slipping underneath his briefs to cup his ass. Lex wriggled his own fingers between them to work on the stubborn top button of Tally's jeans. It seemed to evade his best efforts.

"C'mon. Off," he whined against Tally's mouth, tugging ineffectually.

Tally made a noise halfway between a groan and a chuckle, full of need and want, then he ripped his lips away from Lex's and impatiently yanked the button and zipper down. He stood and pushed at the jeans until they, like Lex's pants, were gone.

Lex tore back his covers and dove onto the bed, sprawling to reach across to the drawer on the other side that had everything they'd need. He was distracted by Tally crawling, hot, velvety skin writhing up his back. Tally ground his hips into the crack of Lex's ass, the fabric that still covered it frustrating and way too thick. Lex wanted to spread his legs and beg Tally to claim him, he wanted to arch his back and let out primal cries of possession. *You're mine. No one else again. Ever.* The urge scared him a little, but not enough that he didn't rummage through his drawer and retrieve the condoms and lube with a triumphant grunt.

"Now, Tally. I can't fucking wait."

Tally paused. "Who's going to…?"

"I don't care, just… oh God, in me."

Lex rolled out from under Tally and ripped his briefs down his legs, wriggling until he could kick them off his ankles. He worked at Tally's too, until they were both naked and he could open his thighs and cradle Tally inside of them. He let out a satisfied sigh. Not satisfied enough, though. His hips wanted to grind, he wanted to feel that hardness slipping in and out between his cheeks, pushing into his body. He gripped Tally as hard as he could and pulled so he could feel the pressure he was so desperately craving.

"Lex, you're killing me." Tally's voice was hot in his ear, only serving to make him want more.

"Then kill me back. I want to feel you everywhere."

TALLY took Lex at his word, slithering down and using his tongue to taste the man he'd wanted since the first second he saw him. He was warm and clean, and he smelled like heaven. Lex moaned and rolled his hips.

"What are you doing? I want you *now*."

"Tasting. I like the way you taste."

With that Tally licked slowly, savoringly, up the length of Lex's painfully hard erection, loving the whimper that his movement produced. Then he opened his mouth and took the tip in, suckling and reveling in the taste of Lex's precome on his tongue.

"Ungh, when I said kill me back I didn't *mean it*. Ah, fuck, that feels amazing." Lex's voice was panicked and sexy, and he arched his hips, pushing himself into the back of Tally's throat. Tally was in heaven. "I'm gonna come if you don't knock it off," Lex grunted.

Tally released Lex's cock with a satisfied pop and rolled him over. He kissed Lex's spine, his lean muscled shoulders, the sensitive skin on the back of his neck. Lex groaned and pushed his ass right into Tally's cock, grinding with all of his strength. Tally pushed right back, just to hear the satisfied groan he loved so much already, then he methodically worked his way down until he could taste the musky skin between Lex's cheeks. The first tentative taste had Lex keening, the next had him scolding, begging, wanting more, harder, everything. It was the hottest thing Tally had ever heard in his life. By far.

After long hot minutes, Tally dragged himself up so he could reach the condom that was carelessly tossed on a pillow.

"Finally," Lex breathed and rolled over so he could watch Tally put it on with hot eyes. Then he opened his thighs again, making room for Tally's hips, and said: "Come here."

Tally had no choice but to listen. Lex's hand slipped around his erection, spreading the slippery lube he'd poured in his palm and guiding Tally closer to where they both wanted him to be. Then he lifted his hips and lined Tally up and pushed, and, *oh God*, there was nothing better in the whole world. Tally's breath hitched, and he squeezed his eyes shut and tried not to scream out loud at the incomparable heat, the tightness, and how he felt so agonizingly close to Lex. It was new and scary and oh so consuming. Lex's legs wrapped around Tally's hips, and strong fingers threaded through his hair, gripping.

"Open your eyes." Tally did what he was told, opening his eyes until he was focused on Lex's golden-green stare. Lex shifted his hips experimentally. "Mmmm... amazing. I want more." Lex's soft murmur was punctuated by a lusty but tender kiss and another roll of his hips.

Tally kissed him again and again as he started to move, watching Lex's face as he moaned and threw his arm back to grab onto the headboard.

"Harder," Lex whispered.

"Hmm?" Tally was too busy spinning in sensation to hear.

"Do it harder. Ugh. Please?" Lex lifted his hips impatiently, panting, mouth open to drag in air.

Tally grinned. He should have known he had a bossy one on his hands. He lifted Lex's hips from the bed and angled his own so he'd rub over Lex's sensitive prostate. Then he withdrew slowly, torturing the keening Lex, and slammed his hips back in until he was buried completely. Lex tipped his head back and groaned guttural and low, his knuckles white from the grip he had on his headboard.

"Like that?" Tally huffed, barely able to speak from the force of the lust that made his head spin.

"*Fuck*... yes. Again."

Tally did it again. And again. And again. Driving into Lex and running his hands all over that smooth peaches-and-cream skin. God, he'd never get tired of touching. Tally felt the tightening start, an orgasm that pulsed down his spine and threatened to explode him into pieces.

"*Lex*. I want...."

Lex gripped Tally's hips with the strength of his thighs. Tally reached between them to palm Lex's erection, finding it hard and slick.

"I know, Tal. Me too. So close. You feel so, *ahhhhh*."

Tally felt it then, the pulsing, Lex's muscles tightening and gripping him until he choked on a wail and came himself, massive waves of pleasure bottlenecking through one intense point of release, continuing until it felt like there wouldn't be anything left of him to let go by the end of it. In shock, he flopped down on Lex's sweaty chest, breathing hard and head spinning.

"Holy shit, that was intense," Lex finally whispered.

"No kidding," he replied.

Tally rolled off of Lex eventually and cleaned up with some tissues from the side table. He was about to turn and ask Lex if he needed a shower when he heard a soft, huffing snore. Lex was passed completely and nearly instantly out, hand over his eyes, legs sprawled on top of the comforter. Tally chuckled and tugged gently until the comforter came loose from under Lex's legs. Lex moaned a little and turned over but didn't wake. Tally simply slid into the bed next to him and reached over to make sure Lex's alarm was set. Then he dragged the covers over his shoulders, tugged the sleeping Lex into his arms, and closed his eyes.

TALLY woke in the darkness to an insistent beeping unlike the one he was used to. It took a few seconds to process. Lex… him… *last night*. Tally grinned and sat up slowly. He turned the alarm off and rolled over to shake the still sleeping man by his side. Just putting his hand on Lex's shoulder made him shudder pleasantly. He wanted to start all over, touch Lex in all the places he missed the night before, make him moan and come and shiver with pleasure.

"Lex, babe, wake up." It felt good to say it, but scary, like he wasn't sure if he had the right. It had been years since he'd woken up in the bed of someone he actually liked. Someone he wanted to be with again and again. He felt something light and achy rise in his chest. It was terrifying and amazing, and he wasn't sure if he wanted to wallow in it or push it away.

"Hmmm?" Lex's voice was disoriented and groggy. It took him a little while to open his eyes and sit up. "Tally? Why are you still…?"

He didn't finish his sentence. He didn't have to. Tally could see the look on his face. Lex was surprised he was still there. Unpleasantly surprised. That tender fragile feeling, the hope that had been growing, cracked and shattered into a million little pieces. *He doesn't see me any differently than anyone else.*

"I get it. Wouldn't want to be caught waking up with the trash. I'll be gone in a minute."

"Tally, that's not what I meant. It just can't be this way, with sleepovers and, oh shit, I'm not making any sense. " Lex sat up and rubbed at his eyes.

Seconds before, Tally would've found the gesture endearing, maybe even adorable. Instead, he wanted to punch the sleepy, sexy look off Lex's face. His gut clenched. If he didn't get the fuck out of there in about thirty seconds he was going to puke.

"No. You're making perfect sense. It's no problem. I've got my stuff, and I'm going. I won't be late to work. I'm not *fired*, am I?"

Lex looked horrified. "No, no… of course not. Tally, wait."

"Gotta go. I'll see you at ten."

Tally slammed his shoes on and ran, jogging through the apartment and down the stairs until he was locking the front door of the shop with shaking fingers. How could he have been so stupid? He'd thought there was real emotion in Lex's eyes when they were together—respect, if nothing else.

Tally had been a low-class trick one too many times back in Seattle—wealthy businessman picks up the hot waiter and leaves a tip before taking off in the morning. Tally'd hated it. It was a scenario he'd never thought he'd be stuck in again. God, Lex must really think he was a fucking asshole. Why would he want to have Tally in his bed for more than the thirty minutes it took to get off? He was the town reject, the jerk who stuffed Lex in his locker, a grown man who had to come live off his grandmother because he couldn't take care of himself. Tally slammed his palm against the steering wheel of his grandmother's car and started the engine.

Great. Now I'm going to have to explain to her where I was too. Just in case having it happen in the first place didn't suck enough. I need to get the fuck outta this town. Today.

The fact that he didn't have anywhere to go made him want to scream.

CHAPTER
Seven

LEX was in absolute agony. What had he done? There were so many levels of stupidity to the previous night, the morning. The worst part was, he didn't know what to torture himself about the most. He slept with his employee; he slept with Tallis effing Carrington, who was, well, everything he was. And the sex? Oh *God*. It was consuming and passionate, tender and raw, and... there really were no words. Lex was still reeling from it. But he hadn't expected Tally to want to stay. He'd been so surprised when they woke up. Lex groaned out loud. He didn't even know how to explain that look he knew was on his face. He wasn't ashamed of Tally; he'd never be embarrassed to have him in his bed, in his life... but that was just it. Tally would never be in his life. Because the second he had a chance, he'd be gone.

If only his brain had been turned on, he could've explained himself, that none of the reasons why they couldn't play house together had a thing to do with Tally not being good enough for him. He only hoped he had a chance. Lex pulled his cell out of his pocket and looked at the time. Nine. He groaned. Could the morning be going any slower? Even the rush, which usually kept him so busy he didn't notice the hours slipping by, had seemed sluggish. The crowds of weekenders desperate for their coffee fix didn't distract him at all. It seemed like every few seconds, he'd see Tally's face from earlier, that crushed look, and he'd want to vomit.

Who'd have ever thought that I would have the power to hurt Tallis Carrington?

It sure as hell didn't feel good.

Tally came in at nine thirty, a half hour early. Lex had looked up when the bell overhead rang, ready to greet a customer, but when he saw that familiar body in that one pair of worn perfectly and almost too-tight jeans, Lex's heart started to race. Tally looked up at him, his face masked. The humiliation from earlier was gone, as was any trace of his usual humor or enthusiasm. Lex opened his mouth to talk, but Tally beat him to it.

"Morning, Mister Barry. I came in early so I could finish the supply room before my shift. I'm sorry I left it in such a mess last night."

Oh, Tally. "Wait. Come here." Lex just wanted to touch him, to make the past twenty-four hours go away. Tally regarded him with an aloof but respectful look. "Tally, about this morning, I didn't mean to hurt you." Tally winced. *Shit, wrong thing to say.* "I mean, I really like you, I'm not—" Lex broke off, feeling tongue-tied and awkward. He didn't know what to say, how to explain any of it. Not to the stone wall that was in front of him.

"Can I go work on the supply room now?" Tally asked, his voice nothing but polite. It was horrible.

Lex nodded miserably. All of the things he wanted to say, the explanation he had planned, evaporated from his mind. It was like they'd reversed roles, Tally being unapproachable and coldly polite, him with his guts twisting, wishing there was something he could do to erase the past.

With Tally in the back room, Lex started to breathe again. He tried, at least. The gnawing, awful feeling didn't go away, though. He had a trickle of customers but nothing to keep him even remotely busy enough to forget. It was the time he was usually the most dead during the day. It didn't take long for him to wipe down the spotless counters or make sure the tables were lined up and clean, chairs tucked under the way they belonged. He could hear muffled thumps from the room behind the shop. Just the awareness of Tally back there working made the hairs on the back of his neck stand. His body was still waiting, wanting Tally's touch, his nearness. *Fuck, shit, fuck.*

Lex strode to the front door and hung his "be back in ten" sign on the door before he locked it. It was something he hated to do, but this, this, *thing* between him and Tally needed to be fixed. Immediately. Lex groaned. *Just in case anyone ever thought it was a good idea to sleep with an employee.* He rounded the corner into the storeroom just as Tally was coming out of it, dusting towel in hand.

"I was just finishing, Mr. Barry. I can get started on my shift now."

Lex held out his arm, trapping Tally in the storeroom. "Tally, shit. Knock it off with the Mr. Barry crap!" He hadn't meant for his voice to come out angry, hadn't meant for a lot of things to happen.

"What do you want me to do, huh? Come in here and act like everything's the same? I'm trying to be professional. I can't afford to lose my job over that big fucking mistake we made."

"Mistake?" Why did it suck so much to hear Tally call it that?

Tally lost it. "Yeah, it was a mistake! It was a mistake for me to think that you might actually have feelings for me. It was a mistake to want you so bad that I risked the one fucking thing that's gone okay for me in the last million and a half years. Don't tell me you don't fucking agree. I saw the look on your face when you realized I was still in your bed this morning."

"Tally, I didn't mean—"

"Do you know they used to leave me tips?" Tally growled.

Lex stared at him silently. "What?"

"When I first got to the city, fresh out of butt-fuck Washington, kicked to the streets by my mother, I used to meet businessmen sometimes, waiting tables or at the bars I snuck into. They were rich, handsome, older than me. They'd flirt and ask for my number. I thought they really liked me. I'd get my hopes up that one of them was going to rescue me from the shit hole my life had turned into, like I was fucking Cinderella or something. But when I'd wake up in the morning they were gone. Every time. You know, sometimes there would even be cash on my dresser. Like I was a fucking prostitute. A few times I was so hungry that I took it."

Lex's throat tightened. "That's awful. I'm sorry." What the hell else was he supposed to say? Lex felt like the biggest ass in the world.

Tally shrugged. "I thought I was past that. I swore years ago that it would never happen again. But the way you looked at me this morning...."

He knew it was probably the wrong thing to do, but Lex couldn't take it anymore. He stepped closer, as close as he could get, and cupped Tally's face in his hands. Then he kissed him, hard and long, not even caring if he got a response.

"It's not like that," he finally whispered, drawing his lips away from Tally's still mouth.

"Tell me then. What's it like?"

He looked so angry. Lex knew it was hurt making his face twist like that, but for a second he thought he saw the boy he used to be terrified of. It would've been easier to run back to the front of his shop and avoid the whole thing, but he'd made the mess, at least part of it, and he knew he needed to be grown up enough to fix it.

"I'm not ashamed of you, Tal. It's just—" He gulped. "—I can't let myself fall for you, okay? And sleepovers, movies, dinners, anything more than just sex—it would be so easy to let myself... kid myself into thinking it was more."

"What if it is more? Why aren't you allowed to have feelings for me?"

"Because you're leaving, Tally! In however long it takes you to get your shit back together, or money enough for a few months' rent, you'll be out the door and back in Seattle. What happens if I've bled my stupid heart out all over you by then?"

Tally's eyes widened. "*That's* what this morning was about?"

"This morning was about me panicking over every single reason why I can't be doing exactly what we did. This—fuck. This morning was a big mess. It *is* a big mess."

Tally was silent for a few long moments. The stillness stretched awkwardly between them. "Doesn't have to be," he finally muttered.

Lex dragged his hand through his hair and looked at Tally imploringly. "And how exactly do you propose to make this not a mess?"

"By doing exactly what you said. No sleepovers, no dates, no feelings beyond friendship, just two guys who haven't had a good time in a while entertaining each other. 'Cause you're right. I am leaving eventually, and it's not fair to you to start anything real."

Lex flinched, then drooped against the door, drained. "How do we know it's not going to make everything worse?"

"We don't. But, hey, it might be fun for a while to find out."

"Fun? You call this fun?"

"I call this a misunderstanding that doesn't have to happen again. We just needed rules. Expectations. Now we have some."

"Rules."

"Yes, rules. You willing to try it, or do you want to go back to constantly torturing ourselves with something we both want?"

Lex pinched the bridge of his nose. He felt a headache coming on. He didn't know if what Tally was proposing was a massive internal hemorrhage waiting to happen or if it would be okay. Tally was right about one thing, though. Not touching after what they had the night before, after knowing what it felt like to have Tally's skin all over his body.... It would be complete and utter torture.

"Okay. We'll try it. Sex only. And it's *not* because I don't respect you."

Tally huffed a small laugh. "I know. Sorry I thought that. It just felt like it always used to, and I hated that, coming from you." He leaned over and gave Lex's lips a small sucking kiss. "Better go open the door. For all we know, they've been out there pounding on the glass."

Lex nodded, drained from the morning. "I'm going to go work in my office, unless you need anything."

Tally gave him a quick smile. "I'll let you know if something, uh, comes up."

Lex chuckled and pushed him on the chest. "Get to work, you perv."

Tally laughed, too, and Lex was glad the tension was broken somewhat. "Yes, sir!" he barked out with a jaunty salute before turning heel and heading back into the shop.

TALLY hadn't known quite how to treat Lex since their conversation in the supply room on that roller coaster of a morning nearly a week before. It would've been impossible for them to go back to being platonic work associates, for sure. Well, platonic in action at least. There had never been a lack of very non-platonic feelings on either of their parts. Not even on that very first day. He was glad they weren't going to try to go back down that frustrating road. As it was, they had a nearly impossible time keeping their hands off each other when there were customers in the store. He knew that a public announcement of their status wasn't something Lex wanted, though. Friends with benefits didn't exactly kiss and touch outside of closed doors.

He'd been with Lex nearly every evening for the past five. They'd kept to their rules: no dinners or romance or, God forbid, sleepovers, but they had still been some of the best nights of Tally's life. The hottest sex by far. Night number six, though, had left him at home on his own. Lex had to go to the town meeting, and Tally thought it was probably a good idea to spend some time with his grandma. She'd gone to the meeting, too, but he was cooking dinner for afterward—enchiladas with rice and beans and a spinach salad. She was due back any minute. Tally was trying not to worry about whether she noticed he'd come in late every night for the past week. There was no point in wondering, anyway. She noticed. She always noticed everything.

He wasn't sure if he should wince when she breezed through the door at quarter to eight. He sure did feel guilty… like he was a kid again caught out past curfew. It had been years since anyone even knew where he was, let alone cared. Even though it was kind of a pain, part of him loved it.

"Good evening, Tallis." She smiled at him. It was pretty obvious, though, that she had something to say.

"Hey, Grams." Tally gave her his best innocent smile… total bullshit, of course, but he tried.

"Tally, do we need to talk about anything?"

"Like what, Grams?"

"Like the fact that Lex Barry couldn't look me in the eye tonight, and you've been out until eight or nine every night since you called last weekend to say you were working in the stockroom."

"I'm just helping him with some stuff around the shop."

His grandmother snorted out a giggle. "Is that what you kids are calling it?"

"Grandma!"

"What? I was clearly born many years before yesterday, and your mother came from somewhere. As long as he's making you happy I have no complaints. You deserve something nice, boy. It's been a long time coming."

Tally tucked his chin into his chest, not sure if he was more embarrassed or profoundly relieved.

"C'mon, Grams. Let's eat these enchiladas before they get cold."

TALLY had Thursday and Friday morning off of work so he could go in and help with the open mic night again on Friday night. It took some willpower, but he didn't call Lex all day on Thursday, not during the day and not even to ask if he could come over at night. Didn't call Lex Friday morning, either, although he was tempted to trump up some excuse of a question so that he could. Tally wasn't even sure if there were rules against it since random phone calls could technically be categorized under friendship.

He grinned at the irony. It probably couldn't be called friendship when he wanted to talk to Lex as much as he did, though. There wasn't anything random about Tally's weirdly desperate need to hear Lex's voice. *Fuck. Friends with benefits, loser. That's all he wants.* He was sure the last thing Lex wanted was a sappy, pining, overgrown barista who would be happiest if he could go to sleep every night curled up in his boss's arms.

And Tally understood. He'd have to be an idiot not to. He didn't want to break Lex's heart—or his own, for that matter. Problem was, Tally didn't know what he *did* want, other than Lex.

Who the hell does?

Tally plopped his load of wet clothes in the dryer so they'd be dry for the start of his shift in a few hours. He reminded himself that he wasn't in a relationship, that what he and Lex had was supposed to be casual and fun, and he needed to quit acting like a moron. Tally stumbled upstairs to take a short nap while the dryer was running. He tried to tell himself that his stomach wasn't getting the flutters every time he thought about the fact that he'd be seeing Lex in a few hours.

THE shop was steamy, packed to the gills, just like it had been for the previous open mic night—perhaps even more so. Tally had been running in circles to make sure that every customer had their drinks and food, all the change was properly counted, and he kept setting up the extra folding chairs so there weren't too many people stuck standing and unhappy. He tried not to stare at Lex, had been trying all night. It was hard, though, not to look at him too much, not to touch him. And the fact that he could touch Lex in private didn't make it much easier. Now he didn't have to imagine what it would feel like to have Lex's skin fill his hands or to have Lex's hands all over him, Tally hated not being allowed to touch him all he wanted. Because he wanted to all the time.

Tally caught a glimpse of Lacey, the girl from the pizza shop, and smiled. She waved as well and made her way through the crowd. Her already curly hair was in tight corkscrews from the rain outside and the humidity in the shop. Tally watched as she shoved it out of her face, a gesture obviously more about annoyance than flirtation. It was refreshing. Sometimes, with the girls, Tally felt like a defenseless guppy being circled by a school of sharks.

"Hey, Tally. How are ya tonight? Am I going to see you in for a pizza tomorrow?"

Tally grinned at her. "I like pizza. Whatchya drinking? The usual?"

"No, it's chilly. I want peppermint. I always feel like peppermint when I'm cold."

"Chilly? It's like a sauna in here."

She chuckled. "Go outside for a while."

"So you want a peppermint mocha?"

She grinned at him. "Sure."

Tally turned to give Lex the drink order and managed to bump right into him. It was amazing they hadn't conked noses, with how fast they were both moving in the small space. Lex blushed and gave Tally a short but decidedly intimate smile. Tally smiled back and passed over Lacey's order. He turned around to ring her up but was distracted by her knowing grin.

"What?"

"Oh, you know what." Her grin widened. "That explains why you're not like octopus hands."

Tally managed to turn bright red. He wasn't sure if he'd had that reaction to anything in years.

"Hey, give me some credit! You're in high school."

"Doesn't stop most of them. Besides, I imagine you wouldn't be interested even if I was your age. But, if I do say so myself, congrats." She tipped her head at Lex. "He's cute," she whispered.

"Lacey."

She just shrugged and smiled at him with her elbows on the surface of the tall pastry case. Lex handed her the steaming mocha.

"Thanks, Lex." She turned her smile on him. He gave Tally a perplexed look.

Just then, another one of Tally's high school customers came up to the counter for, Jesus, was it the third time? Lacey rolled her eyes.

"I'll see you later, Tally," she muttered with a sly grin.

He tried not to sigh. Was he that transparent? Apparently they both were. He didn't have time to think about it, though. One of his other problems was leaning on the counter, cleavage displayed for all who were interested. Clearly, he wasn't. It *was* kind of cute how big of a crush the girl obviously had on him. Or at least it would be if it wasn't annoying. She'd slipped him her number at least four times in the past month. Like he was going to hook up with a high school girl, or any girl at all, for that matter. Ridiculous.

"Can I have another one of those special Tally drinks? They're delicious." The girl, Amber, batted her eyes and tipped her chin suggestively. *Oh, God.* Tally didn't know how he was supposed to react to that.

"Sure, Amber. But aren't you going to have a hard time sleeping tonight with all the caffeine?"

"I know someone who could get me all tired," she told him as she passed him her number for the umpteenth time.

Okay, that was crossing so many lines….

"Amber," he admonished.

"What? I'm eighteen, you're hot. What's the problem? Are you seeing someone already?"

Tally was in the deepest pit of hell. *Somebody rescue me!*

"No, I'm not seeing anyone, but that's not the point."

"Then what is? You think I'm ugly?"

"I think you're very young, and very, um, outspoken, and yes, you're also pretty, but it's not going to happen."

The girl harrumphed delicately, pouting. "Well, a guy like you shouldn't be single. I'm jealous of the girl who finally gets to take you home. You have my number if you change your mind."

Tally waited until she walked away before he let his breath out and chuckled softly. If that hadn't been the most awkward damn thing ever. He went to fill his water glass and walked by Lex on the way. He reached out his hand to touch Lex surreptitiously, a small caress under the counter where no one would see. Lex stiffened and jerked away.

"Lex, no one saw that," Tally whispered. He was confused by Lex's reaction. The man had become downright flirtatious with him the last day or so. Even though crossing the line into actual touch was perhaps pushing it, he didn't think it warranted the jerking away and the small glare that Lex shot over his shoulder.

"I'll be back in a minute. We can start closing down after this last performance." He walked away stiffly toward the supply room.

What the hell? Tally had no idea what he'd done. God, he touches Amy more than that. Speak of the devil….

Amy flounced over with a plastic tub full of plates and silverware. She'd volunteered to bus tables so Lex and Tally could make the coffee and sandwiches and dish out the pastries. She rounded the corner of the counter and headed for the deep industrial sink that was right next to the espresso machine.

"What's up with you two tonight?" she asked Tally after she was done unloading her dishes. "You've been acting about as strange as… well, just really weird." She gave Tally a speculative look. "Is there something going on between you and Lex that I should know about?"

Tally tried to look nonchalant. "Don't think so, unless you know something I don't."

Amy raised her eyes silently and turned to pick up her tub.

"Is that why Lex canceled the date he was supposed to go on tomorrow night—over 'nothing'?"

"Amy, I don't know why he cancelled the date. Why don't you ask him?"

She pursed her lips and walked away with her tub to collect another round of dishes. Tally sighed and went to the sink to start stacking the pile into Lex's huge commercial dishwasher before it got any bigger.

After the last performer, a kid who wasn't half bad, as far as Tally could tell over the irritation humming violently in his ear, Tally started to herd everyone to the door, quickly enough so he could get them the hell out of there and see what Lex's problem was, but without trying to seem like he was rushing anyone. He breathed a sigh of intense relief when the shop was empty except for him and Amy and Lex, who finally emerged from the back room.

"Where have you been, boss?" Amy asked him with a knowing smile.

Aw, shit, Amy, don't start on him too.

"I wasn't feeling so hot, so I just cooled off in the back room for a while. Sorry, guys."

"Just making sure. And you're really not going to go out with Mason tomorrow?"

Lex shook his head.

"But why? He's a sweet guy, and he says he had a great time with you, that you even gave him a kiss goodnight."

Tally gritted his teeth. He thought Lex looked at him for a minute, entreaty in his eyes.

Like I'm going to say anything. I can't believe you fucking kissed him. Tally was stunned by the force of his jealousy.

"It was just a kiss on the cheek, Ames. Mason was really nice, but I don't want to lead him on."

Oh, that's not so bad.

"Shit, Lex. He's not asking for a promise ring, just a movie." Lex looked increasingly uncomfortable. "All right, what's going on? I already asked this one"—she yanked her thumb violently at Tally—"but he said he didn't know what I was talking about."

"And I'm going to say the same thing. You're imagining things, hon."

"You know it pisses me off when you call me hon, *sweetheart*. Fine. Don't tell your best friend what's going on in your life, and don't tell me it's nothing, because I'm not stupid." Amy dropped her apron on the counter and grabbed her jacket and her keys. "I'll see you tomorrow," she ground out before stomping through the back hallway and out the door.

Tally slumped against the counter. "What happened tonight?"

"With Amy?"

"Amy, you, me, whatever. Lex, no one saw me touch you, I promise."

"I know. It's not that."

"Well, then, what? What did I do?"

"Tally, I think you should just go home."

Tally groaned and gathered Lex tightly in his arms. Lex squirmed, but Tally refused to let go. "You have to tell me what I did wrong. I've been waiting all day to see you. I don't want to go home yet."

"That's just it! Do you want to know what it was that made me mad? It was when you told that girl you weren't seeing anyone!"

Of all the unfair—Tally let his arms fall from around Lex's shoulders. "What did you want me to say, huh? You want me to point at you and say, 'See that man? I've spent some of the best nights of my life in bed with him this week and I can't imagine looking at anyone else.' Is that what you wanted me to say? 'Cause it's the truth."

"*Yes*... and no. Shit, Tal, for a few days I really thought this was going to be easy. And then something as little as you saying exactly what I should've wanted you to say just threw me for a loop. I hated it! God, I sound like such an idiot."

Tally pulled Lex back into his arms. "C'mon, Lex, let's go upstairs."

"But can't you see what's happening?"

"Yeah, I can. We like each other. A lot. It's more than just sex to me, and I'm pretty sure it is to you too."

"It can't be. Maybe we should just stop while we're ahead."

"Ahead of what?"

"I don't know." Lex sighed.

"Then why are you making this so hard? I'll come upstairs, I'll touch you like I've wanted to for every second since I left your bed the last time, you can do all those dirty things to me that you're amazing at doing, and we'll have *fun* together. It doesn't have to be all angsty and complicated."

"Angsty?" Lex chuckled. "Way to make me sound like a thirteen-year-old."

Tally raised his eyebrows. "If the shoe fits...."

"Ohh, you're gonna get it!" Lex poked Tally in the side and started herding him toward the steps.

"About that." Tally looked back at Lex. "I was meaning to ask if you wouldn't mind."

Lex stopped in the hallway. "Really?"

Tally grinned. "Yeah, really. Can't think of anything hotter than having you in me."

Lex groaned. "*God.* Start running before I decide to take you right on the stairs."

Tally chuckled and booked it for the front door of Lex's apartment, stripping his shirt off as he went.

CHAPTER
Eight

"Hey, Lex, you mind coming out here? A tour bus just pulled up on the street, and a bunch of people are headed this way!"

"I'll be right out, Tal," Lex called with a smile. Tourist season had begun.

From September until somewhere in mid-April, Rock Bay was a sleepy little hamlet. Only the locals and a few straggling drivers passed through the main street of town on a regular basis. But when the coastal weather warmed up, the tourists started to come. Day trippers out from Seattle or Portland, people driving up the scenic coastline on Highway 101, which went right smack through the middle of Rock Bay, and—the best—tour buses filled with trinket-happy tourists who wanted their own little piece of the Pacific Northwest to take back to wherever they came from. It was when the little town came alive with street fairs and art shows, sidewalk sales and the near constant smell of summer barbecue coming from the grocery store down the street. There was a formal start of summer block party at the end of June, but that was nearly two months away. The block party was big business for Lex, but the whole tourist season was what fueled his little shop through the less busy winter months.

Lex wandered into the front while the people from the bus were still perusing some of the earliest sidewalk stands that the local stores had put out. He casually brushed his hand across the juicy curve of Tally's ass and kissed his neck, comfortable that there were no onlookers.

"Hey. You're gonna get me all excited when I can't do anything about it. Tease."

Lex waggled his eyebrows and slipped his hand around to cup Tally's rapidly hardening crotch. "Doesn't have to be teasing. I'd say we got about two minutes till those tourists hit. You think I can get you off by then?"

"No!" He backed away with a laugh. Lex laughed, too, but he couldn't help but be a bit disappointed. He wanted to get his hands on Tally constantly. "I can't believe I forgot about tourist season," Tally groaned.

Most people in town had a love/hate relationship with the tourists. The revenue was great, of course, and exposure for the little pen dot of a town was good too. The lack of parking, though, and some stranger in your favorite booth at Sandy's diner? That part sucked.

"It's way bigger now than it used to be too. I'll probably have to work a lot of the afternoons. For sure I'm going to need help on the weekends. Maybe I can hire a kid from the community college in Long Beach."

"You know I'd be here every day if you'd let me."

"I wish I could give you that many hours, but Labor and Industries would be up my ass if I did."

"It's not only the money, Lex."

"Tally…." Lex didn't want to hear it. Couldn't hear it. Wanted it more than anything….

"I know. Sorry. Feelings."

Lex gave Tally a slow smile and tried to ignore the warmth melting in his belly. "It's okay this *one* time." He smacked Tally lightly on the butt. "You wanna do the register or make the drinks?"

"Ugh. Drinks. I had enough dealing with people last night to hold me over for a while."

Lex nodded. He totally understood. They'd run an open mic night for the second week in a row because there had been such a long list of people who wanted to perform that they'd ended up with a waiting list nearly as long as the original set list. Open mic nights were always great for revenue but a total zoo. He'd been running the espresso machine so fast that Tally had been stuck at the register the whole night, dealing with flirty girls, nervous musicians, and the usual espresso divas who had to have their twenty ingredient lattes served just right or there'd be hell to pay.

He was about to tell Tally again how grateful he was for the help at open mic night take two when the front door opened and the first few tourists from the bus trickled in. Lex put on his best smile and greeted the customers, getting himself ready for what would be a very busy half an hour or so.

Lex was in the middle of taking a very long and complicated order from one of the city folk when the shop's phone rang.

"Shoot, Tally, can you grab that?"

Tally nodded and reached for the phone. "Good afternoon, Rock Bay Coffee and Sandwich Company, can I help you?"

Lex was busy writing the customer's order and didn't hear the conversation in the background. It wasn't until the last of the tour bus customers were helped and out the door that he finally had a second to ask about the call.

"Oh, it was your mother," Tally answered. "She says your sister's going back to Seattle in the morning and she wants you to come over for dinner."

"Does she need me to call her?"

"She said no. Um, I was invited too."

Lex shook his head. "Of course you were. She remembers you, you know."

"Shit. Does she hate me? I already told her I'd go."

"I told her to back off and that you were the best person to hire. She trusts my judgment, but she's been bugging me to meet you."

"Why didn't she just come here?"

Lex chuckled. "That would've been way too easy. She wants you on her turf."

"Great. Is this going to be an inquisition?"

"Yep. Complete with full anal probing and body cavity search."

"As long as you're doing the probing part, I'm okay with it."

Lex snorted and pinched him on the side. "I'll keep that in mind. You want some help with clean up?"

"If you're not super busy. The city folk made a mess out of my tables."

"The city folk? What are you?"

"Hey! I'm Rock Bay born and raised."

Tally bumped hips with Lex as he grabbed the big plastic tub they usually used to collect dishes on open mic night. Lex smiled as he watched him round the counter and head into the cafe area to clear the tables. His smile faded, though, the further Tally got.

Yeah, but you're not staying....

"OW! SHIT!"

Tally turned at the sound of glass breaking. He'd been in the middle of clearing the last of the tables when the crash came from behind the counter.

"Lex, are you okay?"

"Yeah. Shit. I cut myself on the broken dish. I'm fine."

Tally plunked his tub on the nearest table and rushed around the counter to see if Lex really was, in fact, okay. What he saw was Lex, holding his right arm, which was gushing a bright red trail of blood. The blood was dripping from his elbow to the steadily growing pool on the floor.

"Lex! What the hell? You're not okay. We need to get you to the emergency room!"

"Tally...."

"Can you rinse it off so I can see?"

"What are you, an EMT all of a sudden?"

"Rinse off your arm, Lex."

Lex cringed but stuck his arm under the faucet that he'd turned to low. Even with the extra blood washed away, the gash was deep and long, and he couldn't tell if there were any shards of ceramic in it or not. Before he could even get a closer look, new blood welled up and started dripping down Lex's arm.

"That thing is going to need stitches."

Lex grumbled. "I hate hospitals."

"Well, I can go all pioneer and stitch it up for you, but I'm thinking you'd rather have a doctor do it."

"Ugh. Fine." He gestured to a spot on the counter with his head. "My keys are over there."

"We can take my car."

Lex somehow managed to make a snotty face in between winces. "Yeah, right. I don't care how many times you take your beast into the shop. I'm not crossing the Columbia in that rattrap you call a car."

Tally made a mock outraged face. "Fine, pull my fingernails out. I guess I'll drive the pretty BMW." He sighed long and loud.

"C'mon, let's go. And, hey, will you grab me a few of those towels from the clean pile? I don't want to bleed on the leather."

TALLY made it out to the 101 in no time and was speeding down the highway into Astoria, the closest town with a fully functioning emergency room. They had a small practice in Rock Bay, but the doctor was friends with Tally's grandmother and tended to be on the golf course more than in his office. Tally thought it best to go to Columbia Memorial rather than risk having to sit in Dr. Green's waiting room until he was done with the eighteenth hole. Judging from Lex's comment about the going over the Columbia, it seemed that he agreed. They'd been on the road for a little while when Tally glanced over to see how his suddenly quiet patient was doing. Lex, who'd seemed annoyed but fine at the shop, was starting to turn a rather alarming shade of off-white. Tally gulped and pushed on the gas. He didn't know what was wrong, but Lex didn't look good at all.

He headed onto the bridge that crossed the Columbia River and left Washington behind. By the time they hit land again, they'd be in Oregon and hopefully only minutes away from the hospital. Lex's forehead looked clammy. Little beads of sweat were popping up all along his hairline. The off-white had morphed into a slightly greenish tinge. *Aw, shit.*

"Hey, Lex, don't pass out on me." Tally reached over and nudged Lex gently, hoping to keep him awake.

"Not gonna pass out. I'm fine. Hands on the wheel, please."

"Um, you look like—" Tally stopped. Probably best not to tell the guy he looked like he was about to keel over.

"It's not the blood," Lex groaned and squeezed his eyes shut. "It's the bridge."

"The bridge?"

"It makes me… nervous."

"Nervous? Are you sure that's all?"

"Yeah. It's better when I'm driving, not so good in the passenger seat."

"You gonna puke?"

"No, just get over the damn bridge."

"Almost there. Keep your eyes closed." Tally reached over and put his hand on Lex's thigh, hoping to comfort him. Lex gripped Tally's hand with his uninjured left side. Tally's heart melted a little in that second, but he squeezed back and tried not to make a big deal about it. "Okay, bridge is done."

"We want to get on Marine Drive," Lex mumbled, still pale and sweaty.

Tally chuckled. "I know where the hospital is, silly. Just concentrate on not throwing up."

"Thanks a ton." Lex put his forehead against the cool glass of the car window. Tally saw him breathing slowly, in and out, in and out. He tried to go a little faster, speeding through a yellow light and barely making it.

"It's only a few more blocks, okay? Think you'll be fine with walking in if I park in the lot?"

Lex snorted. "I'm not having a baby, you know."

"Then shut up and look pathetic. The worse you seem the less time we'll have to sit in the waiting room."

Tally pulled into the pay lot next to the hospital and rushed around to help Lex out of the passenger seat. Lex had the mass of quickly reddening hand towels pushed against his arm. He didn't look nauseated any longer, but his face was still really pale.

"C'mon, we've got the walk signal. Let's go get these stitches over with."

The ER wasn't very crowded, thank God. Lex couldn't have handled sitting there watching daytime TV on the monitor, waiting for Amy to see he was there. As soon as she saw his name, he knew he'd be admitted, but if she was busy it might be a while. Turned out to be a quiet day at Columbia Memorial. She came rushing out about two minutes after he signed in, looking flustered and worried.

"Lex! What on earth happened?"

Lex shrugged, feeling a bit embarrassed. "Cut myself on a broken dish. It looks worse than it is. I got sick coming over the bridge." Even to himself, his voice sounded slurry and tired. Amy and Tally exchanged worried looks. "Guys, m'fine. Promise."

"Of course you are. Thanks for bringing him, Tally. Lex, c'mon, let's get you stitched up."

"Babe, can you wait out here?" he mumbled at Tally, knowing only that he wanted to see Tally's face when he got out of the back. It was only when he saw Amy and Tally's surprised faces that he realized what he said. "Shit," he muttered. "Jus' forget—" And with that, everything went black.

WHEN Lex came to he was lying on a gurney in the ER, staring at a heart monitor that was blipping away cheerfully. Amy was standing with her arms crossed over her chest. His arm was numb, but when he went to feel it there was about a mile of gauze wrapped tightly around the area.

"Hey, Ames," he murmured. "Wow. How long was I out?"

"Long enough for them to stitch you up. You're fine. You wanna tell me what that was all about in the waiting room?"

"Great freaking bedside manner, hon. Shit. What was what all about?" He shook his head, trying to clear the cotton from his brain.

"You called Tally babe."

"So? I call you babe all the time."

"It's different."

"I'm in the emergency room, I just woke up. Can you grill me another time?"

"You cut your arm open, not your head, and I'm worried about this Tally thing. What is going on between you two? Don't you remember high school?"

"Yeah, and so does he. I told him who I was."

"And?"

"And he says he's been sorry about that for years."

"And?"

"We get along really well."

"And?"

"He's hot in bed?"

"James Alexis Barry, you did *not*!"

Lex grinned at her. "You said I needed to get laid."

"Yeah, but what does Tallis Carrington have to do with that? He's straight!"

Lex simply shook his head.

"When did you find out? When did… what…." She looked flustered.

"The night I brought him to dinner at your house."

She nearly screeched. "You've been sleeping with him all this time?"

"No. That's the night he told me he was gay. I kissed him. Then I spent the next week trying to ignore the fact that I wanted to rip his clothes off.

"And I made it until the next Friday night." He cringed. "After my date."

Amy chuckled but still managed to swat him on the arm. "You're such a jerk. I can't believe you're dating big bad Tallis Carrington. Just don't come crying to me when you find out he hasn't changed as much as you thought he did."

Lex rolled his eyes. "I won't. Besides, I thought you were the one who said he was different?"

"He is different, but I'm allowed to be overprotective."

"Well, knock it off. Anyway, we're not dating. We're just friends."

"Friends who—"

"Yes, friends who have fun together." He smiled. "A lot of fun." Amy swatted him again. "I really don't want to discuss this any further in an assless gown. Where are my clothes, by the way?" He went to sit up but slouched back when his head spun. All he wanted was to lie in his bed and watch TV—hopefully with good snacks. "And when can I get out of here?"

"Let me call the doctor so he can check you out."

A LONG two hours later, Lex was checked out of the hospital and back in his apartment on the couch while Tally pulled out stuff to make him some food. He'd called his mother to tell her what happened, and they all decided his sister would come by in the morning to say goodbye. He was pretty out of it on the pain medication they'd picked up from the drug store on the way home, so he was glad he didn't have to deal with the collective family and their incessant questions.

"Here you go, sit up, and I can put this tray on your lap. We've got turkey and swiss on sourdough with cream of carrot soup and vanilla pudding. I know you said no dinner dates, but I'm starving. We can just call it a non-date, since I had to drug you first anyway."

"I'd probably say yes to just about anything right now." Lex smiled sleepily and took a lazy bite of his sandwich. "This's good, ba—" *Shit.* Since when was it his instinct to call Tally "babe"? It needed to stop right away.

"Glad you like it. When you're done, I'll get you into bed. I'm going to sleep out here on the couch in case you need something."

Lex chewed his turkey and swiss, finding it almost too much effort, even though his stomach was complaining. "You can sleep in the bed. S'okay, just for tonight."

"Are you sure?"

"Yeah." He pushed away the tray. "I'm done with my dinner."

"You need to eat more than that. The pills will make you sick."

Lex rolled his eyes slowly and took a long deliberate bite of his sandwich. "I ate more."

"Note to self. Percocet turns Lex Barry into an annoying five-year-old," Tally mumbled. "All right. Let's get you to bed."

They walked, a bit crookedly, down the hall to Lex's bedroom.

"You know, some parts of me aren't five," Lex mumbled before he took Tally's hand and cupped it around his crotch.

"Knock it off. You're in no condition to tease me. You need sleep."

"'Kay." He flopped bonelessly onto his bed and closed his eyes.

Lex was vaguely aware of Tally taking off his jeans and gingerly peeling the T-shirt he was wearing over his head. Then he was gently tucked under his comforter before the light was turned off, and he floated in a blissfully drugged state in the darkness.

"LEXIE?"

Lex blinked and opened his eyes to the sound of his sister's voice drifting in from his front door. He rolled over in bed but winced when his arm came into contact with the sheet.

"Hey, Em."

"How are you?" she asked.

"Fine, just a little sore. I guess the cut was really deep." He held up his bandaged arm. "How'd you get up here?"

She smiled. "Tally let me in."

Lex tried to hide his smile. Turned out to be impossible.

"I knew you weren't over him." She nudged him gently with her elbow.

"No, it's not that. It's different now."

Emily nodded slowly. "He really has changed, hasn't he?"

"And you know that because he let you into the back hall?"

She chuckled. "He let me in, told me to make sure you took your pain medication, sent up a muffin and coffee for you to have for breakfast. Honestly, if I didn't know better, I'd think there was something going on between you." Emily raised her eyebrows at Lex. He turned pink and rolled over. How many people could find out about him and Tally before it wouldn't be called "friends with benefits" anymore?

"There's just something about him, Em. I—" He didn't know what to say.

"He's totally sexy. I get it. And weirdly enough, he seems genuine. Nice. Like he had a complete brain transplant at some point after high school."

"He says he hates the person he was back then."

Emily ruffled his hair. "As long as you're happy, little bro."

"I am." And he was. Really, really happy. Lex chuckled softly. "What, that's it? No sage advice?"

"Don't forget to use protection," Emily said with a grin. She'd always loved embarrassing him.

Lex groaned and mimicked looking at a watch. "Aren't you supposed to be in Seattle already?"

"Guess it's time for me to hit the road, since I doled out my sisterly advice already."

"That's all you got for me, huh? Use a condom?"

Emily sobered. "Be happy. That's the most important thing. I don't think I've ever seen you look this content."

"It's the painkillers."

"It's not the painkillers, squirt. You're falling for him. Quit fighting it. Let your relationship just… be what it's going to be."

"How did you know?"

Emily just smiled and kissed him on the forehead. "I *know* you. That's how. I'll give you a call when I get back to the city. Love you, Lexie."

"Love you too, sis."

Lex lay back in his bed, bemused, staring at the ceiling long after his sister left.

Quit fighting it? How was he supposed to do that?

CHAPTER Nine

"UGH, if I never see another red velvet cupcake again, it'll be too soon." Tally placed his newest perfectly made cupcake in one of the huge bakery boxes that lined Lex's living room wall.

Lex chuckled. "This definitely ranks up there with one of my weirder Saturday nights. I still can't believe their oven broke."

It had been the mantra of the night, ever since the frantic call earlier from the bakery that Lex had contracted to make a shit ton of cupcakes—two hundred, to be exact. It had been annoying when Lex thought he could get another bakery to make the cupcakes, but when none had been available, and it became more and more clear that *he* would, in fact, be baking two hundred red velvet cupcakes with cream cheese frosting and sugared orchid garnishes for the lovely ladies of the coastal gardening convention, the annoyance had turned to panic. If Tally hadn't offered to help, Lex didn't know what he would have done. On his own he probably wouldn't have been able to do even close to half of them, especially with his still sore and newly stitch-free arm.

Armed with a large pepperoni pizza, two bottles of Moscato, and more industrial sized blocks of cream cheese than Lex had ever seen in his life, they'd set out on an epic cupcake-making journey. Six hours later, they were nearly done, but they had a messy red pile of screw-up cupcakes nearly as large as the collection of neatly boxed keepers.

"Wait, hold on." Lex counted. *Seven boxes of twenty-five, ten, fifteen....* "Oh my God, Tally. I think we're done." Words he'd never thought he'd utter.

"Hallelujah!" Tally crowed and collapsed onto Lex's brown leather couch, floury ass and all. Lex was so tired and sore from being hunched over squeezing frosting out of borrowed pastry bags that he didn't even worry about the couch he'd spent an arm and a leg on. He flopped on the adjacent couch cushion and brushed a soft kiss on Tally's lips.

"Thank you so much for helping. This whole thing would have been a disaster without you."

"Hey, what are hired sex slaves for if not baking five million red velvet cupcakes until"—he looked at his watch—"three fifteen in the morning. God, what time is the luncheon?"

"It's at eleven. And at least Travis is perfectly capable of opening the shop." Travis was the college kid Lex had hired a week before to open on weekends. He was luckily working out well.

Lex chuckled. "It wasn't as bad as I thought it was going to be, making all those cupcakes. And since the bakery was willing to sell us all the ingredients at below cost, the profit on the whole luncheon will be better than I planned."

Tally groaned. "It *was* that bad. My fingers are going to be cramped forever. Don't get any ideas about doing it again. You already owe me many, many hours of mind-blowing sex for this."

"Which I'll happily start repaying if we can please get in the shower first." Lex made a face. "Every centimeter of me is sticky." He dragged his shirt off, chuckling when it got stuck on his head for a moment before it popped off and was tossed aside.

Tally stood and reached down to haul Lex up with him.

"I'll lick the frosting off."

Lex found himself giggling at the thought… *giggling*. Shit. "Did we drink all of that wine?"

Tally made a show of eyeballing down into the bottles. "Yep."

Lex groaned. "And we forgot about dinner." He eyed the mostly full pizza box on the table. "No wonder I'm feeling kind of loopy. I thought it was from all the sugar."

Tally reached down and dug a finger full of frosting from the mess-up pile and slowly wiped it down Lex's cheek before licking it off.

"Mmmm. Sweet."

"Hey," Lex mumbled, distracted by the spark in his belly. "I'm already all sticky."

Tally waggled his eyebrows, then reached down for another big gooey glop of cream cheese frosting. With one challenging look he wiped it right into Lex's hair.

"Really, Tal, knock it off. My living room is already such a mess."

"Living room?" Tally murmured. "I didn't say anything about getting frosting on your living room. Only on you." Then with a grin he picked up a lopsided cupcake and dragged it down Lex's chest, making a white creamy trail all the way to his jeans. Without warning, he shoved the whole thing into Lex's waistband and ground it in as hard as he could, bursting into laughter.

"Oh, you suck!" Lex chuckled before taking another cupcake and squashing it into the side of Tally's face. "Game on."

Tally ripped his shirt up and over his head, then grabbed two handfuls of messy crumbling cake and squatted defensively behind the oak coffee table. Lex squatted down too, nearly falling, and snaked an arm out to grab his own squishy ammunition. Lex took aim first and fired, catching Tally square in the chest. The moist thud was very satisfying. So was watching red cake and gooey frosting drip down that perfect chest. He got distracted by looking and barely noticed the projectile coming toward his face. Just in time, he dove to the side—but groaned when the cupcake hit one of his newly painted walls instead of his face.

"Hey! I just repainted this room a few months ago," he complained, lunging toward Tally with the hugest pile of frosting he could scrape together. The frosting ended up in a big swath down the front of Tally's chest, getting rubbed into his skin by Lex, who'd managed to fall all the way on top of him. Tally chuckled and wrapped his arms around Lex's back.

"I do believe I've won," Tally murmured with a superior smirk.

"No way! You missed when you threw it at me, and I'm the one on top of you." He leaned over and nibbled the bit of cake that was balancing on Tally's nipple.

"Yeah, but now I can do this."

Lex arched his back in shock as a long, thick trail of frosting and cake was smeared from his neck all the way down his spine into the back of his pants. "See? I totally won."

Lex was squirming and trying to dislodge the hunk of cupcake that had gotten stuck between his cheeks.

"You know, it would be easier if you just took them off." Tally's chuckle made Lex's slightly drunk stomach weak.

He rolled off of Tally and worked at the button of his jeans, which was caked with halfway-hardened sugar. Tally took the opportunity to lick at Lex's chest, cleaning up frosting and nuzzling his nipples while he was at it.

"You're not making this any easier for me, you know," Lex muttered, finally yanking the stuck button free and tugging at his zipper.

"I was hoping to make it harder."

Lex groaned at Tally's dumb joke, then lifted his hips and shoved his jeans down and off. He wiggled then, and brushed as many of the remaining crumbs from his body as he could. Lex saw Tally gulp, and it made him grin. "C'mere." He spread his legs invitingly and reached out for Tally. Tally scrambled to get his own jeans off, then he crawled between Lex's bare legs.

Their bodies came together in a squelching sugary mess that neither of them could muster up much concern over.

"Mmmm, you feel good. Smell nice too." Lex smiled and twined his legs around Tally's hips.

"You always feel good," Tally murmured. "Shower? I wouldn't want to get this shit all over your pretty designer sheets."

Lex poked him and bucked his hips. "I don't hear you complaining about the sheets when you're on them."

Tally gave him a soft smile and kissed him. "Nope. No complaints at all when I'm in your bed."

"Cheeseball," Lex grumbled. "C'mon. This frosting is going to end up sticking my ass cheeks together."

Tally rolled his eyes but stood up. "Such a romantic."

Lex smirked at him and hopped up, swaying dizzily for a moment before scampering off to the shower.

The water was warm and soothing as it slowly rinsed the stickiness of frosting and the grime of a ridiculously long day off of Lex's body. He was exhausted. Being awake from 4 a.m. to after three in the morning with only a short nap in the car while Tally drove them to pick up the baking supplies was enough to make his head swim. Lex was halfway asleep on his feet, head full of shampoo bubbles, when he felt the slick warmth of Tally's skin behind him, enveloping him.

"Hey," he murmured sleepily and laid his head back against Tally's shoulder.

"Hey to you too." Tally leaned over and sucked on Lex's exposed neck, running his hands down Lex's chest, sluicing the soapy water down and away. "So gorgeous," Tally murmured in Lex's ear. Lex arched his back and guided Tally's hand lower until he was cupping Lex's balls. Tally squeezed gently, and Lex moaned.

"Want you."

"Want you too. But you're falling asleep on your feet, babe."

Babe. It had gotten to be a habit between them. One that Lex hated to love… but he did.

Lex rubbed his slippery ass up against Tally and pushed Tally's palm against his cock at the same time. "I don't care. Need you tonight. It's been such a long day."

Tally started grinding his hips, pushing his erection further into the crack of Lex's ass. He enjoyed the feeling for a few minutes, reveled in the slip and slide of their soapy skin, the gentleness of Tally's big hands on him, the way he always felt when they were together. It wasn't enough, though. Enough pressure, enough contact… enough anything.

Lex lifted his leg onto the side of his tub and pushed Tally's fingers closer to his entrance, where he needed to feel them the most. Tally teased him mercilessly, little touches just barely breaching his rim. Lex groaned and covered Tally's hand with his own, pushing on his fingers and rubbing against them. He arched his back and tried to get more. Tally slipped one of his fingers into Lex, finding all the best places to rub.

"That good, babe?" he breathed against Lex's neck.

Lex moaned and leaned his head back to bite at Tally's jaw. The finger felt good, but he was desperate for something thicker. He needed Tally.

"Come inside, Tal. Just for a second. I need to feel you."

"With my—" Tally froze.

Lex rubbed against him, trying to get the pressure he needed, until he realized what he said. "Shit. I'm stupid. Just use your fingers, whatever… *God*, I don't care. I need to be filled."

Tally looked lost for a few moments, then he grabbed the tube of lube that had made it into the shower days before and slicked up his fingers. When Lex felt those fingers start to prod gently, he pushed back with everything he had. He needed Tally deep and hard.

"Fuck, more. I want. Tally…"

Tally had never seen anything so beautiful in his entire life. Lex, all writhe-y and slick, riding his fingers and sobbing for more. He wanted badly to just to dive in and feel the heat of Lex's body squeezing tight on his bare cock. *Damn*, he wanted it. But they couldn't. He wasn't out of his head enough to forget that just yet.

Lex grabbed his own cock and started to stroke. "I wanna come, Tal. It's either gonna happen now, or you need to take me to bed." That last part was released on a groan that shook Tally's spine. He could barely decide between watching Lex ride out his need or waiting until he was inside so he could feel every single aftershock. The thought of that feeling made the decision easy. Tally squeezed his eyes shut, then gently pulled out of Lex, reached over, and turned the water off. He shook himself, then picked Lex up, dripping wet, and carried him the ten steps to Lex's enormous bed.

Without even hesitating a second, Lex reached for his drawer and the lube and a condom, which he handed to Tally.

"Now," he ground out. "No foreplay. Need you in me." He slicked his own fingers with lube and reached between his legs to prepare himself.

Tally shuddered at the sight of Lex's fingers sinking into his tight hole. "God, Lex. Want you now."

"*Yes*. Fuck me."

Lex lifted his legs and slung his ankles over Tally's shoulders. Tally tried to be slow, but the heat and Lex's impatience made him lose it. He thrust deep, holding onto Lex's thighs.

"Oh, God, Tal. Yes!"

Lex arched his back and cried out, rolling his hips frantically. Tally wanted more, deeper, hotter. He couldn't get enough. He pulled out and pushed at Lex's side.

"Roll over, babe. On your knees. I can get deeper that way."

Lex rolled over and rose to his knees, trembling. He reached out and grabbed onto the headboard. His back was damp and glowing, Tally couldn't help running his fingers down the graceful line of his spine. His lips followed, wringing moans and breathy curses from Lex until he spread those beautifully rounded cheeks and delved with his tongue into the tight heat of Lex's body.

Lex shouted hoarsely and reached behind himself to cup Tally's head and tug on his hair. A loud string of curse words, moans, begging cries flowed from his mouth. *"Fuck, Tally, more, shit, need to have you, want you in me, feel your skin, God, please, now, fuck...."* Lex reached down and grabbed his cock, pulling hard, too out of his head to even care. He bucked his hips.

"Tally, gonna come. Want you in me now!"

Tally felt the beginnings of Lex's orgasm shivering around his tongue. He slid up Lex's back and, without even a second of hesitation, lined up and dove in. He grabbed for Lex's cock and found it hard and slick and twined his fist around Lex's. Tally started to thrust hard and fast, helping Lex finish himself off. Lex made a muffled groaning sound, then let go to bring his fist up to his mouth at the same time as he arched his back and shouted out Tally's name. Tally felt the rippling pulses of Lex coming before the wet heat of his release splashed out onto Tally's hand and the sheets below them. His own orgasm tingled at his spine.

"That's it, babe, come for me," he crooned breathlessly, coaxing the last few trembles from Lex with long strokes of his hand.

"T-tally," Lex gulped and shuddered. Then he squeezed Tally one last time, hard, and that was enough to send Tally flying over the edge into oblivion. Lex unwrapped his hand from the top of the headboard, and they slid down until they were flat on the bed, Tally covering Lex's body.

When he realized that he was going to fall asleep on top of Lex if he didn't move, Tally rolled over and, after disposing of the uncomfortable condom, reached down for his jeans.

"Where you going?" Lex's voice was hoarse from shouting and so sexy it made Tally's belly tremble.

"Getting dressed. We've got a long day ahead of us. I've gotta be here at ten, right?" Tally felt Lex's hand on his arm, tugging. He kept it up until Tally lay back down. Lex lifted the blankets and wriggled under them before he attempted to pull Tally underneath. Tally gave in and let Lex pull him into place, facing Lex with Lex's arm slug across his hips, hand cupping his ass familiarly. He stayed quiet for a few seconds until it became apparent that Lex wasn't going to say anything.

"What are we doing here?" he finally asked.

"Just go to sleep, Tal."

"You want me to spend the night?"

Lex smiled and slipped his firm hair-roughened thigh between Tally's legs. "Yeah, what little is left of it. I wanna hold you."

Tally's heart did a double thunk, and he wrapped Lex up tighter in his arms. Was Lex finally admitting that it was way more than just friendly sex between them? Maybe it was just the alcohol, maybe he'd wake up in the morning and Lex would be looking at him accusingly, asking what the hell—

"Tally?" Lex's tired mumble and warm breath made goose bumps burst out all over Tally's neck.

"Yeah?"

"I can feel you freaking out over there. Knock it off. It's fine."

Tally was silent for a few moments, absorbing Lex's smiling but slightly annoyed voice.

"Okay," he finally muttered and wiggled in deeper under the covers.

Lex's lips found his for a sleepy kiss in the dark. "Night, Tal."

"Night, Lex."

Tally hoped like hell things really were fine, because whatever had changed between them that night, he liked it way too much to give it up.

LEX'S head hurt when he woke the next morning to sun streaming through blinds he'd obviously forgotten to close. The light was warm and intense on his face, not a feeling he was used to waking up to. It was usually dark when he— *Oh, shit!* Lex's eyes flew open, and he flailed his arm out in the direction of his alarm clock. Instead of his nightstand, his arm landed on plush empty pillows and the distinct crinkle of paper. He pried his eyes open, blinking in the brightness of the morning, and looked at his clock.

Nine? Shit, shit, shit! He was halfway out of bed, heart racing, when he noticed the sticky note on the pillow next to him.

> Morning, Babe—
> Don't freak out. I got up and let Travis in this morning, and I'm getting all the stuff packed and ready for the lunch thing. You looked so comfortable. I didn't want to wake you. Come down when you get up. No rush.
> —Tally

Lex put the note down, trying not to grin. He stretched, enjoying the slight soreness from the night before and the luxury of waking up in broad daylight for the first time in the over three years since his shop had opened. *I could get used to this.* A little movie streamed through his brain, him and Tally falling asleep together every night, holding hands and watching TV on the couch. Maybe they'd take turns getting up to let the morning kid in, then they'd make each other breakfast and kiss over the toaster, go back to bed and make love…. *Shit. Don't call it that.*

It was a life he'd really like, though. One that was disturbingly easy to see happening. Tally was good for the shop, good for him, fun, sexy as hell, caring and kind. Lex shook his head and hopped up, grabbing some clean clothes and heading for the shower, where he hoped the hot water would wash some sense into him. It didn't help that he kept picturing the night before. How they must have looked all wet and desperate for each other. Lex scrubbed at his hair, enjoying his memories but trying not to make too much of what had happened. It had felt different, though. More intense, hotter than anything he'd experienced before. And having Tally stay? It was pure instinct. His bed had felt cold and empty the second Tally went to leave. Lex hoped he hadn't made a huge mistake.

Clean and dry, Lex made his way out of his apartment and down the stairs to the shop. He found Tally in the storeroom, kneeling on the ground in front of a huge cooler. He had other coolers lined up against the wall and labeled. One for each of the gourmet sandwich varieties, one with the fruit and salads they were setting out, and the final filled with the meat, cheese, and veggie trays he'd ordered from the deli. Tally even had the coffee and tea carafes all filled and ready to be loaded. Lex couldn't help but smile. If he'd been the one getting everything ready to go, there wouldn't be anything near the military precision Tally had going on. He walked closer and waited for Tally to see him. He was so intent on his task, it took a few moments.

"Hey," he said with a smile when he did finally look up.

"Hi." Lex tried to keep the goofy smile from spreading over his face, but it was impossible. He reached down and ruffled Tally's hair.

"I, uh, borrowed a shirt from you," Tally told him, looking mildly embarrassed.

"It looks good on you." Lex followed the shirt's lines with his eyes for a moment before he cleared his throat. "Thanks for doing all of this. It's so far above and beyond."

Tally stood and leaned toward Lex. Lex breathed in the smell that somehow managed to smell like his soap but still all Tally. "Of course I'd do it. I couldn't stand to wake you up when you looked so content."

Content. There was that word again. Don't fight it. Tally leaned over and kissed Lex casually. Lex slipped his hands into Tally's back pockets and leaned against the leanly muscled chest he was growing to love. It felt oddly perfect, standing in the back of his shop and holding Tally like they were at some school dance. He didn't want to let go. It was nice to have a blissful ten seconds where he wasn't worried about feeling too much, or not feeling enough, or whether he should've never asked Tally to spend the night. Lex just concentrated on how right it felt to just *be* with Tally.

"Hey, Tally, do we ha—" Lex's newest employee stood in the doorway of the storeroom, his mouth frozen in a surprised "O."

Lex was mortified. His young, just-out-of-high-school employee found him practically making out with his other employee in the stock room. Who did that? Apparently he did. Shit. Tally hadn't moved his arms from where they were slung around Lex's neck, Lex was still frozen, hands in Tally's pockets. Travis's surprised face slipped into a knowing grin.

"That explains the way you two look at each other," he told them, continuing to smile.

Lex stepped away from Tally. "We don't look at each other any different than we look at you."

Travis snorted. "If that's what makes you happy. Hey, I need a new vanilla syrup. We're getting low, and I didn't want to have to run back here when I had a customer."

Lex grinned. "See, that's why I hired this kid."

Travis smiled at both of them. "You guys look really happy together. Just saying. And don't worry, I won't tell anyone. I know how this town gets."

"Are you—" Lex began before he realized it was none of his business.

"Gay? Nope, but I met a girl at the community college who isn't even mixed with white. My parents are going to have a shit fit, but I'm really into her."

"You really think that's still a problem?"

"Around here? It's probably worse than you two."

Lex shook his head, disappointed. "Probably." He handed Travis the syrup and watched silently while the kid walked back into the front of the shop.

As soon as he was gone, Lex leaned back into Tally's arms for a brief, quiet moment. Tally pressed a tender kiss to the back of his head.

"I didn't want to get out of bed this morning. It was nice to hold you."

Lex's heart melted a little. Why did Tally have to say stuff like that? It wasn't fair. "Tally," he murmured, wishing he could just return Tally's sentiment and not have to worry about getting hurt in the end.

"Sorry. Well, not actually. I'm not sorry. I can't help having feelings for you. It's not just sex for me. Not even close. I think about you the whole time I'm not with you, and when I am with you all I wanna do is smile. Like all the time. Do you know how long it's been since I smiled for real and not just for a tip?"

Lex tipped his head back to look at Tally. "Why are you saying all this when you know you're leaving?"

Tally was quiet for a few very long and painful moments.

"What if I don't know I'm leaving?"

Lex froze. He didn't know what to say, what to think, anything. "I—"

Tally stepped back. "Did I read you wrong? Do you only want me if it's temporary?"

Lex turned and closed the distance between them, wrapping his arms around Tally's waist. "No, you just surprised me. How long have you been thinking about this?"

Tally shrugged. "A while. It really hit me this morning when I woke up in your bed and realized there was nowhere in the world I'd rather be. Not Seattle, not anywhere."

"But the people here—"

"Will get used to me again. Or they won't. But it seems like they're warming up to me. And truth is, my grandmother's not getting any younger. I know my mom's not going to take care of her, which only leaves me. I have a job that I'm actually really liking, and then there's this guy…." He gave Lex one of those blood-heating smiles that he was so good at.

"You can't stay here for me. Things happen, you know."

"I know. I'm not expecting to skip off into a rainbow-colored sunset, but don't you think we're worth trying for? Lex, I'm falling for you. Hard. Am I feeling this alone?"

He wasn't. Not even close. "No, you're not the only one. Are you sure you want to stay?"

Tally closed his eyes and hesitated for a moment before leaning over to touch his forehead with Lex's. "Yeah. I think so."

CHAPTER Ten

THE Coastal Gardening Convention luncheon was one of the best, silliest, most fun afternoons Tally'd had in a really long time. The women were ridiculous, flirtatious, and a bit like an unruly class of fourth graders. The poor presenter who was trying to wrap up her speech as Lex and Tally were setting up their lunch service nearly got drowned out by the constant chattering that was going on. A few of the women even blatantly got up and walked over to another table to gossip. Tally started to wonder how much the women were really interested in gardening. To him it seemed like an excuse to socialize. He supposed it was harmless, but he did feel bad for the supposed speaker.

When lunch finally started, he and Lex stood behind the table dishing out sandwiches, drinks, and the cursed red velvet cupcakes. Tally had never been winked at, pinched, or propositioned that many times in one afternoon probably ever, but he was so happy that he couldn't even bring himself to care. Lex had it just as bad. Turned out that while Tally was getting the flirting, Lex was getting numbers slipped to him so he could be set up with daughters and granddaughters who were "just the thing" for a nice, handsome young man like him. He looked a bit strangled but still managed to laugh and smile more than Tally had seen in the two months he'd been working at the shop.

That smile made it close to impossible for Tally to keep his hands off. All he wanted to do was drag Lex into the back room and have his evil way—or let Lex have his evil way with him. It had only happened a few times that way, but damn, Tally loved it. More than he ever had before.

There was something special about the two of them—and the fact that he could apply the word "special" to them without gagging or making a joke was a testament to how, well, *special* it really was. He hated to use the other word, the one that started with "L" and had been banned to the "never going to happen in a million years" part of his brain for so very long… but there it was, poking at him, saying, "here I am." He'd thought it, even though he thought he *shouldn't* think it. The word was there. And in Tally's experience, once words like that were in a person's brain, it was close to impossible to get them out.

Love.

There it was. Again. Every time he looked over at Lex's adorable flustered smile, every time Lex looked back at him and his eyes melted like he wished they were alone and back in his bed, Tally felt it.

Love. I love him.

Tally's stomach flipped hard. It was the last thing he'd ever expected to feel, and hell if he knew what to do about it other than hold onto Lex as long and tight as he possibly could. Lex glanced over and smiled at him again, bumping hips with him when he was sure none of the women were watching.

"You surviving?" Lex sidled up to Tally and bumped him softly with a hip.

"Yeah, but if that Don Juanita in the purple hat pinches me on the ass one more time, I swear…."

Lex laughed out loud. "Send her my way, and I'll tell her to back off. You're mine."

"Yeah?"

He stuck his tongue out at Tally, then smiled and went back to reorganizing the cursed cupcakes. Tally waited until all of the ladies had been served, then he leaned over and whispered in Lex's ear.

"When can we get outta here? I want you inside of me."

Lex groaned and nearly dropped the tray he was balancing on his hip. "Shit, Tal, it's not fair to do that to me here!" He took a deep breath, then gave Tally a naughty grin. "Clean faster."

"BABE?" It was the second night in a row that Tally had spent in Lex's bed, arms and legs entwined, faces resting right next to each other on the pillow.

"Yeah?" He could tell by Lex's voice that he was halfway asleep.

"What are we doing here? I need to know." He hated how insecure he sounded, how needy.

"I'm holding you." Lex cuddled up tighter and kissed Tally sleepily.

"Lex, you know what I mean."

Tally felt Lex's sigh. "Yeah, I know. What am I doing in the bigger sense? I'm done fighting it, I guess. This thing between us has never been just sex for me—not since the very first night and definitely not after that conversation this morning. It seemed stupid to keep pretending it was."

"So we're…?"

"You want it to have a name?"

"I just…." Tally trailed off. He didn't know how to tell Lex he wanted everyone to know Lex was his and only his without sounding a little nuts.

"You just what?"

"I just want it to be real." He slid his fingers through Lex's honey brown hair.

Lex tightened his arms around Tally. "It is real."

"I know. That's not what I meant. Maybe I need to know that you're mine, for now at least."

Lex chuckled and tightened his arms. "I *am* yours. Go to sleep, Tal. You got, what, like two hours last night?"

"I'm not sleepy."

"Now who's the five-year-old?"

Tally pinched Lex on the butt. Hard.

"Ouch, dork. That doesn't exactly help your 'I'm not acting like a five-year-old' case."

Tally snickered and rubbed a small kiss into Lex's neck. "You felt really good earlier, you know."

"Yeah?"

"Mmm-hmm. I wanna do it again."

"Yeah, me too. But I have to get up early tomorrow."

"You sure you don't want me to work?"

Lex moaned. "I wish. How many do I have you booked for already this week?"

"I'd do it for free."

"I can't do that to you. I already made you my cupcake slave last night. You deserve to have some sort of life."

"Trust me. I don't have one anyway." Lex huffed out a tired chuckle. Tally pushed his hair off his face and kissed his forehead. "Okay, since you won't let me work in the shop tomorrow, you want me to go do battle with MacAuliffe at the city building? I bet I can get the bastard to sign your permit."

"You think?"

"Hopefully. Like I told you before, my ass-kissing skills were legendary when I wanted something."

"And you'll dust them off for me?"

"Of course, babe."

"Awww, how sweet."

Tally pinched Lex again. "You're such a smart ass. You want me to go see him or what?"

"Uh, yeah. I already know the old goat's never going to say yes to me. Might as well try a different tactic." Tally smiled, happy to be able to help, and kissed Lex softly. "Now will you go to sleep?" Lex's voice was tired, yes, but Tally could tell he was more awake then he had been.

Tally shook his head. "Still want you."

Lex groaned, but his hand had already slipped down to fondle Tally. "Who needs sleep anyway?" he mumbled before sliding his thigh over Tally's hip and bringing their lips together for a kiss.

TALLY'S hands were shaking. He'd made it sound so easy the night before. Sure, dust off the ol' ass-kissing skills and get Lex's permit signed. He only wished it was that simple. MacAuliffe had liked him, and he had been friends with his son, Drew. Drew MacAuliffe, actually, was probably the only kid in his high school group that Tally had genuinely wanted to be friends with. He'd thought at the time that he might see a bit of what he was going through in Drew's face, nowhere near sure enough that he ever actually said anything, but still....

He reached up and tugged on the big brass handle of the building that held all the government offices, the police station, the court, the jail, and, well, basically everything else. Rock Bay had never been big enough to have separate buildings for the different offices. Once the heavy glass-paned door had swung shut behind him he looked at the building directory, only to find that Gerald MacAuliffe's office was in the exact same place it had been in when Tally was in high school, testament that nothing in Rock Bay ever changed. Except maybe him.

MacAuliffe was on the phone when Tally paused at the open door of his office. The man was everything he remembered: gruff voice, stomach hanging over the belt of his ill-fitting, permanent press pants, cowboy hat shoved firmly on his balding head. He'd come from somewhere else—Montana, Tally thought, but he'd been in the area at least thirty years that Tally knew of. He wasn't a rancher anymore, that is, if he'd ever been one in the first place. It was time for a new look. Tally waited for MacAuliffe to hang up his phone before tapping on his open door.

"Mr. MacAuliffe?"

The old man swung his chair around and peered at Tally calculatingly. Then his face broke into a big grin. "Well if it isn't young Tallis Carrington. I'd heard you were back in town, boy. You're looking more and more like your father. Too skinny, though. We need to put some meat on you."

Truth was, he'd gained a few pounds since he'd been back living with his grandma. And he knew he looked like his father. Mostly tried not to think about it. He gave Gerald his biggest smile.

"Yeah, I'm here for a while. Got a job in town, helping my grandma out."

The man's face went a bit sour at the mention of Tally's grandmother. She'd never been a huge fan of his father or any of his father's friends. Said they were mostly full of bullshit and thought they were masters of the world. Tally had to agree.

"Well, what can I do ya for?"

Here we go....

Tally cleared his throat. "The job I got, sir, is working down at the Rock Bay Coffee and Sandwich Company. For Lex Barry."

"Oh, Jesus." MacAuliffe didn't try to hide his disgust. "Watch that you don't get sprinkled with too much fairy dust at that place. It *reeks* of estrogen."

Actually, Tally thought the decor, both in the shop and in Lex's apartment, was warm and masculine and inviting. From what he remembered of the MacAuliffe house, it was covered in lace doilies and floral upholstery. *Look who's talking.*

"It's a good job, sir. Pays well. Try to ignore the rest of it." He hated spitting out that last part, but he thought it might help.

"Enough with the 'sir'. You're old enough to call me Gerald."

"Well, um, Gerald, thing is, the job would be better for me if Le—um Barry, made more money, so…." He held up the application. "This drive-through window is benefiting more than just him. I know you were friends with my father. He wouldn't want me working at a place that wasn't going anywhere."

"You can come work for me, if that's what's concerning you."

Tally tried not to gag. He couldn't think of much that would be worse. "Or you could sign the application and Lex Barry would be out of your hair. Plus he wouldn't have to take his complaint to the city council." Okay, so Tally pulled that one right out of the crack of his ass. He hoped Lex didn't get pissed.

"I just don't want that damn *faggot* to get his way. This town is no place for the likes of him. If I approve this application he'll never leave."

Tally gritted his teeth. "He'll never leave anyway, sir—I mean Gerald. His family is here. Rock Bay is his home."

"And you?"

"I'd like to stay, but I need to make sure my job is steady, you know? Somewhere with a future."

"You know my boy Drew's still in town, right? I'd like him to get away from that Brock character. Trouble since you boys were kids. Maybe you can give him a call."

Your son's in his thirties, asshole. He's a big boy. Tally forced a genuine looking smile.

"I can do that. If I'm going to be sticking around, that is."

MacAuliffe sighed. "Give me the damn paper."

Tally slid the application across MacAuliffe's desk, trying not to look triumphant. *Wait until his signature is on the page before you celebrate.* It was hard not to snatch it from those beefy, wrinkled hands.

After heart-bending forever, the paper was in his own hands, and he was smiling and casually waving good-bye to MacAuliffe, when all he wanted to do was run, shouting "I got it!" down the hall.

LEX was startled when Tally's hand slapped down onto the counter of the shop. He was shocked when he saw that instead of yet another rejected application, there was a building permit, shiny and new and signed by none other than Gerald MacAuliffe.

"You got it?" Lex wanted to jump up and down.

"Yep." Tally's grin was pleased.

"Thank you, thank you! I'd have never gotten this without you."

Lex jumped up and gave Tally a big hug, right there in the front room of the shop. They'd never been big on showing how they felt in public. He supposed that all the rules were different after the last few days. Didn't much care about the rules, anyway. Not when he had his arms full of squirmy, happy Tally. Lex loved the look on his face—pride that he could do something for Lex, relief, happiness, and a bit of something more, something unnamed and tender.

"I thought I was never going to get out of that place alive. He grilled me hard about working for you. It was pretty weird. It's usually everyone grilling *you* for hiring me."

Lex made a face. "He's a homophobic prick."

"A homophobic prick who thinks I'm the same as I was back in high school. I hated playing the role, but it got us what we want, right?"

He said "us." Lex couldn't help smiling even harder. Maybe his daydream from the day before wasn't such a dream after all. "Yes, it did. Plus, you're not doing anything wrong if they make you lie, right?"

Tally shrugged, casual and heartbreakingly sexy. "True."

Lex's grin was pushing at the corners of his face. Tally finally chuckled, his arms still slung loosely around Lex's hips.

"What?"

Lex couldn't help doing a little happy dance. "I'm getting my drive-through! I'm getting my drive-through!"

"You're adorable."

"I'm *excited*. I've been trying to get this damn permit for ten months."

"We should celebrate." Tally gave him a sly smile. "Close down early, lock the doors. You've got a few cans of whipped cream that I could put to good use. Mmmm, and the cinnamon. Much more delicious on Lex than on a chocolate muffin."

Lex laughed to cover the insane bolt of lust that flew through him at Tally's words. He jumped up and wrapped his legs around Tally's waist and kissed him, grinning and wishing they were naked. He was halfway listening for the door to open, but Monday afternoons were typically quiet. Oh, who the hell was he kidding? He was so wrapped up in Tally's kiss, in the strong hands holding him up by the ass, and the warmth of the body against him, that an atomic bomb could've gone off and he probably wouldn't have noticed… for a while, at least. Turned out an atomic bomb did kind of go off right about then.

"James Alexis Barry, what the hell is going on?"

It was his mother. *Holy oh my God, how could I have not heard the bell? You were too busy swallowing Tally's tongue to pay attention, that's how.*

"Uh, hi, Ma."

Lex slid down Tally and landed on his feet. He swayed for a second before Tally reached out to right him. *Oh God, face the music, face the music.* Lex was hard as a rock, lips kiss-swollen, hair mussed. He wanted to groan out loud but instead he turned. His mother looked at him with those eyes that had always been able to make him feel guilty as hell.

"Uh, Ma, this is Tally. He… works for me."

"I'll say he was working something, for sure."

Lex's mouth dropped open. His mother had never said anything like that in his presence before. She managed to make it sound incredibly insulting. Tally stuck out his hand. Lex had to give him credit. He didn't even cringe.

"Hi, Mrs. Barry. It's nice to meet you."

"I know who you are, Tallis Carrington. What the hell are you doing to my boy? Don't you think you did enough damage in high school?"

"Mother! I've told you he's not the same person he used to be."

"So now he's the kind of person who accosts his employer in the workplace?"

Lex almost had to chuckle at that. "Actually, I was the one who started it, and it's not what you think." Lex tossed a shy smile at Tally. "Tally and I are together, Ma. We have been for a while."

His mother's jaw dropped. "Is this true?"

Lex didn't know who she was directing the question at, but he figured he'd better be the one who answered.

"Yeah. Of course it's true."

"When were you planning to tell your family about this?"

"I'm pretty sure Em knows… and, well, now you do, so that only leaves dad." Lex reached out for Tally's hand and threaded their fingers together. Tally's warm squeeze calmed him.

"Well, I need to think about this. I expect you over for dinner tonight. Both of you. We need to have a family discussion."

"There's nothing for us to discuss. Jesus, I'm not in high school anymore, Mom. What the hell? I can sleep with whoever I want." Lex saw his mother's eyes widen at that last remark. He realized he may have gone a bit too far.

"As long as I'm around I'm still your mother. Dinner. Tonight."

"What time would you like us there?" Tally spoke up. Lex was about to protest when Tally squeezed his hand. Tight.

"Seven, please."

There was his mother's typical politeness. She must have been a bit mollified by how different Tally was from the bully she remembered. Lex decided to follow suit.

"We'll be there, Mom. Do you want some coffee while you're here?"

"I'd love some, actually."

"You should try the special drink that Tally concocted. It's really good." Why not lay it on thick? He needed his mother to see Tally for what he was, not what he used to be.

His mother raised her eyebrows. She wasn't stupid, and she knew her son well. "I suppose I'll give it a try."

It was the best Lex could ask for.

"ARE you sure we have to go over there? *Ohh*, do that again. So good."

Lex grinned breathlessly and curled his fingers inside of Tally to brush up against his prostate.

"Like this?" Tally's groan was the only answer he got. He bent over and licked at Tally's neck, bit his nipples. He loved making Tally squirm. "I don't want to deal with it either, but she's going to like you as soon as she gets to know you. How could she not?"

"Because…. Oh, I don't know. Fuck, baby. I can't even *think* when you do that."

Lex smiled at the "baby," or maybe how warm and tight Tally was around his fingers, or the way Tally was looking at him, forehead puckered in pleasure, lips moist and parted. Tally was fucking beautiful, and Lex wanted to be inside already, just them, nothing in between.

Why do I keep thinking that?

It hadn't ever been something that Lex wanted before. Not really. He all of a sudden wanted to feel everything he could feel. *You know the reason.* He did. But it was better not to dwell on it. Feelings like that could only end with him hurt. He wasn't quite ready to jump off the high dive with his eyes squeezed shut quite yet. They'd just decided to be a real couple. Lex wasn't going to let himself get deluded into thinking it was forever. If nothing else, neither one of them was ready for love. *Shit.* It didn't matter. Even if he tried not to think it, the feelings were real. They'd been growing the entire time.

Lex distracted himself by leaning over to suck on the head of Tally's cock. Tally's breath caught in his throat, and he made this sexy as hell low moaning noise.

Love you.

Lex swallowed him to the root, and Tally nearly screamed.

Wanna be in you always.

He rubbed firmly with his fingers and used his tongue to tease the nerves all around Tally's sensitive head.

Please love me back. I don't think I could take it if I lost you....

"Lex, please. Come love me."

I already do.

Lex crawled up Tally's body, pausing to kiss all his favorite parts: the tender skin at the top of his thigh, the hollow of his hip, both nipples, his soft lips. Tally moaned and lifted his thighs to hug Lex's hips. Lex wanted to say it, just let the words spill out. *I love you. Stay with me forever.* He bit his lip to keep from doing, or saying, anything stupid and irreversible. Instead he sat up and reached for the condom he didn't want and ripped it open, keeping his eyes on Tally. Tally let his knees drop open, and he arched his back, dragging the heel of his hand down his torso until his long-fingered fist was wrapped around his cock. Lex's breath caught in his throat. He squeezed his eyes shut. It was too much, too fucking hot. He wasn't going to last.

"Lex, *look* at me." Lex opened his eyes and stared down at Tally, watching him touch himself. Lust and warmth and maybe something infinitely more fragile and tender was shining in his eyes. "I need you."

Lex nodded, and with hands that were suddenly trembling, he slicked himself up and scooted until he was at Tally's entrance. Then he pushed, slowly but purposefully, until he was buried all the way in Tally's tight heat.

"God. *Yes.*" Tally's voice was hoarse and incredibly turned on.

Lex bit his lip. He babbled when he was near the edge. Never could be sure of what would come out of his mouth. There was so much he wanted to say. So much he knew he should keep to himself. Instead, he dug deeper into Tally's body with his hips and leaned forward to suck on Tally's neck.

"You feel so good." He couldn't help it. Damn. "I love being like this with you, being here with you. Want it all the time."

Tally made a deep whining sound in his throat and dug his heels into the bed, arching to get more pressure. "Want it all the time too… only with you."

"Just us," Lex breathed, licking at Tally's ear. "Nothing in between." *Aw, shit, I said it.* He was beyond caring. He linked his left elbow under Tally's knee so he could get deeper. It was never deep enough.

Tally trembled hard. "Oh, *fuck*, that would be so...." He gripped Lex's ass and pulled, his hands saying *harder, faster, more*. "I've never... but yeah. With you."

"*Shit*." Lex clenched his teeth to keep from coming. Just the idea nearly sent him flying over the edge. He squeezed his eyes closed again, tried to get some control. If he looked at Tally, he'd be lost.

"Come for me, babe. I wanna watch it." Tally cupped his hands around Lex's neck. "Look at me."

Lex was lost. Tally's gorgeous melty brown eyes were glued to his face, and he was shivering out of control, breaking into a thousand little pieces, and Jesus, shit, he couldn't keep it in....

"*Fuck!*" He felt like every part of him was flying out of his body, and all he wanted to do was grab Tally and hold on for dear life. Tally was shaking too, and coming, warm and wet, all over them.

"Tally I...." He bit his lip just in time and covered it with a low groan. He dropped onto Tally's chest, panting and clutching at the sheets.

"I know, babe. I know."

Lex didn't want to move, didn't want to do anything other than stay wrapped up in his warm man, but he reluctantly detangled himself to go to the bathroom and clean up. He brought a warm cloth back for Tally when he was done and wiped him off before crawling back in bed and drawing the comforter over them.

"How long till we have to leave?" Tally's voice rumbled under his ear.

Lex peered at his clock. *Damn.* "Twenty minutes. I don't want to get up."

"Me neither. Better to get this over with, though. It's not going away until we do."

Tally went to sit up, but Lex held him down. "Let's just stay here a few minutes, then we'll get up." He waited until he felt Tally's muscles relax, then he kissed his chest and relaxed himself.

Just a few minutes....

CHAPTER Eleven

Lex threaded his fingers through Tally's when they got out of the car in front of his parents' house. He didn't want to be there, dealing with his parents, when he could be at home, in bed, holding Tally, talking and kissing. He knew his mother was going to be confrontational, maybe even borderline rude, but there was no way in hell she was going to make Lex act like he was ashamed of Tally. They were there together. Nothing was going to change that.

"Let me do the talking at first, okay?" he murmured. He brought Tally's hand up to his mouth and kissed it.

Tally nodded. The poor guy was nervous as hell. It didn't look like it was going to be much of a hardship for him to keep his mouth shut.

"Here goes nothing," Lex muttered. He tried to give Tally a reassuring smile. "It'll be fine, you know."

Tally said nothing, but smiled, cupped his chin, and gave him a small tender kiss, one that reminded him of every reason why he had to convince his mother that Tally was the perfect guy for him. Because he was. They hadn't talked about, well, what he'd said earlier, what they'd decided. But damn, he wanted it—wanted to feel the wet tight heat on his bare skin, wanted the intimacy that it implied. Fuck, he was a goner.

The door opened before Lex even had a chance to knock. His mother was standing there, dressed in one of her nicest outfits, with the pearls Lex had gotten her for Christmas draped around her neck. Rather than her usual sunny greeting, she simply stepped aside and let them pass.

"Hi, Ma," Lex murmured and kissed her on the cheek. He was damned if he was going to act like he'd done anything wrong.

"Dinner is on the table, why don't you two go and sit."

"Aren't we going to talk about this first?"

"Sit. The macaroni and cheese will get cold."

Lex bit back a small smile. She'd made macaroni and cheese. He would bet the side dishes would be applesauce and tuna salad. They always were. It was his favorite dinner, and his mother knew it. Hopefully, it was her way of saying she wasn't that upset. Hopefully.

"So, Tallis, how is it that you ended up back home after all these years?"

Lex sighed. The diplomacy that had lasted until dinner was served was apparently over. He reached under the table and laid his hand on Tally's knee.

"I ran into some hard times in Seattle. My grandmother generously offered to let me live with her if I help around the house."

"Hmm. That was nice of her."

Lex glared at his mother pointedly. She wasn't making a damn bit of effort to be welcoming.

"And how did you go from Lex's employee to making out with him in broad daylight?"

"Mom, shit!"

"Watch your tongue, James Alexis," his father snapped. Dad didn't care much if Lex swore, but not in front of his mother. His father was old-fashioned that way.

"Alexis?" Tally grinned. "I always thought Amy was kidding."

Lex squeezed his knee. *Don't make fun of it here.* "It's an old family name."

"Really? Where did it come from?" Tally smiled at Lex's mother without a hint of laughter in his face.

Thank God he got the picture.

"Lex's great grandfather was James Alexis, and all of the first-born males have been since."

"I wish my family had traditions like that." Tally couldn't have said anything more perfect. Flattery would work with his mother every time.

"Who were you named after? Tallis is very unique." She actually sounded polite and genuinely interested. The flattery *had* worked after all.

Tally blushed. "I think she got it from a romance novel, actually. She tells everybody now that I was named after her favorite composer, but my mother doesn't listen to classical music any more than she reads the Russian epics."

"You were named after a character in a romance novel?" Lex couldn't help chuckling.

"Yeah, some duke or knight in shining armor from one of those bodice rippers. It's embarrassing."

"You could pull off the regency look." He poked Tally in the side. "Hey, at least you can lie and say it was the composer. Thomas Tallis, right?"

Tally shot Lex a surprised look. "How did you know that?"

"Uh, he was on The Tudors. I can't *not* watch Jonathan Rhys Meyers."

"You're already cheating on Zac Efron?"

Lex laughed under his breath. "I'm going to kill Amy."

Tally gave him a small bump with his shoulder. It was then that Lex realized he and Tally had been having their own conversation right in front of his parents, teasing and smiling and not paying a bit of attention to the way his mother was watching them appraisingly. As soon as he noticed her watching, he also realized she was smiling as well.

Yes, Mom. See how nice he is?

"You two act like you've known each other for years." Her smile was real and aimed at both of them.

"It feels like we have, Mom. I—" *love him. More every day.*

The moment hung awkwardly for a second, but his mother saved it.

"Dig into the food, boys. My macaroni isn't very good cold."

"YOU know we're probably going to have to do this again with my grandmother. Her questions are getting more pointed by the day."

They were walking back to Lex's car, hand in hand. Lex couldn't have been happier with the way the meal had turned out. His mother, just like nearly everyone else, had been at least mostly won over by Tally's charm, by his politeness, the genuine interest he showed in people. Lex had known Tally could do it if he only had the chance. It seemed like one more obstacle had been removed from their path.

"I like your grandmother. I'm a little scared of her, but I like her."

Tally chuckled. "I think everyone's a little scared of her. She already knows, babe. She just wants to make sure I'm happy."

"You are happy, right? Things have changed a lot in the past few days. They've gotten awfully—"

"Real?"

Lex hesitated. He would have said serious. And it was true. They had gotten serious, for him at least. "Yeah, real."

"I like real." Tally reached out and curled his warm hand around Lex's neck, pulling him in for a kiss. "It feels good."

"So what I said earlier today—um, when we were in bed." Lex's stomach fluttered nervously, but he didn't want the conversation to be forgotten.

He could tell the moment when Tally figured out what he was talking about. An uncharacteristic flush went up his neck. "Um, can we at least get in your car before we start talking about that? I feel like your mom is still listening."

Lex chuckled. "You never know with her. That's probably a good idea." He unlocked his car, and with suddenly trembling hands he got in. It had been so easy to let it slip out in a moment of heat, but to discuss the matter rationally wasn't quite so easy. He'd started the car and pulled out on to the main road before either of them managed to spit out the first sentence.

Tally reached over and laid his hand on Lex's thigh. "So. What you said. I don't want to be with anyone else so… I think we could… make it just us."

Tally's answer was slow and hesitant, but Lex could tell he meant it. They'd be just that much more… *real*.

"Have you ever before?" Lex saw Tally shake his head out of the corner of his eye.

"No. I haven't really been close enough with someone, well, since high school. And back then it just never occurred to me. Have you?"

Lex shook his head. "My boyfriend in college wanted to, but I said no. I'm really lucky. It turns out the bastard was cheating on me."

"You got tested just in case, right?"

He snorted. "About a million fucking times. I'd have gone after him with a baseball bat if he'd given me anything."

"And recently?"

"There hasn't been a 'recently'. Not for a long, long time. I'm good. I can show you the papers."

"I trust you." Tally smiled. "How long was it before me?"

Lex groaned. *About a million years.* "I don't want to talk about it. It's a miracle I didn't spontaneously combust."

Tally chuckled. "It had been since November for me. I'd gotten so tired of dating by then that I just gave up. I was fine last time I got a test. I just need to make sure."

"And then we can…." Lex couldn't help the smile that snuck onto his face.

"*Yeah.*" The heat in Tally's voice was enough to make Lex's blood rush between his thighs. "I'll take care of it on my next day off. I can't wait to feel you."

Lex gulped. "I think you might have tomorrow morning off."

Tally gave him a quizzical look "No I don't."

"Yes. *You do.*"

TALLY was at Gianelli's again, waiting for his Saturday night pizza. On the outside, things seemed like they had every other day. No one looking at him would've been able to tell that he was barely keeping it together, but *nothing* seemed the same. He'd gotten his results back that morning. He was fine, which wasn't a big shock. But that one piece of paper burning a hole in his wallet meant everything was going to be different between him and Lex. It wasn't the actual physical act, although he knew it was going to be that much more intense with just them and no condoms. The big difference was mental. It was him and

Lex telling each other with their bodies that it was only going to be them. No one else. Ever. It was scary and exhilarating, and he was feeling everything that went with making those kinds of promises. He wanted to tell Lex, but he didn't know how many new and slightly terrifying things he could possibly fit into one night.

"Here's your pizza, Tally." Lacey slid a hot cardboard box across the counter.

"Thanks, sweetie."

She cocked her head and gave him a sly look. "What's up with you tonight? You seem nervous."

Tally cleared his throat and tried to shrug nonchalantly. He felt like he was fifteen years old again. "Nothing."

"Yeah, right. You going to ask Lex to go steady or something?"

She was flipping him shit, but the little brat was perceptive. He cringed. "Something like that."

"My guess is whatever it is you're too chicken shit to say to Lex, he's trying to find a way to say it to you too."

Tally felt his eyes go wide. "What?"

"I might be a kid, but I pay attention. He is so obviously, like, ass backward over you. That's what this is about, right?"

Tally nodded, bemused. Who was this kid, the psychic hotline?

"Just tell him how you feel." She grinned. "Why do men have to make things so difficult?"

Just tell him. Sure. Easy as pie. Tally nodded and picked up the pizza.

"Have a good night, Lace."

"You too."

Tally simply chuckled softly and shook his head as he walked out the door with his pizza.

When he got back to Lex's place, he heard the shower running and couldn't help but grin at the thought of naked, wet Lex. He poked his head into the bathroom.

"Hey, I'm here. I brought pizza." Tally tried to keep his voice casual. He hadn't told Lex about the paper in his wallet yet. He wanted it to be a surprise.

"Hi, babe. I'll be out in a minute." Lex stuck his soapy head out from behind the curtain and winked. "That is, unless you want to get in here with me."

"After dinner. I've got something I want to show you."

"I like show and tell." Lex's slow smile made Tally's heart race just a little faster, but then Lex ducked back behind the curtain and under the water. "Will you get out plates and stuff?"

"Sure. Hurry, though."

Lex's head popped out again. "Do I get a kiss?"

Tally smiled. *Anytime.* "Of course." He walked over and cupped his hand around Lex's dripping hair, dropping a small nibbly kiss on his wet lips.

"What do you want to show me?" Lex turned the water off and shook his head like a puppy.

"Patience. I'll have the plates and drinks ready by the time you're dry and dressed."

Lex gave Tally a little pouty look and tried to snap him with his towel. Tally laughed and escaped the stinging towel by inches.

"Nice cheeks," he threw over his shoulder as he jogged back out to the dining room area.

Tally was still smiling as he set out plates and glasses and grabbed two bottles of beer from the fridge. He wanted to shake his head at himself. There he was again, as usual, smiling like a lunatic for no other reason than he couldn't stop just… dorking out over how happy he was. Lex came wandering out of the bathroom, shirtless and wearing a pair of low-slung track pants. Tally had a hard time not following the line of sandy hair down his perfect abs… who was he kidding? He was totally doing it. More than anything he wanted the annoying pants gone so he could taste Lex like he wanted to.

"Okay, I got mostly dressed, and I was sort of patient. What is it that you wanted to show me?"

Tally thought he might draw it out a bit, for fun, or maybe because he was nervous, but then he looked at Lex's face, and he didn't want to wait another second. He pulled out his wallet and took the envelope and handed it to Lex.

Lex saw the return address and flashed a shy smile at Tally. "This what I think it is?"

Tally simply nodded and watched while Lex skimmed the paper. Then he handed it back and stepped closer until his bare chest was right against Tally's suddenly too-hot T-shirt. He slowly wrapped his arms around Tally's shoulders and kissed him, heat growing every second.

"Can't wait to feel you. Just us."

Tally kissed Lex and slipped his hands underneath the waist of Lex's track pants to cup his perfect round ass.

"I can't wait either." He was silent for a few moments while he tried to gather himself back together. "You, um, want some dinner?"

Tally was surprised by Lex's breathless laughing groan. "*No*. But we probably should." He brushed a fingertip across the warm dry skin around Lex's entrance. Lex tipped his head back and moaned lightly. "You're not making dinner sound any more appealing."

Tally grinned. "Isn't pizza better cold anyway?"

"I was hoping you'd say that."

Tally removed his hands from the warmth of Lex's sweats and held one out to Lex. "C'mon, babe. You ready?"

Lex shuddered. "Definitely ready."

They were quiet in Lex's room, which was bathed in the glow of an early summer sunset. Lex tugged his track bottoms down his legs and dug in his drawer for the lube. No condoms. Tally tried to keep his stomach from trembling, told himself it was just like all the other times. He knew it wasn't. It was different. More. It meant everything to him. Tally realized he was standing there, naked, staring at Lex, who was sprawled out golden and beautiful on his pale comforter. He never wanted to stop looking.

"Aren't you coming?" Lex asked, reaching out his hand.

"Not coming just yet," Tally answered with a grin, recovered from his emotional moment. "I've got big plans before anything like that happens." Then he kneeled on the bed and crawled up until he was kissing Lex. And then it *was* just like always, the fire between them that was usually just barely banked exploded into scorching flames, and they were fighting to get closer, closer, each one wanting to sink into the other's skin.

All they had to do was look at each other and it was fucking perfect.

Lex made a choked growling noise and threaded his fingers into Tally's hair, tugging hard.

"*God*, every damn time. You barely have to touch me."

"Me too. Never felt anything like it." Tally slung Lex's leg over his elbow and ground their hips together, taking Lex's mouth in a deep kiss. "Not even close."

Lex dragged his nails down Tally's spine and grabbed his ass, hauling Tally hard up against him. Tally laid his face on the pillow next to Lex's ear and started whispering. It was usually Lex that talked, and *damn*, Tally couldn't think of anything hotter in his whole life than Lex's voice all cracked with passion, whispering dirty things in his ear, but he couldn't seem to help it.

"Wanna be in you, baby," Tally moaned. "Want you all hot and tight around me."

Lex moaned and arched his back. "*Yes*."

"Need you in me too. Wanna know what it's like when you come."

Lex convulsed below him. "Oh *fuck* yes."

Tally shimmied lower to suck on Lex's nipples. Lex rolled his hips insistently, pushing his erection into Tally's stomach.

"C'mon, babe. What are you doing?"

Tally grinned up at Lex. "Tasting. I like the way you taste."

Lex let out a strangled moan when he remembered those words. Tally could tell by the moan that followed that he obviously remembered what had happened after them. Torture. Pure torture, and only the best kind.

"Oh, God, are you going to make me wait?"

Tally's only answer was a huge smile. "What if I did this instead?"

He licked his fingers and pushed them deep into Lex, whose keening cry and arched back were the only answer Tally needed. God, did he love this man. And then the talking started, flowing from those pouty sexy lips and making Tally want to purr. "Come inside me, baby… need you in me, fuck, do that again, now… love, oh God. Please."

It was the *please* that did it. Or maybe the *love*. Tally wasn't so out of his head yet that he missed it. His heart melted, and he wanted to do anything, *anything*, to make Lex happy.

"You need me now?"

Lex's breathless laugh rippled through his body. Tally could almost feel it from inside. "Lube," was the only word Lex was able to squeeze out.

Tally reached for the lube, popping open the flip cap and accidentally pouring a big pool into his palm. "Oops, shit. Too much." Lex reached out and took some from Tally's hand, spreading it all over Tally's erection, then his own, before he opened his thighs invitingly. Tally spread the rest of the lube on Lex's tight entrance, then reached back with slick fingers and readied himself as well. He had meant it about wanting to feel Lex come inside.

"Don't come, okay?" he whispered as he lined himself up, slippery and hard and dying to feel Lex's heat.

Lex bit his lip. "Are you kidding?" he gasped. "I'm about a heartbeat away already."

"Not till you're in me."

"Aww, fuck." Lex trembled and squeezed Tally's hips with his thighs. "Hurry, then. I'm gonna die."

In a motion made easy by slick lube and weeks of practice, Tally slid into Lex's body, not stopping until he was buried to the root and shaking to keep from flying apart at the seams.

"Oh my—" His voice was choked. He was on fire. There was nothing, *nothing*, like it in the world. "You've gotta try this, babe."

Lex's head was tossing back and forth on the pillow. "It's incredible."

Tally took one long stroke, angling his hips to hit Lex's prostate. "So *warm*. So fucking good." He leaned forward until his chest was on Lex's again, heated skin against skin, hearts pounding together.

I love you.

It wanted to come out so desperately. Tally had to close his eyes and bite his lip. Didn't want to say it for the first time like this. He spread his thighs between Lex's for better leverage, pushing deep, needing more. Lex's nails dug into the skin of his butt when he yanked hard.

"I'm not gonna last much longer, Tal," Lex stammered, his voice hitching. "Come. Now."

Tally didn't need much encouragement. Only a few more strokes into Lex's tight, hot body and he was coming, frozen, and watching Lex's eyes go wide.

"Oh my God, Tal. I can feel it," he whispered.

Tally stroked experimentally. If anything, it was warmer and wetter, and it felt like fucking heaven. He slid out reluctantly.

"I wanna feel you now," he murmured in Lex's ear.

Lex shifted and giggled softly.

"What?"

"I'm dripping."

"We'll take a shower later. Come here."

He lay back and let his thighs drift open. Lex scrambled closer, weird new sensations forgotten.

"I can't make this slow." He was coating his cock with more lube, looking at Tally with an indescribable look of tenderness on his face. Lex knew the look was there. He felt it on his face.

"I know, babe. Just… inside."

Lex lined himself up and pushed inside, eyes squeezing shut. "Holy *fuck*."

Tally could barely breathe. He was so full of Lex and a million damn emotions that all he could manage to do was wrap his legs around Lex's hips and squeeze.

"I can't—oh my God."

"Come inside me. Do it."

Lex started to move, rolling his hips slowly at first, then with more speed and desperation. He leaned over, kissing Tally sloppily, too turned on to worry about technique. Tally loved every second of it, loved the faint smack of their skin, the smell of sex and Lex's clean sweat, the way Lex arched his back and shouted out when he filled Tally with his hot, wet release.

It was them and it was perfect and it was everything he'd never dared to dream.

After a few minutes, Lex sighed raggedly and tipped his sweaty forehead against Tally's. "How much better do you think it can get before one of us blacks out completely?" he asked with a soft chuckle.

Tally pressed a long tired kiss on Lex's well-loved lips. "I don't know, but I'm definitely willing to try."

"All in the name of research, of course."

Tally grinned. "Of course."

TALLY was humming while he wiped down the espresso machine. Sun was pouring into the windows of the shop, warming everything with the first real wash of summer. It was still May, but there were always days like this, when the air smelled like summer and the warmth was gorgeous but not intense. He'd woken early, right as the sun was poking its way up, and kissed a soft, sleepy Lex before heading down to open the shop. He loved that Lex didn't even blink, just let Tally go with a smile like they'd been running the shop together forever.

The morning had been busy. Fridays always were. He'd been dishing up twenty-four ouncers since right after the doors opened at six. Sometimes he wondered if it would be more efficient to simply set up an IV drip so their customers could just inject the caffeine right into their veins. Or perhaps people could actually sleep instead of relying on coffee to keep them awake. Not that he'd been sleeping much. He'd been in *bed* early most nights but not actually sleeping.... Tally grinned and turned the sound system in the shop up just a little. It was always a little slow between the before work crowd and the people who snuck out to grab coffee at lunch.

He was dancing, not something he usually did, but the Latin beat on the radio was cheerful and sunny, and the permanent good mood he'd been in for close to a month wanted to flow out of his feet. Lex was out talking to the contractor who was going to work on their drive-through window. *Their drive-through.* Tally stopped where he was standing. God, he didn't even hesitate to think of the shop as theirs. He wanted nothing more than to blend their lives together, stay with Lex, live in his apartment, run the coffee shop together. Tally could barely believe a life like that was possible. He'd thought he would spend his life drifting, never belonging to anybody. It was a little scary how much he wanted to belong to Lex.

It took Tally a few minutes to realize someone was watching him. Not just *someone*. He felt the usual flutter in his stomach.

"How long have you been standing there?"

"A minute or two. I like the way you dance." Lex came up and slid behind Tally, putting his arms around Tally's waist and kissing the back of his neck. Tally melted, just a little, and covered Lex's arms with his own.

"We've gotta stop meeting like this." He felt the chuckle against his back.

"One of the customers is going to get the shock of their life someday soon if we don't."

"Wonder if any of them know?"

Lex shrugged. "It didn't take Lacey long to figure it out, or Travis. My guess is a few others probably have our number too."

"Do you care?" Tally turned in Lex's arms to look at him.

"Not really. Well, actually, not at all. I don't think it would be good for one of them to walk in on us like this, but that would be true no matter who I was with, even if it was a woman."

Tally grinned and patted him on the butt. "Yes, that nice young man Lex Barry would never make out with someone in his perfect shop. It would be unheard of."

"Shut up." Lex said it with a smile and followed up with a kiss, so Tally didn't take him too seriously.

"What's the status on the drive-through window?"

Lex wiggled happily in his arms. "The contractor says he can start in two weeks. I can't wait. Hey, I'm starving. I'm going to make myself a sandwich. You want anything?"

"Nah, I'm good. Thanks anyway, babe." He let his hand slip slowly off of Lex's hip as Lex turned to go to the refrigerator for sandwich fillings. He was still watching that sexy little walk when the bell on the shop door jingled. Tally turned to greet his customer, but the friendly hello he had planned froze on his tongue. He felt his stomach turn to ice water.

"Mom?"

CHAPTER
Twelve

"WHAT on earth are you doing back in town, Tallis?"

His mother looked at him just like he knew she would: cold, superior, irritated by his very existence—and clearly not expecting to see him there. He was surprised by how much it still hurt. Lex had frozen behind him, head in the fridge, probably unsure of what to do. Tally had barely spoken to his mother since that god-awful day when he was eighteen, but he was already sick of her.

"I could ask you the same thing, Mother."

"Since when do you call me Mother?"

"Since—" He broke off with a sigh. Tally didn't feel like getting into it with his damn mother. He'd been having such a good morning. "What do you want? You weren't surprised to see me, so I'm guessing you're here for a reason."

She smoothed her expensive skirt and sat on the edge of one of the bistro tables. "I came to visit your grandmother for the day and was surprised to learn that you've been staying there for over three months without my knowledge."

"Yeah, Mom. Grams said I could move in with her for a while. I ran into a tough patch back in Seattle."

"Tallis, don't you know how inappropriate it is for you to be in this town, what with your being—" His mother broke off like she couldn't even stand saying it.

"My being what, Mother? Dad's son? *Your* son?"

Lex came up behind him and put a comforting hand on the small of his back. All Tally wanted to do was lean into that touch and push his mother's voice as far from his mind as possible.

"You know why I don't want you here. Don't make me say it."

"And you came to the place where I *work* to tell me that? This conversation ends right now. If you'd like to continue it, I'll come to Grandma's house after I'm done today."

"Of course you will. Where else could you possibly have to go?" Tally stiffened at her caustic tone and the implication that he had no friends… which might have been true a few months ago. But not anymore. Lex curled his fingers around Tally's arm and slid them down until their fingers were threaded together. He had so much more than just friends.

"I'd be here. With Lex."

The look of outrage on his mother's face was almost funny. Almost. But it was too horrible to be funny. He hated that he still cared.

"You wouldn't!"

Lex smiled at her, deceptively sweet. "He does. Regularly."

Lex couldn't have picked a more perfect thing to say. Tally had to bite his lip to keep from grinning. His mother, on the other hand, pointed one of her perfectly manicured talons at them before huffing through the front door, which she slammed so hard the bell fell with a clatter to the floor.

"Sorry if I goaded her. She just made me so *mad*. I know what she was implying."

"It was fairly obvious, wasn't it?"

"So what now?"

Tally rolled his eyes. "I have to go over there tonight and deal with her. Hopefully I'll get her to go back to Seattle and leave us the hell alone."

Lex kissed the hollow below Tally's Adam's apple. "Want me to come with you?"

"*Yes*. But I'm not going to put you through that shit."

"Tal." Lex squeezed his hand hard. "Are we just fucking around here, or are we for real?"

"You know we're real."

"Then standing by their guy is what *real* boyfriends do. There's no way in hell I'd make you deal with her on your own."

Tally crushed Lex in his arms. The back of his throat was suspiciously tight.

"Thank you," was all he could manage to whisper.

LEX could've killed the bitch. To see Tally's face go from teasing and happy to frozen solid in the blink of an eye. He wanted nothing more than to vault over the counter and break his long-standing rule of never hitting a female. As it was, he planned to stand quietly by Tally's side no matter what she said to him. He was going to let Tally deal with his family, be respectful, and… *shit*. It was going to be such a pain to hold back when all he wanted to do was fight to protect the man he loved.

They were standing outside of Tally's grandmother's house. He was watching Tally breathe deep and try to relax. It sure as hell wasn't the scene Lex imagined when he thought of the first time Tally would bring him to "meet" his grandmother. He'd imagined answering questions about how they realized they were interested in each other, maybe talking about the shop or trading stories about town. He'd never imagined being the fire buffer between Tally and his bitch of a mother.

"Do you really care what she thinks?" he asked Tally quietly. It sucked standing there and watching Tal tear himself apart.

"I thought I was years beyond caring. But it hurt this afternoon, the way she assumed that I wasn't wanted."

How long has he been carrying this thing around? It hurt Lex to even think it. "Don't listen to it. You're *so* wanted, and not just by me. Think of how much Lacey likes you, or even Amy. She laughs at your jokes and tells me that she likes us together."

Tally winced. "She told *me* if I hurt you she'd tear my balls off."

Lex couldn't help but laugh. "Amy's never seen a pair of balls in her life. She wouldn't even know where to start."

"I am so telling her you said that."

Lex rolled his eyes. "You want to go get this over with?"

"Yes, please. Let's send the wicked witch back to the emerald city."

The atmosphere in Tally's grandmother's house was nothing like it was the few times Lex had been by. It was like Tally's mother had brought a wave of glacial air with her that permeated the entire place. He had a hard time reconciling the cold superior woman with his Tally or even Tally's grandmother, with her opinions and frank, down-to-earth nature. Neither of them seemed to match Tally's mother at all.

When they'd gone in, she was sitting on the sofa reading, not "visiting with Tally's grandmother" which was her supposed motive for being there in the first place. Tally's grandmother was out in the kitchen, and from the amazing smells, Lex decided she must be making cookies. If she was anything like his mom, that meant she was worried about something. They stood there for a while before Tally's mother deigned to acknowledge their presence. And then it was only with a snide look and a rude question.

"Why is he here? This is a family matter."

Lex clenched his teeth.

"Let's just get this over with, Mother. You can tell me all the reasons why I should disappear, I can tell you that I'm staying no matter what you say, and you can hissy fit your way back to Seattle where you belong."

Other than a flared nostril, there was no reaction. She continued to sit, crossing her legs at the ankle. *How did Tally stand her all those years?*

"Seattle is where you belong too. This town is no place for you."

"What do you know about where I belong? I had nothing in Seattle. Here…. Here I have family, and—" He broke off and looked at Lex. The look Tally gave him was so tender and honest that Lex's gut clenched. *He has someone who loves him.*

"People here hate our family enough. What happens when they find out you've been carrying on with the coffee shop boy? Don't you think you did enough damage to my name?"

"Me? What the hell did I do?"

"You were horrible! Do you think I had no idea how the people talked about you? Between you and your father I can barely show my face in this town. And now this… this *gay* thing. It's unseemly."

"It's not a thing, it's who I am." Tally looked frustrated. "Why are we even bothering with this? I told you last time I was never going to change."

"It's disgusting. Go do it somewhere where nobody knows you—or me."

"It's not disgusting, it's...." Tally's voice faltered. Lex could see he was still a little scared of his mother, no matter how much he tried to stick up for himself. Lex decided he'd had enough.

"It's love," Lex said quietly.

"What?" Tally's mother stood and walked closer, getting in Lex's face as much as a pampered society madam would dare to do.

"I said it's love," Lex burst out. "Your son is... is *wonderful* and caring and kind, and I'm so in love with him that it's hard to breathe sometimes! There's nothing wrong with that."

I can't believe I just said it. Not how I wanted him to hear it the first time.... Apparently, it wasn't what Tally's mother wanted to hear either. Her face twisted into a genteel sneer.

"Do you think that little... *tirade* made me see the error of my ways? So you're a filthy pervert. Just like Tallis. Maybe you two belong together. Just take your perversion somewhere far away where no one can see you." Her words came out in a low, silky purr. It was the ugliest thing Lex had ever heard.

"Why do you care anyway, Mom? You don't live here anymore."

She shrugged delicately. "This is where I came from. It might be a bit common, but I do have to show my face every once in a while. I can't have people talking about me."

"No one gives a *shit* what you do anymore. Dad's been gone for years! You've been gone for years."

"And now you'll be gone too. I want you to remove yourself from this... situation"—she gestured at Lex like he was some kind of parasite—"and pack your things. You're leaving."

"The fuck I am. *You're* the one who's leaving. Now get out." Tally moved to stand between his mother and Lex, like he'd protect Lex from any more of the negativity that she spewed.

"You can't kick me out of my own house."

"No, but I can." Tally's grandmother came from the kitchen, where she'd been diplomatically avoiding the whole conversation. "I can't believe a daughter of mine would treat her son so atrociously, even if there are things about him she disapproves of. I was hoping for more out of you. Unfortunately I was wrong. I'd like you to leave."

"But, *Mother*—"

"Out." Tally's grandmother pointed to the door, her face leaving no room for argument.

Lex saw Tally wavering between horror and laughter, hurt and awe, somewhere close to the edge of a breakdown. Tally's mother was stomping around the room, gathering her purse and her keys, cheeks pink with rage.

"Hey, do you want me to go outside? I can wait in the car." Lex reached up and rubbed the pad of his thumb on Tally's heated cheek. Tally shook his head as if trying to shed the shock.

"No, stay. Please. You… you love me?" His voice was happy and shy and scared and everything Lex was hoping to hear. The shadows behind his happiness weren't good, but Lex could only hope he would be able to make them go away someday soon.

Lex smiled softly, the little nervous flutters in his stomach melting into a gentle warmth. "Of course I love you. I didn't mean for you to hear it like that, but yeah, I do."

"I do too. L-love you, that is," Tally stammered.

Lex didn't care where they were, he didn't care that Tally's mother was still stomping around, making a big show out of gathering her things. All he cared about was grabbing on to Tally and holding him as hard as he could, kissing him until they could barely breathe.

When they drew apart for air, Tally's mother was gone, and Lex noticed that his grandmother was standing, arms crossed, looking at them placidly. Tally noticed too, and turned a bit pink.

"Uh, Grams, you know Lex, right?"

"Of course. How are you, Lex?"

Lex snickered. He couldn't help it. Not the question he'd have imagined coming from the grandma who just caught them making out in her living room.

"Um, I'm good." *I'm fucking amazing. He loves me.* Lex knew everything he was feeling was all over his face.

"Hey, Grams. Do you mind if Lex and I go? I have some things to think about."

"Yes, dear. Go ahead. But I'd still like to see you two for dinner."

"Tomorrow?"

"Yes, that's fine."

Lex wondered how many times he and Tally would have to explain themselves. To their families, their friends, the town at large. All he wanted was to love Tally and live like everyone else got to and not wonder who was saying what about them behind their backs.

When they got in the car, it was quiet and filled with emotion. Not uncomfortable exactly, but different then it had been on the way there. The air was swirling with everything Tally's mother had said to them. Everything they had said to each other. Lex was worried that the bad side was going to take over so that everything good about the past hour would come to mean nothing. Slowly, though, Tally's hand crept across the gearshift until it was curled around his thigh. Lex hadn't realized he was holding his breath until he could suddenly breathe again.

"I'm sorry about everything my mom said. She's awful." Tally winced, his eyes pinching up on the sides.

"Hey." Lex put his hand over Tally's. "It's okay. It's not what matters about today."

Lex looked over to see a slow smile spreading across Tally's face. "No, it's not." He brought Lex's hand up to his face and kissed his palm. "I love you," he murmured, then he put his hand back on Lex's thigh.

"I love you too, Tal. I really do."

Tally fell silent again, and although he didn't move his hand from Lex's leg, Lex could tell he was still dwelling on what had happened with his mother. Lex let him stew in silence, thinking he might need a few minutes to think. Lex wasn't going to let it go on for long, though.

When he unlocked the door of his apartment, Lex took hold of Tally's hand and pulled. Tally followed him meekly to the bedroom where Lex stripped him down to his briefs and pushed gently until he was lying down. Then he stripped himself and crawled under the covers to wrap his arms around Tally.

"You okay?" he whispered.

Tally made a suspicious sniffling sound. "I feel like shit, and it sucks that I do because I should be happy, I should be *so* happy right now. Most of me is."

Lex slung his leg over Tally's hip and hugged him close. "I'm happy for us." He kissed the side of Tally's neck. "You can't let her get to you, babe. I know she's your mother, but sometimes that's not all that matters."

Tally buried his face against Lex's neck. Lex thought he might feel dampness, but he didn't want to. He didn't want Tally to be hurt.

"Why do I let her do this to me?"

"Because you're human, and a good man who cares about people."

"I want to be good."

"You are. And you have people who love you. Me, your grandmother, my family soon enough if they don't already. We love you *because* you're you, not in spite of it. Don't let her make you think less of that."

Tally tugged Lex until they were lined up, chest to chest, forehead to forehead.

"I'll never think less of that."

"Good."

Lex kissed him and dug his fingers into Tally's hair, which had grown charmingly shaggy over the past few months. Then he let his hand drift down to rub up and down Tally's spine, comforting and light, until he could hear the even sounds of Tally breathing in his sleep. Lex relaxed back against his pillow and stared at the ceiling. The afternoon had been awful and wonderful, and he couldn't help but feel like he had his whole world right there curled up next to him, dented a bit, but hopefully not damaged.

Even though it was still light out, Lex figured they wouldn't be going anywhere else that night. He set his alarm for the morning and draped his arm over Tally, hoping that, if nothing else, he could at least get some sleep.

CHAPTER Thirteen

TALLY was in the grocery store picking up beer and stuff to make nachos for the movie night they were having with Amy later. It was Saturday, and he'd talked Lex into letting them host for a change. It felt oddly domestic to be walking through the grocery store, list in hand, getting supplies to host his first little dinner with the man he lived with—and Tally had to admit that he and Lex were living together. He hadn't slept at his grandmother's house since the night that they made all those hundreds of cupcakes, and most of his meager belongings had migrated into Lex's closet and dresser. Tally still couldn't believe it was real. He'd never even come close to having a boyfriend since high school.

He'd felt guilty about ditching his grandmother at first, but she seemed to be perfectly happy with visits and even happier that he'd found someone as nice as Lex. Even the dinner, which he'd been halfway dreading, had been fine. She told him basically the same thing Lex had said before, that people loved him and it didn't matter what her horse's ass of a daughter thought. Okay, maybe Lex hadn't called his mom a horse's ass, but the idea was there. And he felt better about that. Mostly. It still nagged at him when he ran across someone who didn't know him from the coffee shop and he got that old "I hate you Tallis Carrington" look. At those times, he found himself thinking that maybe his mother was right, and it was a bad idea for him to be back where his family's name was a cussword. And then he thought of Lex, and his heart practically burst from the sheer volume of happiness it was trying to contain.

He loves me. Me. How is that even possible?

Tally picked through the tomatoes, trying to find ones that were ripe already. He was excited to see Amy that night, and weirdly enough, he was worried even more about what she thought of him than he had been before. He didn't know what Lex had told her—about their sex life, about his mother, about what they'd said to each other the week before....

He tried to talk himself out of being paranoid, but it seemed like he was constantly waiting for people to hate him, waiting for the day that he'd wake up and Lex would look at him and say "what the hell was I thinking?" God, he hoped it never happened. The thought of not having Lex was like an arrow to the gut.

"Tally?"

Tally nearly dropped the onion he'd been about to bag. He looked over and blinked. *No way.*

"Drew?"

Drew McAuliffe looked *amazing*. He'd dropped about twenty pounds of beefy muscle that he'd carried in high school, and like Tally himself, he'd become lean but still healthy looking. The guy could've walked right off the pages of J. Crew. The golden-boy-gone-to-seed look that Brock seemed to have going on must have passed right over Drew. Didn't mean Tally was attracted to him. More like proud.

"I was hoping I'd run into you soon. My dad said you paid him a visit."

Tally chuckled softly. "Yeah, I did. You know, I have to say it. You look really good."

"You do too. Kinda lost that beefcake look."

Tally sputtered and nearly laughed outright. He'd forgotten how Drew didn't hold much back.

"That's exactly what I was thinking about you," he said with a smile.

"What *are* you doing back in town? The rumors circulated back when you first got here, but I know most of that shit is never true."

"What were the rumors?"

Drew laughed and added a head of lettuce to his basket. "Let's see, cancer, scorned lover, coming home to take care of your dying grandmother, who looks healthy as a horse to me."

"Would you believe plain ol' broke?"

"That's not very soapy of you."

"Boring but true. I lost my job in Seattle and ran out of cash. My grandma said I could stay with her until I got my feet under me again."

"How come you're still around?"

Tally shrugged. "Things are better here than I remembered, sure as hell better than I had them in Seattle." He didn't know why the first thing out of his mouth wasn't "I fell in love." Maybe he wasn't sure of his old friend yet. Maybe he wasn't sure of himself.

"Hey, do you want to drop that stuff off at home and go get coffee or something? It would be great to talk, and I hear that place down on Old Main has good desserts."

"You mean Lex Barry's shop?"

Drew blushed. "Yeah."

"How come you don't go there, then?"

"How did you know that I don't?"

Tally elbowed him. "Because I work there. It's my day off, but that's okay, we can go anyway. Lex is probably bored. He's been in his office all day working on the computer."

"Oh, you want to meet in a half an hour or so? Give you time to get home and put your food in the fridge."

Tally opened his mouth up to say that the coffee shop *was* home but instead said, "Sure. I'll see you there."

TRAVIS was bustling around behind the counter, cleaning, when Tally came down from putting his groceries away. A pretty girl with gorgeous skin the color of rich French roast was sitting at the counter, school books spread out.

"Hey, Trav. Is this the Cheri I've been hearing about?"

Travis looked embarrassed. "Yeah, this is Cheri. Cher, this is Tally."

"Hi, Tally, you're Lex's boyfriend, right?"

"Yeah." *Why did that feel weird to say out loud? It shouldn't have felt weird.* Tally changed the subject. "What are you working on?"

Cheri groaned. "Calculus. It's horrible."

Tally chuckled. "Wish I could help you there. I never even took that class."

"Cheri's going to be pre med." Travis's voice was full of pride.

"That's great." Tally smiled. "I'm going to go say hi to Lex really quick. If someone comes in looking for me, tell him I'll be out in a minute."

Travis raised his eyebrows, and Tally rolled his eyes at their young employee. "He's an old friend from high school. Give me a break."

Travis stuck out his tongue. Tally laughed and wondered when he'd managed to acquire a little brother. It was kind of nice, actually. He was still smiling when he walked into Lex's office to find him buried in a pile of papers and tapping frantically at his keyboard. He was wearing those wire-rimmed glasses that drove Tally insane. He had fantasies about those glasses sometimes: the glasses, Lex, a button-up shirt halfway undone and falling off his shoulders, head thrown back in ecstasy while he rode Tally in that rickety old computer chair. Tally shuddered. That was going to have to happen. Soon.

"Hey, babe."

Lex jumped, then he looked up and smiled. "Hey, you scared me."

He got up and stretched. His shirt came up to expose a few inches of golden skin and just the hint of a treasure trail. *Mmmmm.* Tally reached out and rubbed Lex's abdomen. He wondered if he would ever be able to keep his hands off. Lex draped his arms over Tally's shoulders and gave him a leisurely kiss.

"Did you get all the stuff for tonight?"

"Yep. Even avocados for homemade guacamole." Tally kissed him and massaged his lower back.

Lex groaned and leaned into Tally's touch. "That feels amazing. I wish it was dinner already. I'm starved."

"Want me to get you something from out front?"

"Nah." Lex kissed Tally's neck and patted him on the hip. "I'll wait."

"Hey, Tally, your friend is here." Travis's voice drifted through the hallway.

"Friend?"

"Yeah, Drew MacAuliffe. I ran into him at the grocery store." Lex made a face. "Drew's really cool, actually. He's not like Brock or the rest of them."

"Hmm." Tally could tell Lex didn't believe him. "I'm glad those guys don't want to be infected by my homo juice, or I'd have to look at them every day. They already give me enough trouble when I run into them in town."

Tally snorted. "I like your homo juice." He leaned over and nuzzled Lex's neck. "And I'll deal with Brock if you want me to."

Lex chuckled. "What did I do before I had you in town to fight my battles for me?"

"Suffered nobly?"

"Something like that. Hey, I'm going to get back to these so I can have fun tonight instead of worrying about all this crap that needs to be done."

"See you in a little bit?"

"Yeah, when I drag myself out from under this pile of papers."

Tally leaned down for one more kiss before turning to go back out to the shop.

Drew was waiting with a muffin and a huge latte. "This is awesome. Travis makes really good coffee."

Tally smiled at him. It was hard not to. The guy had always been so friendly. "You should come in more often."

Drew rolled his eyes. "Brock would never let me live it down. He calls the coffee here fairy juice."

"He must be hanging out with your father."

"No, actually, for as much as they have in common they don't like each other."

"Why do you care what Brock thinks, anyway?"

Drew chuckled disbelievingly. "Oh, man. You've been in the big city for too long. He runs this town."

"Brock?" From what Tally remembered, he'd been a bit of a moron, and his encounter with him a few weeks back hadn't done anything to refute that. The guy was a douche. A douche who hit on high school girls. Tally shuddered.

"Yeah, his dad basically owns the country club. They're the money in town ever since, well...."

"Ever since my dad died. It's okay. I've had a long time to get used to it."

"I've always meant to say sorry about that, and about the way I acted, or didn't act is more like it. I should've been a better friend back then. I was a follower."

"It's okay. Like I said, it was a long time ago."

Lex came wandering out of his office and went rooting around in the pastry display until he came up with a muffin.

"Hey, I thought you were waiting for dinner?"

Lex gave Tally a little sideways smile. "I thought I could, but my stomach started growling." He waved at Drew, hesitant, but it looked like he was prepared to be friendly.

"Lex, you remember Drew, right?"

"Yeah. Hey."

"Hi, Lex."

"You don't have your usual entourage with you."

Drew actually smiled at that. "They're not *my* entourage."

"Yeah, technically they're mine," Tally added with a grin.

Lex shook his head, but he was still smiling. Tally hoped he could separate Drew from the rest of them. He really was different. "Hey, I've gotta get back to those accounts before they start having babies."

"Let me know if you ever need help. I'm a CPA." Drew smiled at Lex, also nothing but friendship in his face. Tally felt hope well in his stomach. Maybe everything would be easier than he thought.

Lex shrugged and took a big bite out of his blueberry muffin. "I wish I could afford you," he mumbled around the food in his mouth.

"Well, hey, I've been friends with Tally for years, and he works here, right? I'll just call it a friendly favor."

Lex looked surprised. "That's really nice of you."

"It's no problem." Drew beamed.

And that's when Tally figured out what was going on. *I knew it!* Tally had always thought there was something… recognizable about Drew back in high school, and he clearly had the hots for Lex, not that it was *ever* going to happen, but still. Tally waited until Lex went back into his office before he turned to face Drew.

"You so want to get in his pants!"

It was a good thing they were the only people in the shop. Drew's face turned red. The poor guy was mortified. Tally hadn't really meant to blurt it out like that, but he felt a little vindicated that he'd been right all those years.

"I don't—it's not...." He looked like he didn't know what to say.

"D, just spit it out."

"Fuck. Yes, okay? I think Lex is hot."

"And you're gay?"

"No! I mean, no, I'm not." Tally simply looked at him. "I'm bi, but it's not something I advertise. You're not going to tell Brock, are you?"

"First of all, what makes you think I talk to Brock, and second of all, no. I don't tell other people's business."

Drew breathed more easily. "So, is Lex single, do you know?" It seemed like it was hard for him to spit it out.

"You just said no one knew you were bi."

"I know, but...."

"Lex isn't really into closets." Tally deliberately gave Drew a slow satisfied smile. "Besides, he's not single."

Tally saw the comprehension dawn on Drew's face. "You? Tallis Carrington?"

"Yep."

"Since when?"

"A month or so."

Drew looked a bit flabbergasted. "No, I mean since when are you gay at all?"

"Always."

Drew's jaw dropped, and Tally burst out laughing. "Wait, so you knew this in high school?"

Tally nodded. "I had a boyfriend in high school."

"No way! Who? Please tell me it wasn't one of the guys on the team."

Tally groaned at the thought of sleeping with one of his old football teammates, not that some of them weren't kinda hot, but that wasn't an image he wanted in his head.

"You didn't know him. Not very soapy of me again, but he lived out of town. In Astoria."

Drew grinned. "Hey, secret gay is soapy enough for me—doesn't have to be a hidden football romance."

"There could've been even more to the story. I was secretly gay, you were secretly bi…." Tally wiggled his eyebrows and smiled.

"I'm still secretly bi."

"I know, which I don't get."

"You haven't lived here every day of your life, haven't tried to do business."

"Lex does."

"Yeah, but isn't he hassled all the time? Like from my father?"

"Not really. I mean your dad didn't want to give him that building permit, but he isn't actually bothered by anyone."

"How 'bout the fact that none of the parents around here wanted their kids to work for him?"

"What are you talking about?"

"I know Lex was looking for someone for a long time before you came, and I'd heard some whispers about how none of the kids' parents wanted them working for him."

Tally was outraged. "Lex would never touch a kid!"

"People here are still really small town, Tally. Hence my closed mouth. I guess if I was completely gay then I'd either move away or come out. Since I'm still attracted to women, I've always taken the easy road."

"But are you happy?" Drew's face turned pink. *Shit.* "Sorry, dude. Sometimes I think I should've become a reporter."

"It's okay. Happy's a strong word. I'm fine with the way things are. I'd have to fall for a guy pretty hard for it to be worth it. I doubt that's going to happen."

Tally shrugged. "You never know. I didn't think I would ever really fall for anyone."

Drew smiled. "So it's pretty serious between you two?"

"Yeah." Tally couldn't help his smile. He had a sudden thought. "Hey, listen. I don't know if it's weird, but Lex and I were going to watch movies with his friend Amy tonight. You want to come?"

Drew looked unsure. "Um, is she single?"

Tally couldn't help but to laugh. "It's not a hookup. She's not into guys at all."

Drew chuckled. Tally could tell he was relieved. "So is this the Rock Bay gay squad or something?"

"Something like that. You should come, though."

Drew shrugged. "Why not? Where is it?"

"Right upstairs. Lex's apartment is over the shop. I was going to head up there and get snacks started pretty soon, actually. You could always just stay here and hang out with me."

"Can you make sure it's okay with Lex first? I don't want to intrude."

"Yeah, I'll go make sure, but he'll be fine with it."

THE self-proclaimed gay squad of Rock Bay was having a good time, better even than Tally had imagined possible. After some initial standoffishness, Drew and Amy banded together in their efforts to give Lex and Tally shit, and by the time they were done with a movie and a game of Trivial Pursuit, they were well on their way to being friends. He still had to pinch himself every once in a while when he started thinking there was no way any of this could really be his life.

They'd made their way through a couple bottles of wine and at least two six packs of beer. Tally was lying back on the couch with a mostly sleeping Lex between his legs. Amy was sprawled on the floor beneath them, and she and Drew were embroiled in a game of speed on the oriental carpet. Tally was busy trying to inch Lex's shirt up so he could touch the soft skin of his belly.

"Knock it off, Tally. I don't want to watch my best friend get it on." Amy didn't even pause in her game. She slammed down her last card and flung both of her hands in the air.

"Damn it!" Drew growled. "I give up."

"I told you no one ever beats me." Amy tossed him her signature self-satisfied smirk.

He sighed. "I want a rematch. But sometime when my eyes aren't drifting shut."

Tally shot Drew a concerned look. "Hey, D, are you cool to drive?"

"Maybe. I guess I could always walk home, but I need my car in the morning. Do you have any coffee?" He looked surprised when Amy and Tally started laughing, then he realized what he'd just said. "Wow, that was dumb."

"What's happening?" asked Lex, his voice a sleepy grumble.

"Drew asked if we had any coffee." Lex smiled at the irony. "Babe, do you care if he crashes on the couch for a few hours? I think we managed to get him a little drunk."

"'Course not. There are extra blankets and stuff in the closet."

Tally kissed Lex on the back of the head and scooted around so he could stand and go look for the blankets.

"Hey, Lex, walk me out."

Tally noticed that Amy was giving Lex a significant look. She was clearly trying to be casual, but even Tally, after only knowing her for a few months, could see right through it.

"Sure, Ames. Let me get a sweatshirt on." Lex pressed a short tired kiss on Tally's lips and rolled his eyes a little when he was sure nobody but Tally could see. "Be right back. Don't fall asleep without me."

"I won't."

As soon as he waved good-bye to Amy, Tally got Drew settled on the couch with a few blankets and a down pillow. Drew looked like he was still spinning a little, but he didn't seem too bad off. He was just turning to go to bed when Drew spoke.

"You guys seem really happy, Tally. I'm glad."

"Yeah? You don't disapprove of our evil gayness?"

Drew sighed. "Fuck off. You know that's not me."

"I know, I was just giving you shit. Hey, it was really nice to see you, man. Give me a call soon if I'm still passed out when you wake up. Thank God it's Lex's turn to get up and let Travis in tomorrow."

Drew gave Tally a sly grin.

"What?" Tally asked.

"You, dude. I never thought I would see badass Tallis Carrington in love and all domesticated and shit and *happy* about it to boot."

Tally shrugged. "Guess it took the right guy."

LEX shivered. He'd been so warm lying on the couch, cuddled up to Tally. The brisk night air was a bit of a shock. He hopped from one foot to another while he waited for Amy to get her keys from her self-named manbag. Lex had made the mistake of calling it a purse once, and she nearly bit his head off. Apparently the word "purse" was far too girly for her. Didn't matter. The damn thing was like a bottomless pit, and wherever her keys were it was taking forever for her to find them.

"C'mon, Ames, I'm freezing! What's taking so long?"

"Found 'em. They were stuck beneath my makeup bag."

Lex snorted. "If you have a makeup bag in there, it's a purse. I'm not buying that manbag shit ever again."

"Whatever." She was uncharacteristically lax in the defense of her butchness. "Hey, listen, Lexie, I don't want to be too overprotective, but I have to ask."

Ah, shit. This isn't going to be a short conversation. Amy only called him by his sister's nickname for him when she was ready for a heart to heart.

"What's going on, Ames?"

"You and hottie up there are getting awfully cozy looking. I thought this was just a friends with benefits thing."

Lex felt his cheeks turn pink. "Not anymore." He took a long breath. "He loves me, Ames," Lex told her quietly.

"And what, this is a summer love affair, fun until he moves back to Seattle? I just don't want you to get hurt, babe. I had to pick up the pieces when Eric cheated on you. I don't want you to go through that again."

Lex shook his head. "He's not going back to Seattle. I think—" He didn't know how to say it. He hadn't really even said it to himself. "I think he might be it for me."

"It?"

If anything, Lex's cheeks felt hotter. "Yeah. *It.* Like I love him. Like I can't imagine waking up for the rest of my life without him next to me."

Amy froze in place. "Shit, Lexie, when did that happen?"

He shrugged. "Slowly, or maybe it's been there from the beginning, and I was trying to ignore it. I don't know. All I know is when he told me that he didn't want to go back to Seattle anymore, my heart stopped for a second, and then I was happier than I've ever been in my life. The whole thing felt… *right*. I can't describe it any other way."

"Does Tally know how you feel?"

"I don't know. I think so. He knows I love him. I guess the rest of it was implied."

Amy made a face. "Just be careful, all right?"

Lex shook his head. "I'm thinking this might be the one time in my orderly, careful life that I'm going to let go—just let things happen, you know?"

"And if it ends badly?"

"Then it ends badly. He's worth the risk."

And he was. Lex knew that, no matter what, he'd never regret feeling the way he did right then, totally in love. She squeezed him in an uncharacteristically tight hug.

"I'm happy for you, hon. Love ya."

"Love you too, Ames. Hey, are you sure you're cool to drive?"

"Of course. I stopped after two glasses of wine. I knew I didn't want to spend the night camped out at the love nest."

Lex gave her a playful shove. "Then I'm going to go back up now, 'kay?"

"Yeah. Have a good day off tomorrow. What are you going to do?"

Lex grinned. "*Sleep.*"

"Hey, at least you'll have someone to sleep with."

He nodded. That was probably his favorite part of being with someone, lying quietly together, kissing, being close. He was glad that Tally seemed to like it just as much as he did.

"Night," he called softly from the stairs that led to the back door of his building. Lex glanced over as Amy was pulling out and saw his BMW pulled right next to Tally's old, dented, rattrap, piece-of-crap car. Oddly enough, they seemed to go well together. He smiled. That was the way it was supposed to be.

CHAPTER
Fourteen

TALLY was cleaning up from the early morning rush on a rainy Tuesday. Lex had driven down to Astoria earlier for what he claimed was a much-needed haircut. Tally actually liked that Lex's hair was getting long, kinda skater-boy adorable, but he could tell it was driving Lex nuts so he said to go and he'd watch the shop. Lex had gone with a kiss and a promise to bring fish and chips back from the Bowpicker, one of Tally's favorite places to go eat when he was in high school and visiting Jeremy. After years of working at Cutter's in Seattle, the smell of fish and chips had stopped appealing to him, but lately he'd been craving that old familiar flavor. Must've been something to do with being home.

The overhead bell rang, and Tally looked up to see Drew walk through, looking a bit nervous but well put together in a suit and tie.

"Hey. What brings you here? Isn't Brock back in town?"

Drew had finally confessed that the only reason he'd had the courage to walk into Lex's shop in the first place the week before was that Brock was in Seattle for the weekend with his wife for the Nordstrom's Memorial Day sale. Tally had been to one of those before. Torture of the highest degree.

"Well, I kind of told him you work here. Um, I wouldn't be surprised if you see him around."

"Aw, shit. Thanks. You know I was trying to avoid him."

Drew cringed. "Sorry. I wasn't thinking, and I let it slip that I saw you, so he wanted details. It doesn't matter, Tal." Tally noticed that Drew seemed to have picked up Lex's nickname for him. He was surprised by the fact that he liked it.

"I just don't want to get involved with him. I'm really happy, you know? It's been years since my life was this nice. So what can I make for you?"

Drew blushed. "Just an Americano. And, um, about that?"

Tally chuckled. "What is it?"

"Brock told me to invite you out for guys' night next weekend. I was hoping that you'd come, and then, well, if he knows about you, then it might be easier for me."

Tally rolled his eyes. "And what makes you so sure that he'd be cool with me being gay?"

"Because you're you. Brock totally worshiped you in high school. We all did. I swear, every time that one of us does something that he doesn't like, his first reaction is to tell us what he thought you would do."

Tally rolled his eyes. "What would Tally do? You've gotta be kidding me. I'm not Jesus. Besides, I was a total fuck-up then. There wasn't anything to worship."

"You weren't all bad. There were lots of times when I could see this Tally peeking through. It's what I liked about you. The possibility that you weren't what you seemed."

"And here I thought all these years that no one saw through my bullshit back then."

Drew shrugged. "If it makes you feel any better, I don't think anyone else did. I wanted to. I wanted to believe there was more to you."

"Drew?"

"Don't ask. You don't want to know the answer. Besides, it was a long time ago." He sighed.

"And now? What makes you all of a sudden want to be out?"

"You know that guy that I'd have to fall pretty hard for?"

"Yeah?" Tally raised his eyebrows and smiled.

"I may have met him last week."

"Really? What's his name?" Tally was happy for his friend, but he didn't want him to push himself into anything until he was ready.

Drew shook his head and laughed. "You know, I have no idea. I saw him at a restaurant when I was down in Astoria grabbing dinner with my aunt. All we said was hi, but I swear...." He unconsciously laid his hand over his midsection. Tally knew exactly what he meant.

"How are you going to find him again?"

"He was wearing scrubs. My guess is he works at the hospital."

No way. Tally smiled. "If that's the case, then I'm sure Amy can help you if you want."

Drew looked nervous all of a sudden. "Don't say anything to her yet, please. I'd feel like an idiot if I was imagining the whole thing. He could totally be straight, there's just—"

Drew was interrupted by the door to the shop swinging open. Instead of the gentle jingle the bells usually made, there was a crash.

"What's up, fucker? D-dog told me I'd be able to find you here! I've been waiting for you to call me."

Fuck. Brock.

"Hey there, Brock. You, uh, want some coffee?" *How can I get him to leave?*

"Sure, dude. At least with you serving it up, I can be pretty sure it's not that fairy juice that Barry makes."

Drew laughed nervously, and Tally gave him a long look. That was not the way to start easing Brock into the idea that he might like men. Tally turned and rolled his eyes at Brock.

"I got the same beans that he has, *dude*. You want coffee or not?"

Brock's cheeks got red. He looked a bit embarrassed. "Yeah, but no sugar. The wife's got me on a diet."

Tally poured Brock his cup of drip coffee. Drew was making significant eyes at him, like he wanted Tally to blurt out the fact that he was gay right then and there. Tally waved him off with a small gesture. All in good time. If he'd learned anything at all during his long years in the city it was how to work it with a jerk. Brock fell under that category, and past hero worship notwithstanding, Tally knew the whole thing had to be handled delicately and at the right juncture—not to mention the fact that he wasn't particularly looking forward to doing it. A replay of the scene with his mother wasn't the way he wanted to start off his afternoon. Brock tossed a few dollars down on the counter.

"Thanks for the coffee, man. We're going to see you this weekend, right? Golf and drinks at the club. We might even check out the action down at Fox's on the highway."

Golfing, drinks, and the strip club instead of spending his night with Lex. Hell, cleaning the apartment would be better than what Brock had planned. Tally could've gagged at the thought of it. Drew shot a pleading gaze his way, and Tally sighed internally.

"Yeah, I'll be there."

"Sweet!" Brock raised his hand for a high five. *You've gotta be kidding me.* Tally didn't know what to do, so he gave Brock a weak high five in return. "C'mon, D. I'll give you a ride to work." He turned to Tally. "This one insists on being some granola munching tree-hugger. He never drives to work."

"It's only ten blocks!" Drew protested.

Tally wanted to tell Brock that perhaps if he walked to work more often his wife wouldn't have him on a diet, but he figured that wouldn't be the best plan when he was trying to be diplomatic for Drew's sake. It was beyond him why Drew wanted to keep being friends with Brock and the others, except for the fact that they were the only friends he probably had to choose from since everyone else managed to get the hell out of town. He could only hope that, by the end of it, Drew got what he wanted and Tally would be left alone to be with Lex.

"ARE you really going out with Brock and his friends? I hate those guys."

"I'm not a big fan of them either, but Drew asked me to do this for him."

Lex tried not to sound annoyed, panicked, everything that was pushing around inside of him. "What good will it do Drew for you to start hanging out with Brock and Rick again?"

"He hopes that once Brock finds out that I'm gay, he'll be a bit more accepting, and it'll pave the way for Drew to tell them he's bi."

Lex didn't understand any of it. "Why now, after all this time? Why does he care?"

Tally grinned. "I guess he met someone—well, sort of met someone, anyway. But he wants to be able to be with that guy if it ever comes to anything."

"And he really thinks hanging out with you for a night or two will make Brock Peterson more tolerant?" It was the stupidest damn thing Lex had ever heard.

"Listen, I don't know if it's going to work or not. But either way, I'll hang out with them once or twice, tell Brock about us, then I'm done. I'll have done what I told Drew I would do, and everyone can go on their merry way, including me and you."

Lex shook his head. He didn't want Tally anywhere near those guys again. Sometimes he could still see Tally's face back in high school, the way he looked when he was angry and closeted. He hated to admit it, but he was scared that Tally would turn into that guy again if he spent too much time with his old friends, getting pressured to conform. Lex didn't want that for either of them. He also didn't want to drive a wedge between them unnecessarily by starting a big fight over what he hoped would be nothing.

"I guess as long as you have a plan," Lex muttered. He tried not to hang his head, but he couldn't help it. He was worried about what could happen if Brock got his dumb, bigoted claws into Tally again.

He felt the pressure of Tally's fingers under his chin lifting it up. "Babe?"

Lex's throat tightened. He was annoyed at himself for getting so emotional. It was just after years of dealing with those... *assholes*, he thought he was finally done, and there they were, right back in his life, potentially causing havoc with the one thing he loved the most.

"What?" he whispered.

"I love you. *You.* I'm just doing this as a favor to Drew. I don't want to be friends with those guys again. I only want to be with you, okay?"

Lex sighed. "I'm being such a chick. Sorry."

Tally wrapped him in one of those big warm hugs that he loved so much. "You're not. You're worried, and jealous, and I love that you care. You didn't see how much I lost it when you went on a date with that nurse guy."

Lex smiled. "Yeah?"

"Hell yeah. If I'd been in my place instead of your shop there probably would've been some damage done. I felt like I was going nuts." He rolled his eyes.

"You know I only went out with him to talk myself out of wanting you so bad."

"Yeah. Didn't help. I still hated it."

Lex tugged on Tally's hair. "And I hate this. But I trust you."

Tally kissed him long and hard, not enough to erase his doubts but more than enough to distract him from thinking about them.

"How long until you have to leave again?"

Tally gave him a sly smile. "At least an hour."

Lex tugged him back toward their room. "C'mon."

He wanted to leave his mark on Tally somehow, to make sure he remembered that Lex was home waiting for him and nothing else was more important. He kissed Tally long and deep, biting Tally's lip hard enough to make his breath catch. Impatiently, he tugged at Tally's shirt, wanting to feel only skin, to taste him and bite at the lean muscles just underneath the surface. Tally growled softly and fell back on the bed, pulling Lex after him. Their legs and arms tangled together

"Maybe I don't have to leave for an hour and a half."

TALLY couldn't decide if the whole hanging-with-his-old-friends experience was infinitely worse than he imagined or quite a bit better. Even though he wanted to roll his eyes at two thirds of the things that Brock said, in an odd way, it felt like no time had passed at all. The minute he was surrounded by Brock, Rick, Kyle, and Drew, he was transported back to high school, back to the place where he was king, and they hung on his every word. He couldn't believe they still did.

The guys were simple, yes, and with the exception of Drew, they hadn't really ever grown out of their football-god mentality, even though he doubted a single one of them could sprint fifty yards even one time. But they treated him exactly the same as they always had: no stares, no condescending looks, no sympathetic pats on the back when they learned he was (supposedly) living with his grandmother. Although disconcerting, it was actually a bit refreshing.

That wasn't to say that Tally wasn't in the middle of his worst nightmare, because he was. He was living the life of a straight married man, desperate to escape the ball and chain for some hijinks with the boys, and it was driving him nuts. The golf game had been an eternity. He'd remembered how to golf from years before when he used to go out with his father and his father's friends. That didn't mean he liked it. Golfing still sucked. It was boring as hell, and the golf course was still the biggest good ol' boys society in the whole damn town. It made him want to gag.

After golf they'd changed and had just met at the lounge for dinner and drinks. The worst part was it was just the *beginning*. There would be more drinks after dinner, perhaps a strip club, ugh, pouring their drunk asses into the twenty-four hour diner for coffee and eggs, and *shit*. He still had hours left of the night, hours that could've been spent with Lex, who had tried to hide it but was probably way more hurt than he'd even let on that Tally was choosing his old friends over him.

"Yo, T, what are you having for dinner?"

Tally cringed at the old football nickname. He'd been given shit (respectfully of course) for his name in school. Brock used to tell him it sounded queer, which in the past had driven Tally insane. Now he honestly could care less. He sure as hell didn't want to be called "T" anymore.

"Don't call me that, Brock. We're not in high school anymore, and last time I saw I didn't wear a neck full of gold chains." He rolled his eyes and laughed so the moment wouldn't get too awkward. "And I think I'll have a chicken Caesar."

"Dude, that's chick food. You've been working at the fairy queen for too long. Get it? Instead of Dairy Queen it's Fairy Queen?"

Drew rolled his eyes and for once spoke up. "That's really dumb, Brock. Lex is a nice guy. You should leave him alone." He looked back down at his menu, like he couldn't quite believe what he'd said. "Um, I think I'm going to have a salad too. Didn't make it to the gym much this week."

"Are you cracked out, D? Why the fuck are you defending Sexy Lexie's fag ass? Are you in looove with him or something?"

Tally cringed when he heard Brock call Lex "Sexy Lexie" with that condescending hateful voice. He opened his mouth to say something but found it was stuck in his throat.

"Shut the hell up, dude." *Thank you, Drew*. "I went in there to see Tally, and Lex was there." *Oh. Well, not as good as defending Lex, but at least "shut up" was part of it.*

Tally knew lying about knowing Lex wasn't the best way for Drew to start his inch-by-inch journey out of the closet, but Tally let it go. The guy clearly wasn't ready for full disclosure. He was glad that Drew put Brock in his place, though, even before he had a chance to decide if he could.

"Whatever." Brock looked annoyed, but his face brightened when he spotted the server heading their way. "Here comes the waitress." He whistled low. "Damn, look at the tits on her! My dick tells me she's new to this joint."

Rick and Kyle whistled too, as she came closer, and Drew gave Tally an apologetic grimace. He looked embarrassed. Brock, Rick, and Kyle must've behaved the same way everywhere they went. It was the most ridiculous setting for it too. The poor girl had a button up shirt with a vest and long pants. The country club was clearly not Hooters, and she *clearly* wasn't looking to flirt with some mostly drunk assholes. Tally knew that if he made a big deal about it the guys would leave their waitress alone. He liked that, for some unknown reason, broke-ass barista and all, he was still powerful in their little tribe. Like he realized earlier, it was like nothing had ever changed.

Everyone ordered, Tally and Drew got their salads, the rest of the guys got steaks and burgers. Tally groaned at the pure quantities of meat that were coming to the table. He'd never been what you'd call a vegetarian, but he felt like a little went a really long way, and the thought of a big thick steak was nearly enough to put him off his salad. He wondered for the hundredth time what Amy and Lex were doing and vowed not to get stuck at another boy's night out the next weekend. Maybe he'd say he had to work. Maybe he'd say he had malaria. Drew apparently didn't really need his help to stick up for himself against Brock.

He sat and ate his salad silently, wondering to himself how he'd managed to get to this place: eating with old friends he didn't really like to help someone who was practically a stranger while he left the man he loved at home. If he said it like that it sounded like the stupidest thing in the world he could possibly do. *Not again.* Tally made a promise to himself. After this first night, Drew was on his own.

"Hey, Tally, what do you want to do after this?"

Why the hell are they asking me? Tally smiled. *Because they actually care what I think.* He felt a perverse thrill from the power. He wasn't used to it, for sure. At least if he was in charge of the plans there wouldn't be a damn strip club. Thank fucking God.

"You know, it's been forever since I went bowling."

"Hey, babe, you're home late." Tally had just crept in after hours of drunken bowling and the requisite trip to the diner for late night breakfast and coffee. Lex rolled over and looked at him with sleepy half-closed eyes. *He's so beautiful.* Tally had missed him, even after just one evening.

"Yeah. Sorry I woke you up." He leaned over and gave Lex a soft kiss.

Lex made a face. "Beer and maple syrup? That's not the best combo."

Tally chuckled. "I'll brush my teeth before I come to bed."

"M'kay," Lex mumbled and rolled back into the pile of pillows he'd made.

Tally had to wrestle one out from under him when he crawled under the covers. "Hey, you stole all the pillows," he teased as he tugged ineffectively.

"Can't sleep when you're not here." Lex scooted into Tally's embrace and pulled an arm around his waist. Tally's heart did a little double trip, then settled happily. He wriggled until Lex was nestled perfectly against him, back to chest, toes tangling together. Lex traced little patterns along the back of his hand. "So how did your night out with the Brock squad go?"

Tally hesitated. "It was okay. They haven't changed much."

"How did Brock take the news?"

"Um, didn't tell him. Next time."

Lex stiffened slightly. "Next time?"

Tally petted his hand along Lex's stomach, trying to make him relax again. "Yeah, I said it would be once or twice. I guess it's going to have to be twice. Tonight didn't seem like the right time."

"Hmm." Lex didn't say anything more than that, but Tally knew he was annoyed.

One more time. That was all he was going to do. He didn't really like his old friends… but at the same time he did. It would've been impossible to explain the feeling to Lex of wanting to roll his eyes at their stupidity while liking how he was treated like no time had passed. Shit. Didn't matter. He'd still pick Lex any day. Tally tugged Lex closer and kissed him on the neck.

"Love you," he whispered. He was answered only by even, deep breathing. Lex was asleep.

IT WAS dark still, but Lex had been awake for a while. He hadn't really slept, actually. Too busy worrying about his relationship. Shit. He'd thought that wasn't going to happen this time, not like the last time he'd given someone his heart and had it wrung out and stomped beyond the point of recognition.

Lex didn't know what was up with Tally. It started after the first night he spent with Brock and his old cronies. He'd come back smelling like cigars and looking half-annoyed and half-bemused, but he'd lain down next to Lex and pulled him into his arms like he was happy to be back where he belonged. Lex had ignored the weird feeling in his gut that things weren't quite the same as they'd been before Tally left.

When he was woken up the next morning by tender lovemaking, he convinced himself that everything was perfect. That was until Tally went out with Brock again. And again. It had been, what, four times? And every time he came back, Tally acted a bit more squirrelly, more distant. He'd have moments where he was exactly like he'd been for the past four months, and then moments where he was almost the Tally he'd been in high school. Lex didn't know what to make of it, other than the fact that he sure as fuck didn't like it.

He knew that Tally hadn't told Brock about them, and it bothered him… it did. But after what he'd been through with his mother, Lex understood that things were feeling unsettled for Tally, that he needed some source of confidence. A place to belong. He only wished there was some way he could show Tally how much *he* loved him and how much they belonged together, and that it didn't fucking matter if Brock liked him or approved of him or whatever the hell it was that he seemed to be looking for.

Lex's alarm went off, and he reached over Tally to slam the sleep button. Tally grumbled and turned toward him.

"Morning, babe." He reached over to cup Lex's face so he could give him a slow kiss.

"Morning." Lex almost didn't kiss Tally, but *damn*, he couldn't help it. Those morning kisses had quickly become one of his favorite things in the world. He wanted to be able to pull away, though. He felt like he needed to steel himself. He didn't want to lose the one millionth of a percent of his heart that didn't already completely belong to Tally in case he ended up turning on Lex like every other fucking guy he'd dated seemed to. Lex went to get up, but Tally pulled him back down.

"Where you going?"

He chuckled. "Open the shop, of course. I've gotta get up now."

Tally rubbed his eyes, then reached out and curled a hand around Lex's waist. He slipped his thigh around Lex's hips and hugged him close. It was moments like that when Lex thought that maybe nothing had changed between them, and it would all be just fine.

"What time you want me down there?"

"Ten is fine." He leaned over and kissed Tally again because kissing him felt just that good. Then he dragged himself out of bed and went to shower.

The morning rush felt good. He managed to get his maybe problems with his boyfriend out of his head and concentrated on whipping up drinks for the long line of customers that he saw every day. He went through the motions, not concentrating on anything but the drink orders and the gossip and the smiles that came from his customers. But then he noticed Tally's apron draped across the counter where he'd left it the night before, and his mind was filled with everything he'd been avoiding.

He's acting like a shit, hanging out with his old friends, digging himself back into the closet. He still comes home to you every night. No matter what. And he holds you like he never wants to let go.

There goes the not thinking about it. Lex wanted to growl. He angrily yanked on a bag of beans. He didn't notice that they were caught on the cupboard door's hinge until the damn thing ripped open and beans flew everywhere, spilling and spewing all over his hardwoods, blending in so it would be nearly impossible to clean them all up. He gave an apologetic look to the last of his morning customers. Luckily the line was gone, or else he'd be slipping and sliding on the beans while he tried to pump out all those drinks.

"Don't worry about it, sweetie," Mrs. Reynolds, the old school nurse, assured him. "Where's Tally, anyway? Doesn't he usually help you in the mornings?"

Lex didn't want to hear about Tally. Or think about him. Did he want to see him? He wasn't sure. "He doesn't come in until ten most weekdays."

"Oh, well that's good. Gives you some time off, I suppose. He really is a nice young man now. I'm glad he's changed so much."

Not the conversation Lex wanted to be having. He made Mrs. Reynolds her latte and all but shoed her out the door so he could spend some unfulfilling time cleaning up coffee beans that wanted to skitter around everywhere. He nearly dumped the whole dustpan full on the floor when his overhead bell jangled violently.

"Sexie Lexie! Where's T?"

He knew that voice. He hated that voice. *Oh, Jesus. Brock.* Lex looked up. *And Rick. Fantastic. Does the world hate me today?*

"T? Do you mean Tally?"

"Yeah, I mean Tally. Does the fairy juice make you deaf as well as a cocksucker?" Brock laughed and slapped hands with Rick, who was also snickering. Lex wanted to tell them what they could suck, but he tried to be an adult. As much as he could, at least.

"Brock, this is my shop. You need to go if you're going to act like an asshole."

"I thought you liked assholes, fag. Isn't that your *thing*?"

Lex clenched his fists and counted to five.

"Tally will be in later today. I think it's best that you leave."

"Awwww, are you going to cry, little Lexie? Too bad there isn't a locker to shove you into. Tally sure did like doing that when we were younger. I bet he hates the fact that he has to work for your fruity ass."

"Leave, Brock. Now."

"You know I told him he could come work for me so he didn't get tainted by your...." Brock made a prissy face and flopped his hand around limply. Rick burst into laughter. Lex wasn't sure if he was laughing with Brock or at him. Lex would've laughed at how big of an ass Brock was making of himself if he wasn't so angry. But he was. Tally was acting weird because of these guys, these *jerks*, and Lex was mad. Mad that the man he loved was letting his life be run by a pair of overgrown morons. Morons who dared come into his shop and treat him like he was less than they were.

He stormed around the counter and brushed past them as rudely as he could without actually pushing. Then he yanked open the door to his shop and gestured to the sidewalk.

"You're not welcome here. Leave, before I call the police."

"I golf with the chief, you fucking ass-pirate. But I'm going. I wouldn't want to be in here any longer than I had to. Tell Tally we're on for drinks this Friday. And tell him to get a phone while you're at it. I'm tired of coming into this dump."

He left, followed by his stooge, Rick. Lex slumped against the counter, exhausted. He hated confrontation, and he thought he'd been done with Brock the Rock years before. Now it seemed that the only way to get them out of his life would be to remove Tally as well.

What am I going to do?

THE alarm blared noisily. Tally reached for it, slamming his hand against the clock radio. God, it seemed like he was always waking up. The hours when he was blissfully asleep were shrinking on a daily basis. His head was pounding. He had to have said no to at least five drink offers from Brock, but he'd still managed to have enough that his brain felt like it was going to rupture. He glanced over at Lex, who was curled around his pillow, sleeping. Lex looked exhausted… and beautiful. Tally missed him, to tell the truth. He'd been with Brock, Drew, and the guys so much in the past few weeks it felt like he barely got to see Lex anymore, and usually when he did they were both at work or sleeping. They hadn't made love in over a week, and it felt like each morning he woke up with Lex further and further away from him in the bed.

Tally knew he was being stupid, but he didn't know how to get out of the situation he'd managed to entangle himself in. Every time he left the house, every night he went out, he told himself: *This time I'm doing it. This time I'm going to tell Brock I'm with Lex and then leave Drew to do whatever he feels like he needs to do.* It hadn't happened yet. He was a damn chicken. Why was it so hard for him to admit that he didn't want one more person looking at him like he was a leper? He reached out and smoothed the tangle of Lex's hair with a smile.

"Mmpph." Lex opened his eyes blearily. "Is it time to get up?"

"I'll let Travis in, baby. Go back to sleep."

"M'kay," Lex mumbled, turning back onto his stomach.

Lex was stretching in bed and yawning by the time Tally came back up from getting Travis started for the day. "Morning," he murmured. "Sorry I was so passed out when the alarm went off. I know it was my turn today."

Tally smiled at him, loving his sleepy morning voice and the way his eyes drooped, like his eyelashes were too heavy to hold up. "It's okay. I was awake anyway." He sat on the edge of the bed and reached out, running his hand down the golden expanse of Lex's flank.

"Hey, it's a gorgeous day. We should drive down to Cannon Beach." Lex slipped his fingers under Tally's shirt and rubbed at his lower back.

Tally cringed. Cannon Beach with Lex sounded like exactly what he wanted to do that day or any other. It would've been perfect. Shit. "I kind of already promised the guys I'd go fishing." The soft, swirling caress on his back stopped. Lex drew his hand out from under Tally's shirt.

"Oh."

Shit. I should cancel. Tally *wanted* to cancel. He wanted to sit on the beach with Lex and bask in the early summer sun. He wanted to feel Lex's touch again. He'd been missing it so badly. But if he canceled, Brock would want to know why. He didn't want to get caught in a lie, didn't want to deal with the drama of a showdown with Brock. *Shit is right. What the fuck am I doing?*

"Babe, I'd really rather go to the beach with you. I would. I just already promised."

Lex scooted away, swung his legs over the side of the bed, and stood. "Nah, I get it. It's fine. I have paperwork to do anyway."

He grabbed some clothes and a pair of new underwear from his dresser and walked, without another word, into the bathroom. The sound of the door closing and the shower starting shocked Tally out of his momentary trance. He stood as well and went to the bathroom door, ready to get in the shower with Lex. He was canceling on Brock. He wasn't going to keep doing this to Lex or himself. Only problem was, when Tally went to turn the knob it was locked.

"Lex?" he called, loud enough to be heard over the water. "I was going to get in the shower with you."

"Just go fishing, Tally. I'll see you tonight."

"Lex...."

Tally stood at the door for a good five minutes but got no answer. *Shit.* How had things gotten so weird? His stomach coiled, and for the first time he started to feel a bit panicked. Lex had *never* shut the door on him like that.

I need to talk to Drew. This has got to end.

TALLY wasn't paying attention to what was going on around him. The guys were fishing, he supposed, and drinking beer and flipping each other shit, but all he could do was think about Lex. He could almost smell the saltwater in the air, feel the sun on his face, the comfortable weight of Lex's head resting in his lap. He imagined they were lying there, napping, enjoying their day together. Maybe his hand was in Lex's hair, or brushing along his collarbone. Maybe after the beach they'd head home, shower together all warm and wet, dry off and meet

Amy and Drew for pizza. God, what the hell was he doing fantasizing about something that easily could've been his? *Moron....*

"Tally. Yo, where the hell are you?" Brock reached over and poked him with a pepperoni stick. Tally had to suppress his eye roll at the irony.

I'm at the beach with my man instead of sitting here with you. "Just thinkin'. What's up?"

"You've been a space case all day, man. What's your deal?"

"Just work stuff," Tally lied.

Brock gave him an odd look. "Dude, you work in a coffee shop. You worried about the chocolate syrup?"

Tally shook his head. "Nah, just thinking about stuff. Where'd Drew go?"

"He went back to the car. Probably forgot his mascara or something." Brock rolled his eyes.

"I'll be right back."

Tally struggled his long frame out of the camping chair and went in search of Drew. He found him texting on his blackberry behind Brock's car.

"Whatcha doing?"

Drew jumped and nearly dropped his phone. "Just doing some work e-mails. My office is never really closed."

"I hear that. We're never closed either."

Drew smiled.

"What?"

"Nothing, I just like the 'we'. It's nice to see someone having what I want, you know. Makes it seem more possible."

"So what, have you found the guy?"

"No. I know he works at Columbia Memorial, though."

Tally chuckled. "You're not following him, are you?"

"No, dork. I do some work for the hospital. I saw him there."

"And you didn't get his number? How 'bout a name?"

Drew shook his head. "I'm a fucking chicken."

Yeah, I know how that feels. "Speaking of chicken...." Tally looked up at Drew. "I can't do this after today. Lex is getting pissed, and I'm not going to risk my relationship over fucking Brock."

Drew smirked. "You're fucking Brock? That should make my life easier."

Tally punched him on the shoulder. "Shut up, D, I mean it. Lex is seriously getting mad because I keep hanging out with Brock. You know how much of a dick he is to Lex. It's gotta feel like I'm being disloyal. I need to end this today. This fishing thing has gotta be it."

Drew looked panicked. "Listen, how 'bout tonight? We'll get him a drink or two, you can tell him about Lex and then take off. It should be cool, right?"

"Truthfully, I'm not sure he'll ever be okay with it, but I'm starting not to care. I could've been at the beach with Lex today, D. I actually caught myself fantasizing about spending time with my own damn boyfriend. I don't *want* to be here with Brock."

"Okay, so tonight, then you're out. We'll take him to the bar, get him a little loose, then you can lay it on him. If he's cool, then I'll be next in line."

"And if he's not?"

Drew cringed. "I'll get there when I get there."

Tally gave Drew a glare. "Tonight. That's it, right?"

Drew nodded. "For better or worse, that's it."

"Why are you going out with them again? You were with Brock last night *and* all day today." Lex looked a bit hurt, actually he looked more than a bit hurt. Tally tried not to concentrate on it.

"Tonight's it, babe. I promise. Drew just wants me to be around one last night so I can smooth things over when he tells Brock that he's bi." *Or whatever his plan is. I better not have jeopardized things with Lex over nothing.*

"Have you told Brock about *you* yet?"

Tally felt nauseated. "No, but that's going to be tonight too. I told Drew I wanted to be done."

The hurt turned to flustered confusion. "Why the hell does he need to be friends with them, anyway? Both of you should tell Brock to fuck off and come eat pizza with us."

Tally sighed. "It's not like that for Drew. He can't run his business on high school kids and moms in tracksuits. He needs the assholes of Rock Bay to send clients his way or he'd go under. You've gotta understand that."

"But why does he need you?"

"Because for some reason Brock loves me." Tally rolled his eyes. It was true, but he still didn't get it.

Lex sneered. "Yeah, but he's not going to when he finds out that you're a fucking fag just like me."

"Jesus, Lex. I just want to help Drew, okay? He was actually decent to me back in school. I want to be decent back. It's nice to have someone need me, anyway."

"*I* need you."

"No you don't. You've got your shop and your family and Amy. You don't need me."

"I love you. Isn't that the same thing?"

Tally's stomach still fluttered when he heard it. He stepped closer and wrapped Lex up in a tight hug. "I love you too, babe. I really, *really* do. I just need to do this for Drew, okay? One more night, let him come out, and then I'm back with you where I belong."

"You haven't even told them you're gay yet."

"No, but I said I'm going to tonight. I wanted to before, but you can't rush things with guys like Brock."

"You mean total assholes?"

Tally huffed out a laugh. "He's not that horrible."

"Yes he is, and you've been acting differently ever since you started hanging out with him. I don't like it."

"I haven't been acting differently at all!" *Had he?* "I think you've just been expecting me to turn back into the guy I used to be this whole time so now you're seeing it when it's not there."

"I'm not! You're acting distant, and you don't touch me as much as you did just a few weeks ago. It's like all of a sudden you're ashamed of us. *Are* you ashamed of us?"

"No! Hell no. You're the best thing that has ever happened to me. Ever. You've gotta know that."

"Then why are you doing this still?"

Tally hesitated. He wished he knew the real answer. "Because I have to," was all he could think of to say.

Lex backed away from Tally and squeezed his temples. "I'll see you later." His voice was soft, resigned. It sucked having Lex pull away. Again. He wondered if that was what Lex had been feeling for the past weeks—like Tally was pulling away. He hadn't meant to. *Shit.* He wished he knew what to do. He'd never had anyone before who gave a shit what he did one way or another. It was a bit overwhelming to want to make everyone happy. *God, what happened to Tallis "I don't give a fuck" Carrington?*

Tally went to leave but couldn't do it. He didn't *want* to do it. What a mess. Either way he turned he was going to disappoint someone. It was going to have to be Drew. He turned back, ready to take Lex into his arms and tell him he was staying home. Too late. Lex was walking back toward their room. "You're never going to tell him." He heard Lex say softly before closing their bedroom door. He heard the distinct click of a lock shutting him out.

Lex was wrong. He was going to tell Brock. He *was.*

He plodded out the door and down the stairs and practically ran into Amy, who was on her way in.

"Hey, Tal. Where you headed? Aren't you going to pizza with us?"

Tally hesitated. He didn't want to tell her that he was going out with Brock again. He knew it didn't sound good. "Not tonight. I'm meeting Drew and the others for a drink."

Amy gave him what could only be a stare down.

"What the hell are you doing, Tally?"

"Going out for drinks?"

She rolled her eyes and shook her head at him. "I know you're not stupid. That's not what I asked. What are you *doing*?"

Tally sighed. Fuck if he knew. "Drew asked me to help him out with Brock. He wants to come out, but he thinks that Brock will make a huge problem for him. He's hoping I'll ease the way."

Amy shrugged. "As long as you have a plan." Didn't *Lex say that exact same thing?* "You do know it hurts Lex when you're out with those guys. They're total assholes to him."

Tally winced. "I just had to get in with them. To help Drew. After tonight I'm going to back away."

"Are you sure that's all this is about? Helping Drew?" She eyed him shrewdly.

Of course it's all this is about. Liar. You like how they look at you like you're not a fuck-up. You like the attention. You like not having to work for their respect. Still not worth it.

"I'm ending it. I love Lex."

She poked him in the chest with one of her little poky fingers. "You better. You're a fucking idiot if you choose those assholes over him."

"I know."

Another poke. "He'd do anything for you."

"I know."

A third poke, even harder. "And if you hurt him, I'll rip your balls off."

Tally winced. "I *know*."

Amy backed off and gave him a smile. "Just as long as we're clear. Have a good night. I'll probably see you at the shop on Monday."

Man, she's crazy. "See you Monday."

Tally knew his voice sounded tentative. He *felt* tentative. What the hell was he doing? Tally turned for the second time to go back inside and tell Lex he was staying with them that night, always, not going out with Brock again. Ever. But he had promised Drew, or maybe he really just liked the way his old friends treated him, or maybe he was a big flaming moron. Hell if he knew. *Fuck.*

LEX was sitting on his bed wondering what the hell had just hit him. He wasn't sure what he thought Tally was going to say when he asked him not to hang out with Brock again. Was he delusional when he thought that maybe just this one time a guy would pick Lex over his friends, his latest trick… his weird and inexplicable agenda with the assholes in town? Guess not. He still wanted so desperately for Tally to be different than the others.

He didn't know why he hadn't just opened his mouth and told Tally what Brock had said to him earlier in the week. Tally would've stayed with Lex. There was no way he'd have chosen Brock after that. Hopefully. Lex only wished he could be sure—sure that if he opened up a vein and showed Tally his humiliation that Tally would actually do something about it. Days before, when Tally had offered to deal with Brock for him, Lex believed him outright. But now? He wasn't sure if he could. And it was breaking his heart.

There was a not-so-subtle banging on his door.

"Lex, are you in there? I'm starving!"

Lex dragged himself to his feet and unlocked the door, then he went back to his bed and sank down tiredly. Amy followed him in and stood, watching him expectantly. He tipped his head to look back, not really all that interested in moving. "I'm just tired. You ready?"

Amy regarded him for one more long moment. "You know what? Get up. Fuck him. He's being an ass, and you don't have to put up with it."

Lex squeezed his eyes shut. "I hate this. Things seemed so good there for a while."

"Hey, maybe Tally will pull his head out of his butt. You never know. But for now, you're not moping. We're going to have pizza and go watch a movie. Oh, and Mason is meeting us at the pizza place."

"Mason? Amy! Hanging out with him is the worst thing I could do," Lex moaned. Like he needed that complication.

"Yes, Mason. He asked if I was doing anything tonight. He understands that you're in a relationship. It's not the big deal you're making out of it."

"Fine." Lex drilled Amy with a mutinous stare and slowly peeled himself off of the couch. "But just to be clear, I think this is an awful idea."

Amy rolled her eyes and shoved his jacket into his arms. "Yeah, yeah. Let's go."

"Hey, Tally! What are we doing tonight?" Brock looked like a big dorky puppy when Tally knocked on his door. He saw Lindsay, Brock's wife, in the kitchen reading a book with a cup of tea.

"Do you want to see if Lindsay wants to come with us?" That was nerves talking. Tally knew if Brock's wife was there he'd never be able to go through with it.

Brock scoffed. "Are you kidding? It's just us guys, right?"

"Yeah, but it was just us guys last weekend. Don't you want to do something with your wife?"

"Not really." He rolled his eyes and lowered his voice. "I have to see her every other night when I get home from work. I need a night off."

You've been with us half the weeknights too. Tally didn't get it. He never felt like he needed a night off from Lex. Lex. Shit. He shouldn't have left him. He'd thought it a million times. Fucking stupid. "Did you call Drew and the others?" It was time to get the show on the road. He wasn't going to drag it out any further.

"How 'bout just me and you this time? Like in high school. We can even go to the cemetery."

Brock wiggled his eyebrows and pulled a joint from his pocket.

Tally laughed. "You've gotta be kidding me."

"I thought it would be fun."

Tally was saved by Brock's phone ringing in his pocket. He pulled it out and looked at the caller ID. "Shit. It's Drew. I was hoping to get away from him tonight. He's such a kiss ass."

Actually, you're the kiss ass. He's just a nice guy. Tally was kind of annoyed. The follower act that he'd been kind of flattered by at first was suddenly grating.

"Tell Drew we'll meet him at O'Toole's. Let's grab a few beers."

Brock made a face but passed on the message.

It wasn't all that late when they were done at O'Toole's. Brock had predictably gotten drunk off his rapidly spreading ass, and Tally and Drew were propping him up as they made their way to Drew's apartment. He hadn't managed to tell Brock before the guy was completely sauced off his gourd and not willing to listen to anything, but Tally didn't care. It was over anyway, confession or not. No more.

Tally was excited to get home. He was tired, and he'd had enough of Brock fun to last him for weeks. Forever, actually. Besides, after what Brock had said about Drew earlier, he wasn't sure if it mattered what he did. Brock wasn't ever going to respect Drew, and after he learned that Tally was gay he wasn't going to respect him either. *Fuck it.* All Tally wanted was Lex. In his arms.

The small park that served as a town square was cluttered with booths, already being set up for the start of summer block party that was in a week. Tally had always mocked it when he was younger, choosing instead to get high at the cemetery with Brock and the others. He was actually looking forward to it this time: working in the booth with Lex, handing out drinks, and smiling, touching each other when no one else was looking. *Lex.* Every time Tally thought about his face earlier, the way Lex looked at him like he was being betrayed, he felt a shot to the gut.

They were stumbling by the small movie theater with Brock getting heavier with each step. People started streaming out, first slowly, then more and more. The ten o'clock movie must have just gotten out. Tally and Drew stopped walking and waited for the crowd to dissipate.

"Why we stoppin'?" Brock slurred.

"People, Brock. We're waiting for the people."

"Oh, look. Ith's Sexshie Lexshie!" *Fuck a duck.* Tally looked up and, sure as can be, there were Lex and Amy coming out of the theater with another guy who had dark brown curls and an adorable smile. *What the fuck?* "Ooooh, Lexie!" Brock called. Lex stopped and looked. Tally mentally willed him to turn and keep walking, but it didn't work. "Which one of them is your date, the fag or the dyke? I bet she'sh got a bigger cock for you to sit on."

"Brock!" Tally yanked on the drunk ass. Amy gave him a pointed stare as if to say "what are you going to do now?" A couple of people on the sidewalk stopped to look. "I'm sorry, Lex," Tally said, his voice polite but nothing more than friendly. "Brock's just a bit drunk, and he's acting like an *asshole.*" Tally pinched Brock under the armpit. He knew it was his moment to drop Brock and walk the few short steps it would take to pull Lex into his arms and never let go. He didn't move. *Shit....*

"Ouch, fucker! Why did you pinch me?" Brock looked drunkenly outraged.

"Say sorry to Lex. He didn't do anything to you."

"'Cept maybe turn him down for a date," Amy muttered with a low laugh.

Lex clenched his jaw. He looked angrier than Tally had ever seen him. He elbowed Amy in the side. "Amy, Mason, let's get the hell out of here." He didn't even look at Tally. *Mason? The nurse?* Tally saw red. What the hell was that guy doing with Lex? Lex was his! He glanced over at Drew, who'd been silent for the whole exchange. Drew was standing there with his mouth open.

"Your name is Mason?" Drew whispered.

Mason the nurse was staring right back at Drew, looking shocked and clearly a bit disgusted at the fact that Drew would been seen with the likes of Brock. *Oh, of course it was the same guy.* Tally's stomach hurt like hell. Could the situation suck any worse? Lex didn't even look at Tally. He just turned and walked away, right toward his building. Tally felt like the air was sucked out of his lungs.

"Drew, let's go. We've gotta get Brock to your place. I need to talk to Lex."

"Yeah, that kinda sucked, Tally. I would be pissed if I were him."

"Thanks a fucking lot, Drew. Listen, I'll make sure Brock knows about me, but like I said. After tonight, I'm out."

"Knowsh whatt?" Brock asked, tipping his head.

"Never mind, dude. We'll talk about it tomorrow."

WHEN Tally got back to the apartment, Lex was sitting in the dark at the dining room table. He had his head in his hands and didn't even turn around when he heard Tally walk up behind him. *Shit.*

"Hey, babe." Tally nearly whispered it. He was afraid of the reaction he was going to get.

"Don't 'hey, babe' me! What the fuck was that out there?" Looks like he was right to get worried. Lex was angrier then Tally had ever seen him.

He wished he had a good answer. "I don't know." He wanted to say more. It was dumb, he was dumb, he loved Lex more than anything. He was scared to open his mouth, even though he knew he needed to right at that moment. *Speak before it's too late, asshole.*

"Listen, I think it's best if you go back to your grandmother's place."

"Tonight?" Tally's heart was pounding so hard he could swear it was visible even through his shirt. How could he have fucked everything up so badly?

"No. I think you should go back to your grandmother's permanently."

"Lex. What... *why?*" He felt like he was going to throw up, and the worst part was he couldn't even get mad. The whole damn thing was his fault.

"You know why. We're not going to work as long as you're friends with Brock. I hate seeing you with him, can't stand there and listen to him talk like that and then have you look at me like we're just... acquaintances. That was fucked, Tally, and you know it."

"I know, Lex. I'm sorry, I—"

"I can't do this right now. The guy I saw out there tonight, well, it wasn't you. To be fair, it wasn't the guy from high school either, but 'not quite an asshole' isn't who I want to be with."

"Lex, please—"

"Tally, can you please just go?"

"But—"

"*Go.*"

Tally looked at Lex, afraid to walk out the door, afraid to even move for fear he would never be back in this place, back belonging to Lex and happy and in love. It would've been one thing if he never had it in the first place, but he *had*, and it was amazing and comfortable and nothing like he expected. He didn't know if he could give it up. Tally turned slowly toward the door, hoping like hell that Lex would say something to stop him. He didn't. *I'm not taking my clothes. I need a reason to come back.*

"Don't forget your stuff."

Fuck. "Can't I get it tomorrow?"

"I'd rather you took it with you right now." Tally felt his heart crumble. "I'll just see you on Monday."

"*Lex.*"

"I need to not see you for a couple of days, Tally. Then maybe I can try to just… go back. To the way things were. Before." He stood up and went to his closet where Tally's duffle bags were sitting on the floor. He picked them up and handed them to Tally.

"Can't we talk about this?"

Lex shook his head. "Not tonight. I need to think."

"Are you really ending us?"

He squeezed his temples. "Right now? Yeah, I think so."

Tally crumbled inside. He didn't know what to say or do other than pack his things and go silently. It wasn't what he wanted. All he wanted was to hold onto Lex and never in a million years let go. It didn't look like he had a choice. He felt the pressure of tears building up behind his eyes. *Fuck. Don't you dare fucking cry.* He started piling shirts, socks, and underwear into the bags with shaking hands.

This isn't the end. It can't be. For once in my lame-ass life I have something to fight for, and I'll be damned if I let him go.

CHAPTER
Fifteen

TALLY'S stomach quaked as he ran down the street to Drew's loft. Fuck tomorrow. He was dealing with this shit now before it was too late and he lost Lex forever. The pavement was hard under his feet, jarring and solid, each step he took away from Lex and the life that he might have ruined felt like it echoed in his knees. *Love you, babe.* He was going to get Lex back, or at least show him that he was more important to him than some old friends who weren't worth a tenth, no a millionth, of what Lex was to him.

The blocks disappeared under his shoes. He practiced his words in his head. *Brock, I'm gay, Brock, you're an asshole, and we're not friends and oh... I'm gay. Brock, I love Lex. Stay the hell away from him.*

Tally was glad Drew's loft had exterior stairs. He didn't much care about waking Brock up and figured Drew fucking owed him, but getting a bunch of neighbors involved in the scene wasn't his big fantasy. He pounded up the metal stairwell toward Drew's top-floor condo. He was glad that he'd driven Drew home a few times after one of Brock's drunken evenings or else he'd be screwed trying to find the place. Tally pounded on the door of Drew's condo, hard and continuously, until he heard a shuffling from the other side. The door creaked open cautiously, and a woozy looking Brock stuck his head out.

"T? What the fuck are you doing here, I thought you went home." He stepped aside anyway and let Tally into the apartment.

"I did go home, but I got kicked out. We need to talk."

"Kicked out?" He rolled his eyes. "Your grandmother always was a crazy bitch. You can sleep on my couch."

Tally gritted his teeth. "This has nothing to do with my grandmother. I haven't been living there for weeks."

"What the fuck are you talking about, dude?" Brock slurred. He lurched into Drew's kitchen and came back with a glass and a bottle of whiskey.

"Don't you think you've had enough?"

Tally went to grab at the glass, but Brock snatched it up and away from him. "What are you? My fucking wife? Bitch is always nagging me about my food, how much I drink, telling me to exercise."

"Maybe she just wants to take of care you." Tally wasn't about to get in some heated debate about Brock's poor wife. He had his own problems to deal with. "But that's not why I came." He watched Brock down the finger of whiskey.

"What's going on out here?" Drew came out from his room looking sleepy and confused.

Tally gave him a significant look. "I'm dealing with it now, D. Lex just ended things with me over this. It's not fucking worth it. I'm not losing him."

"What the hell are you two girls talking about?" Brock looked bleary and confused.

Tally turned on him. "I'm gay, Brock. *Gay*. Lex isn't my boss, he's my boyfriend. I've been with him this whole time. He just broke up with me because I've been being a dumbass to him because I'm too stupid and insecure to rock the boat with you. Not doing it anymore. I want my real life back."

Brock squinted at Tally, his confusion turning a bit hostile. "I know it's not April Fools. You can't be serious."

Tally walked closer, until he was right up in Brock's face. "About Lex? More serious than I've ever been about anything in my life. I'm going to walk out of here right now, and I don't want to hear from you again." He looked over at Drew. "It was never going to work the way you wanted it to. You know that, right?"

Drew nodded silently. Tally clenched his fists one last time, and without hesitating even one more second, he turned and jogged out the door.

He was calmer on the way back to Lex's place... *his* place too, damn it! Lex would take him back; he had to take him back. Tally didn't know what he would do if Lex said no.

I'm such a fucking idiot.

How anything could've seemed more important, even for a few brief weeks, than what he had with Lex baffled Tally. It was so clear to him as he jogged back to the apartment he thought of as home, the man he thought of as home. Tally slowed and let himself in the back door. His car was still there in the gravel lot right next to Lex's. It looked right sitting there. *They* were right. Lex loved him, he loved Lex. They would work it out. Tally was sure of it. He'd ditched Brock, right? So why was he standing outside instead of going up and proving himself to the man he loved?

Tally took a deep breath and walked quietly up the stairs to the apartment and let himself in. He started to creep across the living room toward the hallway that led back to their bedroom.

"What are you doing here?" Lex's voice was quiet but unexpected. Tally jumped. "I thought I asked you to go to your grandmother's house?"

Tally felt his chest constrict. He turned. Lex was sitting on the couch. He looked pale, and even with only the light from the moon, Tally could tell his eyes were red and puffy. "Lex, babe. *Please*. I don't want to lose you."

He sat down on the couch where Lex had been sitting, slouched in the dark. He tried to reach out for Lex's hand, but Lex drew it away. "I need you to go. I'll talk to you on Monday."

"But Lex, I *told* him. I told him everything: that I love you, that I don't want to be friends with him anymore. It's done."

"Why'd you do it, Tal? What was the point if we were already over? Was it that you really just can't stand to lose?"

"I can't stand to lose *you*. This isn't some competitive thing. When you kicked me out earlier my fucking heart broke."

"It broke *my* heart to watch you being friends with some guy who's been a total asshole to me my whole life. Don't you understand that?"

"Yeah, I do. I'm not stupid, you know."

Tally didn't understand what was going on. It wasn't supposed to *be* that way. He was supposed to apologize to Lex, tell him about Brock, and they were supposed to already be in bed kissing and making up. He didn't know what to do with this Lex who was sitting there so stoic and unemotional.

"I never treated you like you were," Lex murmured. He was right. Lex may have, rightfully so, treated Tally like an asshole, but he'd never acted like he was dumb, less than worthy… all the other shit people seemed to think of him. "Why were you doing it, Tal? If you knew it hurt me, why did you keep going out with him?"

Tally sighed. "I don't know." And he didn't. He'd liked the attention, but how could he have ever thought it was worth hurting Lex over?

"Lex, can't we fix this? I don't want to do it without you."

"Do what?" His voice was still quiet, dull.

"I don't know. Life… everything. I love you."

"I love you too, Tal. That's why this sucks so much. Can we just… *not* right now? I can't deal with it. I need to think."

"Think about what?" Tally was panicking. What was there to think about? They loved each other, right? It was a stupid fight, and it was over, right? He couldn't have messed things up that bad, could he?

"I jumped into everything so fast with you, you know?" Lex said quietly. He was fiddling with the hem of his shirt. "I was ready to just… I don't know, give you my heart, the rest of my life, share this place with you, the shop, everything." Tally reached out for Lex again. He couldn't help it. Lex had just said everything he wanted to hear so bad that he could barely believe it was real. And then he said exactly what Tally was afraid of hearing. "But what if this whole thing was a huge mistake?"

It took Tally a few moments to breathe. "Baby, we can't be back there again."

"I am." Lex looked unsure, concerned. Tally's stomach twisted up. "Listen, I'm not saying I'll give us another shot, and I'm not saying I won't. I just need some time. Please go."

"I'm not giving up. I'll see you on Monday, okay?"

There was a long silence. Tally was afraid he'd pushed it too far and Lex would say no. He was about to get up when he heard a quiet "Okay."

Tally couldn't help it. He had to touch him, if only just once. He reached out and cupped Lex's face in his hand. He wanted to do so much more, hold him, kiss him, take back the last few weeks so he'd never made such a dumb mistake in the first place. For a second, Lex brought his hand up to cover Tally's, fingers intertwining, but then he seemed to remember himself, and he pulled Tally's hand away from his face. Tally nodded and stood.

"I love you," he said again as he walked toward Lex's front door.

Lex didn't answer.

WHAT a fuck of a night. Lex was still sitting on his couch, head in his hands. He missed Tally. Already. The thought of going back into his room and sleeping in a cold bed all alone didn't appeal to him at all. Why didn't he just say okay? Tally had done exactly what he wanted, he told Brock about them, he told him that he didn't want to be friends. Why was Lex sitting alone in the dark when he could be wrapped up in Tally's arms in the middle of amazing make-up sex? They were meant to be together. He felt it in every cell of his body. Too bad he couldn't talk his mind into catching up. It was still all pissed about the Brock thing.

You're gonna take him back. Why'd you even bother hesitating?

Lex sighed. He *was* going to take Tally back, wasn't he? It was the only way to get rid of the burning ache in his chest. Damn truth was he loved the dumbass too much to not give him a second chance. He just needed to breathe for a few seconds before—

Was that a crash?

Lex stood, almost afraid to hear what he knew he'd heard. It was the sound of glass breaking—a window, to be more correct. *What the hell?*

He was out his apartment door and running down the stairs to the shop before he could even think that it might not be the best idea for him to go prancing in there unarmed when there was clearly someone in his shop who shouldn't be there. He wasn't ending this awful damn night with a robbery, though.

Lex pulled his phone from his pocket and dialed the local 911, waiting on the line for a few tense ring tones until the operator connected.

"I just heard a window break in my shop," he said forcefully the moment an operator picked up the phone. "There's someone in there."

He gave his address in quick whispers, creeping down the hall toward the front room. Lex was worried, but he was also just plain confused. There weren't any *burglars* in Rock Bay, and even if there were, what would they want with a coffee shop? Lex pushed the door open cautiously, ready for who knows what. He wished he had a broom or a bottle of syrup to use as a weapon. Anything. Lex did a quick scan but saw nothing he could pick up, only the gaping hole where his shop's glass-paneled front door used to be. His heart thunked in his chest before it started pounding hard and fast. More than anything, he wished Tally were there.

"Who's in here?" Lex knew his voice sounded shaky. *C'mon, cops. Put your foot on the gas.*

He squinted into the darkness, trying to keep from trembling. There, right by the broken door was a figure, pale and puffy. Lex turned on the lights. *Brock? What the hell?*

"Brock, what did you do? Why are you in my shop?"

Brock had a bottle in his hand, vodka, maybe. Lex couldn't tell. He was swaying, but he looked angry. Irrational.

"It'sh your fault."

"Brock, you're drunk. Let me call Drew."

"Fuck Drew. And fuck you!" Brock stepped closer, feet crunching on broken glass and swinging the bottle in his hand until alcohol sloshed over the side. "You tookth Tally and turned him into a fucking fruitcake."

Oh my God. Tally really did tell. Lex was getting scared. Brock's eyes were red-rimmed and a bit wild, like he'd lost whatever small amount of reason was knocking around in his brain.

Lex backed away as Brock lurched toward him. "I didn't turn Tally into anything he hasn't always been." Brock was standing close enough that Lex could smell his breath. Ugh. Whiskey.

"You're fucking lying, you pansy ass chocolate jockey. Tally's not going to pick you!" Brock swayed closer, and Lex leaned away again, not wanting to be anywhere near that toxic breath.

"That's not true." He tried to be reasonable. "Tally's always been gay. He told me himself that he had a boyfriend in high school." Brock made a growling noise and teetered a little, clearly so drunk and angry he couldn't concentrate on standing straight. "Listen, Brock. Sit down before you fall over. I'm going to call Drew."

Lex didn't see it until it was too late. The bottle, that damn bottle of whatever the hell it was that Brock had was heading for his skull, and if he didn't move in about—

Too late.

"Fuck you, faggot!" The sound of glass breaking was the first thing Lex noticed. Then the pain slammed through his consciousness for about two seconds, and he thought he saw flashing blue lights before black spots took over his vision, and he felt himself slumping to the floor.

TALLY woke to his grandmother pounding on his door.

"Tallis! Wake up!"

The distress in his grandmother's voice penetrated his sleep-fogged mind, and he sat up, instantly alert. "Come in, Grams. What is it?"

His grandmother's face was tense with fear. "Drew just called the house. Something terrible must've happened." She looked scared and worried.

Instantly, Tally's stomach clenched. "Grandma, just tell me. What did Drew say?"

"Brock's in jail, and Lex is at the hospital. Brock must've… attacked him. Lex isn't waking up, Tally."

The wave of dread that hit him was immense and black. He was frozen solid.

Lex. No!

He bolted out of bed and reached for the jeans and shirt he still had draped over a chair in the corner of the room. It took a few tries to jam his legs into the jeans, he was shaking so bad. His stomach started to twist and turn, nausea rising fast. He had to sit down, get a grip. No. No time for that. He needed to go, to get to Lex.

He looked up to see his grandmother standing at the doorway.

"Calm down, son. You won't be any use to him if you're a jittering mess."

Tally could barely even answer. "I've gotta go, Grams. Now."

"I'm going with you, son. I don't want you on the road like this."

Tally turned in circles, looking for his keys. He was getting frantic when he noticed them sitting on the dresser where he'd put them for weeks before he'd moved in with Lex. *Lex.* How could Brock hurt him? Was he totally fucking nuts?

Tally knew it was his own fault. He shouldn't have left Lex alone. *I love you, baby. Please be okay.*

He waited by the door for a few brief moments before his Grandmother came down, dressed in jeans and a sweater. "Why don't you let me drive, Tally?"

Just the thought of that long car ride, only able to think and not act, made him panic. "I need to do *something*. I can't just sit in the car."

"Well, getting us in an accident isn't a good something. Call Drew back."

Tally turned to the phone and stared at it for a few seconds before he shook his head. He couldn't stand to know. Not until he was there, touching Lex with his own hands.

"Let's just go. I need to be there now."

As expected, the ride to the hospital was excruciating. It felt at least ten times as long as the last time, when he'd had a green but not dying Lex seated next to him, trying not to vomit. That was nothing. Back then there was nothing about Lex *dying*, about him being so hurt the doctors couldn't wake him up. *C'mon, Grams. Get there.* Tally clenched his hands to keep from drumming on the windowsill. He wanted to crawl out of his skin.

"You sure you don't want me to drive?" he asked. It probably wasn't the first time he'd asked. He didn't even know what was coming out of his mouth anymore. The only thing he could process was sheer panic.

"We're almost there," his grandmother replied patiently.

"I know, Grams. I'm sorry. I'm just—"

"I understand, darling. You love him. I never thought I'd see you like this."

Tally laughed mirthlessly. "I didn't either." *Hurry!*

Thankfully, his grandmother elected to pull through the ambulance turnaround instead of parking. He was sure she could sense his desperation.

"I'll see you in there. Go get your boy."

Tally nodded gratefully and vaulted himself out of his grandmother's old boat of a car before sprinting through the sliding-glass emergency-room doors. The first thing he saw was Drew huddled next to Amy, who was white-faced. Any traces of her usual sarcasm were lost.

"Where is he?"

Amy looked at him. Tally thought he saw accusation in that glare. He didn't blame her. "He's in the ICU. No one's allowed back there. They're trying to determine if he had any brain damage."

"Brock hit him that hard?"

Amy's face grew pinched, like she was holding something back. Drew put his arm around her. "Yeah, he was drunk and unreasonable. I guess he swung really hard. Why weren't you with him, Tal? I thought you were going back there."

Tally ground his thumbs into his eyes. They ached, and his throat was tight, and fuck if he was going to lose it in front of Amy and Drew. "I did go back there. He told me to go back to my grandma's house. He said he needed time to think. God, this is my fucking fault."

Drew shook his head. "It's Brock's fault, or if you want to blame someone else, then blame me. Lex is going to be fine."

"We don't know that," Amy spat out.

Tally was going to reply, but Drew shook his head. He understood. Amy was scared just like he was, and she needed someone to blame. He was rubbing his eyes again when Lex's parents came running in, followed by his grandmother. Lex's mom was wearing sweats, and her hair was pulled into a haphazard ponytail that leaned over the top of her head.

"Tally, dear, how is he?"

Tally's heart sank. God, it hurt. He didn't want to have to confess that he hadn't been there when it happened.

"He's still under. They're going to let us know when he comes around."

Everyone huddled in the uncomfortable emergency room chairs. Drew and Amy sat next to each other, muttering quietly. Lex's parents sat silent, staring at the waiting room TV, unseeing. Tally sat next to his grandmother, unable to do anything but worry. There was no way he wasn't going to see Lex again. His life couldn't be that fucked up. He sat, and sat, and watched the minutes tick away on the clock. It was starting to get light. Shit. It was going to be time to let Travis in soon. There was no way he was leaving. No goddamned way.

"Hey, guys. Someone's gotta go take care of the shop, get the window patched. Make sure the customers know it's closed." He hated being practical, but he knew Lex would be pissed off if his precious shop wasn't taken care of.

Drew sighed. "I'll go. You just want me to make a sign or something?"

Tally nodded. "It's the best we can do right now. The shop needs to be cleaned up, and I just don't want Travis to have to deal with all of this. Hopefully...." He didn't say it. Hopefully Lex would be fine the next day, fine enough so Tally could leave and take care of the business for him. He wasn't leaving until he was sure.

THERE was daylight coming through the emergency room doors when a doctor came out and called for the family of Lex Barry. Lex's mother rushed over, his father not far behind. Tally wanted to shoot out of his chair, get as close as he could to hear what was happening. Lex's mother was smiling, though, and that may have been the first time

Tally breathed, really breathed, in hours. She wouldn't have smiled if he wasn't okay.

"He's awake," she finally said, tears pooling in the corners of her eyes. "So far it seems like he has a concussion and some cuts and bruising but nothing else."

Thank fucking God.

"Just the parents for now." Tally stayed seated. He understood.

It seemed like they were back in that room forever but finally came out, both smiling but looking a bit concerned.

"How is he?" Tally couldn't wait to find out for himself.

"Sore," Lex's mother answered. "And a bit tired, but he's going to be fine."

Tally stood. He assumed he'd be next. He *had* to be next, had to see Lex.

"Um, Tally, he says he'd like to see Amy and to tell everyone else to go home and get some rest."

Tally felt like he'd been stabbed. "I've gotta see him," he protested.

Lex's mother shook her head. "He's not ready."

She knows. He felt like throwing up for the hundredth time that night and wondered what he could do to make it right. He couldn't say any more, though. Lex's mother wasn't going to go against her son's wishes for *him*. He hadn't been wanted in the first place. Sure, before all the stuff with Brock he'd been tentatively making progress with Amy, with Lex's family. He couldn't imagine what they thought of him now. He was having a hard time not hating himself.

"Okay," was all he said. Tally could hear the rejection in his voice. He felt pathetic, like a dog that the owner kicked out of bed. Lex's mother spared him a tired, understanding smile.

"Go home, everyone. They're going to release Lex in a few hours, and we'll take care of him."

Tally sighed and gestured for his grandmother. He felt defeated, but there was nothing he could do. Lex would see him when he wanted to see him. Until then… well, until then he could feel like the biggest asshole on the planet.

LEX'S head hurt like a motherfucker, he felt the stitches over his eyebrow pulling every time he moved his face, and the daylight flooding into his apartment made his headache even worse. He was sore and angry and doped up. He wanted desperately to complain, but everybody had been so *nice* he'd feel like a jerk doing it. Even Tally. Especially Tally.

He'd run the shop without complaint for four days so far, dealt with the customers, cleaned up the mess, even coordinated with the contractors who were starting work on the drive-through window to do the repairs on the front door. Lex knew he was running the place open to close with whatever help Travis could provide. He wasn't even clocking in his hours.

Lex had been sneaking downstairs after all the do-gooders were gone and checking on everything. He wanted to get back to his normal routine, to be done with the pain meds, the police reports, the hovering, concerned females. He wanted his shop back, his life back. His boyfriend....

He missed Tally. A lot. Shit, it was awkward, though. They'd talked about the shop a few times, and he could swear they were both giving each other these sad little looks, but he didn't know what to say. After the whole Brock mess, it seemed like neither one of them knew what to say to each other. There was so much, it was just hard to start talking. Part of him just wanted to kiss Tally until his eyes rolled back into his head and just get it over with.

Lex stood gingerly from his couch and walked to where a zip-up hoodie was draped across one of his dining room chairs. He had to get the heck out of his apartment before he went nuts. His clock read 4 p.m. The shop was still open, but he wasn't dressed for customers. He looked scruffy and unwashed and not ready for action at all. He'd just sneak down for a minute… just to see what was happening, of course.

Lex heard voices when he got to the doorway of the shop. Well, one voice at least. Tally. It sounded like he was on the phone. Lex stood really still, trying to tell himself he wasn't completely eavesdropping. Yeah, he was.

"Mom, why did you call here? Yeah, of course I know what happened to Lex." Tally listened silently for a long time, then he sighed loudly. "You're right. It's my fault." He sounded defeated, sadder than he was even at the beginning. Lex's chest felt tight. *It wasn't Tally's fault. Not really.* Part of him wanted to rush out there and yank that bitch's voice away from Tally's ear. A bigger part of him still wasn't ready to be near him any more than necessary. Lex was about to retreat to his apartment when Tally's voice started to rise.

"I'm not leaving here, Mom. No, you listen for once. You're never going to approve of me, so why don't you leave me alone?" Lex bit his lip, waiting for Tally to back down, to take it back, but apparently he had no intention of doing that. "I love him. That's not going to change. Ever. I don't care what you want." He was silent for a long time. As far away as he was, Lex could hear the braying coming from the earpiece. That woman may have acted genteel, but she had the screech of a damn harpy. Tally must have eventually had enough, because the next thing Lex knew he was yelling, something Lex had never heard him do. "Well, fuck off." More yelling. "Yeah? Don't call again!"

Lex heard nothing else other than the phone crashing down onto its cradle. His heart was pounding, just as he was sure Tally's was. It had been good to finally hear Tally stick up for himself—stick up for them, actually. Lex smiled a little but froze in place. He didn't know what to do. Did he turn and book it for his apartment? Tally would be sure to hear him. Did he stay and admit that he heard the conversation? The awkwardness between them wouldn't get any better if he did. *Shit.* Lex decided on truthfulness. Anything else would've made the weirdness between them even worse.

"Um, hi." He stood in the doorway between the back hall and the shop. It felt… different being there after even a few days.

"Lex!" Tally's face bloomed red. He looked embarrassed but happy to see Lex. "How are you?"

"Better, I guess." He automatically touched the spot where stitches still held his head together.

"Does it still hurt, babe?" Tally asked. He went to reach for Lex's face but stopped himself and turned away. "Sorry. I keep forgetting."

"Tal…." Lex didn't know what to say; he just didn't want Tally to walk away.

"Yeah?"

"I heard you. With your mom."

"I figured. Sorry. I didn't know she was going to call here again."

"It's okay. I'm... I'm proud of you for sticking up for yourself."

Tally shrugged, looking uncomfortable. "It doesn't matter what I do. She'll never see me as anything but an embarrassment. I might as well try to make myself happy if I can't please her, you know?"

Lex nodded. "Hey, listen. Um, thanks. For everything you've done this week. I mean, I know I'm not paying you enough. We should talk about that."

Tally hung his head a little. "You really came down here to talk to me about money? I'm not doing this to get paid."

"I know. I mean—" Lex felt flustered and awkward. He started backing toward his hallway. "I just wanted to thank you." Tally stared at him silently. "Um, I'm going back upstairs. I've got to rest."

"Lex—"

It was his turn to stare silently. There was too much in that silence. It was full of want and need and weird awkward feelings, neither one of them knowing how to say what they both wanted to say. Lex figured he'd have to make the first move if they were ever going to try to be like they were for those few amazing weeks. The question was, what the hell was he going to do?

"Um, Lex?"

God, get me out of here before this becomes any more painful. "Yeah?"

"The block party is the day after tomorrow. Do you want me to coordinate everything with Travis?"

Oh. Lex was relieved and disappointed. "No, I'll be fine dealing with it tomorrow. I'll get it all set up if you're willing to put in one more day at the shop."

"One more day?" Tally looked panicked.

"Tal, I meant one more day without taking a break. That's all."

"Oh. Well, um, I was going to work the block party. I don't mind."

Lex wanted to hug him. He looked kinda sad and lost. But he couldn't. Not yet. "It's okay. You need a break. Just get through tomorrow, and I'll see you Monday, okay?"

Tally nodded reluctantly. "Okay."

"So, um, I'm going to go up now. Let me know if you need anything."

Tally nodded. Lex knew he wouldn't call up. He didn't need any help, and he seemed to be almost afraid of talking to Lex. *It was when I wouldn't see him at the hospital.* Even he didn't know why he did that, other than the fact that he just hadn't been ready to get into all the drama again. Lex backed into the hallway all the way and turned, booking as fast as his aching head would let him back up the stairs and into the blissfully angst-free zone that was his apartment.

It worked for about five seconds, until the memories of the last few minutes started creeping in, and Tally's face, that sad little face, was the only thing he could see.

CHAPTER Sixteen

TALLY fucking wanted to kill Brock. Kill. That asshole bashed his boyfriend, knocked him out cold, and got off with a fucking *fine*? Two hundred dollars? He would have paid more money if he'd been speeding in a school zone! But according to the cops, Brock had been "brawling." *Brawling.* It was the stupidest thing Tally had ever heard. He had to pay to get Lex's door fixed, and other than that it was back to life as usual. The news had spread around town like all news did, with the speed of a flash flood. People seemed to be regarding it with a chuckle and a "boys will be boys" kind of headshake. It was infuriating. Tally was ready to go to war for his man.

Only problem was, Lex wasn't his man. Not anymore.

Tally had no right to defend him as much as he wanted to. They hadn't really spoken in the week that Lex had been home. Lex had thanked him for watching the shop and had asked for a rundown of daily activity, but they hadn't *spoken*, spoken. Tally was getting nervous. Starting to think that it might actually be over. He didn't know what he'd do if that were the case. Just the thought made him want to keel over.

Tally didn't even look up from scrubbing the counters when the bell rang on the front door. He assumed it was one of the groups of high school kids who usually came for their second fix right before closing.

"We're closed, guys. Getting ready for tomorrow."

"Tal, it's me."

Tally looked up to see Drew standing there. He looked as uncertain as Tally had felt the past week. They hadn't spoken since right after the hospital. Great. 'Cause that conversation with Lex the day before hadn't been awkward enough. "Hey, D."

"Listen, I'm really sorry about all this. You don't hate me, do you?"

A little. "No. It's not really your fault. I could've said no."

"Are you and Lex doing any better?"

Tally shrugged. "He says hello. He asks about the shop. He told me he doesn't need my help tomorrow." *Like I'm just an employee again.* Any real partner would tag along to lend a hand if nothing else, just because that's what you did when you were with someone.

Drew cringed. "You want me to say something?"

"Like what? I dug my own hole. I'm going to have to try to get out of it. I'm just hoping that he sees I'm not going anywhere."

"I get ya." Drew nodded.

"What about you? What are you going to do with Brock now that… well?"

Drew shuddered. "I can't even look at him. What an asshole."

"I can't believe he got off so easily!" Tally couldn't keep the disgust from his voice.

"He's friends with the police chief. His dad is friends with everyone. Lex didn't have a chance." Tally was glad to hear the disgust in Drew's voice, and he was glad that he'd not chosen Brock just out of political correctness. It seemed that Tally would have one friend, at least.

He took a deep breath. "People are acting like it was just a brawl. Lex doesn't brawl!"

Drew rolled his eyes. "He doesn't, but I might be tempted. When I was on my way over I saw Brock walking into O'Toole's with the guys, laughing like nothing was wrong. It turned my stomach, Tal."

"Brock's at O'Toole's right now while Lex is walking around with *stitches* in his head?"

"Yeah, what are you going to do?" Drew shot him a wary glance.

"What do you think?" Tally had never understood the term "seeing red" until that very moment.

"Aw, don't be stupid, Tal. I was kind of kidding before. As much as I'd like to introduce Brock's face to the floor, nothing bad ever seems to touch him."

"*I* can touch him." He tossed his rag in the sink and strode over to the front door that was still temporarily boarded up. He slammed the lock down and closed the blinds on the windows. "I'm going to go have a chat with our buddy Brock. You can either come with me or run the other direction. It's up to you."

He turned, then, and stormed down the back hallway of the shop. It felt *good* to lose it a little. He'd been so together all week, so rational and efficient, when inside he was a rapidly growing pool of seething lava.

It was time to let off a little bit of steam.

Tally wasn't surprised when he heard the crunching of footsteps behind him. "What the hell are you going to do, Tal? He practically owns that bar, along with everything else around here. Everyone in there is his friend. You saw that the last time we were there."

"I need to do this. *Someone's* got to tell him what he did was fucked up and crazy."

"You know why he did it, right?"

Tally slowed down. "No. General small town bigotry?" He shrugged.

"Try general *jealousy*. Lex told me that Brock accused him of stealing you away."

"What the...?" Tally was flabbergasted. "We've only hung out a few times. I haven't seen him in years!"

Drew shrugged as well. "Who knows? That's just what he said to Lex when he was drunk off his ass. The guy kind of idolized you back in the day."

"I always figured he was jockeying to take my place." Tally continued to walk, drawing closer to O'Toole's and Brock.

"I don't think so. Tally, why don't you just let this go?"

"I'm not leaving unless Lex finds someone new, and I have no chance of getting him back. Until then, Brock and I are going to live in the same town. I won't be able to do that until I get this out of my system."

Drew sighed and followed him wordlessly.

It was a bit dead in O'Toole's. The place was a total dive, but popular with the local ex-frat-boy crowd. Tally guessed it was too late for the happy hour but too early for anyone but the seasoned drunks to be out. That list included Brock. He was over by the pool tables with a few beers already lined up waiting for him to drink. Tally could tell he was buzzed, but he hadn't had the time to work his way up to drunk just yet.

Tally walked slowly closer, waiting for the moment when Brock would look up and notice him there. It was going to be a good time, for damn sure. Asshole. If it wasn't a total cliché, Tally would've been cracking his knuckles already. He grinned when Brock looked up and noticed him, his face turning to a sneer. He cocked his head toward the entrance, a blatant invitation for Brock to meet him outside.

"Tally, are you nuts?" Drew was pulling at his shirt. "He's huge!"

"I'm fine, Drew. Follow or run away."

Drew looked a bit panicked. "Fighting is so juvenile! This isn't the way to win Lex back. He's going to think you're an ass."

Tally shook his head. Drew was wrong. "Lex would be standing right where I am if Brock had done anything to hurt someone he loved."

Tally watched Brock put his beer down and place his cue on the table. Then he walked slowly past Tally and Drew and outside. Tally brought up the rear with Drew behind him whispering heatedly at Tally, trying to get him to stop.

"This isn't going to prove anything!"

"It will to me," Tally muttered back.

"Jesus, Tal."

They emerged from the bar into the waning early evening sun.

"What do you want with me, Carrington?"

Brock was in the grass on the side of the bar.

Tally chuckled. "Apparently the pleasantries are over. So soon?"

"C'mon, fag. Let's get this over with. I don't want anyone to see me with you and think we're... together." He made a face.

"Okay, let's get this over with. Good idea." Tally stepped closer. "This is all I wanted." And with that, before Brock could move, he drew back his fist and punched Brock as hard as he could.

Brock stood there stunned for a moment before he reacted by punching Tally back. Tally swerved to the side, but Brock still managed to clip him on the jaw. It hurt like hell, but he didn't even care.

He whaled on Brock with his other hand and brought his knee up and jammed it into Brock's balls as hard as he could.

"Fuck! That was a fucking girl move if I ever saw one!" Brock hunched over for a second. Then, without warning, he reached out for Tally's shirt and yanked him onto the ground. The next thing Tally knew, he was under Brock, and he had pain shooting from where Brock was repeatedly slamming his fist into Tally's face.

Tally bucked his hips and shoved to get Brock off of him. It didn't work at first, but he got some momentum and managed to tip them enough that Brock fell off his perch. He rolled out and got to his knees before Brock lunged at him again. Catching Tally off guard, Brock slid his arm around Tally's neck and squeezed. Shit! He couldn't breathe. Tally used every free limb he had to pummel Brock's stomach, the backs of his knees—anywhere Tally could reach. When Brock finally let go, Tally collapsed to the ground, breathing hard. He felt like his lungs were filled with fire.

"Are you happy now?" Drew was standing over Tally with his hand out.

"Yeah." He took Drew's hand and stood.

Brock backed away, clutching at his stomach and holding his eye. "What the fuck, dude?" he asked, wincing.

Tally got up in his face and poked at his chest. "Don't ever fucking touch Lex again, you hear me?"

"Who the hell do you think you are? The gay avenger?" Brock rolled his eyes.

"I think I'm defending the man I love. And I'm serious. Stay the hell away from him."

"I don't wanna hear about you and your butt buddy, Carrington. In fact, get the fuck away from me. I don't want to hear about you or your faggy friend." Brock pushed roughly past Tally and Drew and went to go back inside.

"What if I'm one too, Brock? What if I'm a big fag just like Lex and Tally?"

Brock just laughed. "I should've known you took it up the ass. You're such a fucking loser."

Tally hoped Drew hadn't been hoping for a different response.

"I'm not the loser, Brock. You wanna see one of those, just take a glance in the mirror." Drew turned and walked the other direction, away from the bar and bleeding Tally. He paused and looked back. "You coming?"

Tally smiled, feeling sore and bruised but all of a sudden so much better. "Yeah, I'm coming. I think we're done here."

THE block party was loud and colorful and everything it had always been. Didn't much matter. Lex felt like he was seeing things through a black and white lens. The people moved slower. Sounds seemed to be coming from the other end of a long tunnel. No matter who he looked at, they weren't the one person he really wanted to see. Tally. The party was almost over. He could tell by the band that was warming up for the last hour of the night, which was usually a dance right in the middle of the street. *Jesus*, it had been a long day. He'd had Travis and his girlfriend Cheri to keep him company, Amy had been by multiple times on her breaks from volunteering at the first aid tent, but nothing seemed to make the hours go by any faster. The last few days at the shop had been painful, but at least he could watch Tally, hear his voice, smell him if he dared to get close enough.

Lex didn't know what he was supposed to do. He still loved the guy. Desperately. He wanted the whole awkward situation to just be over without him having to make any grand gestures.

"Lex." He looked up at Travis, who was waving a flyer from the local radio station in his face. "Earrrtth to Lex," he droned, then started walking around stiffly, making little beeping Martian noises. Lex huffed out a small chuckle.

"Yes. I'm here. Sort of."

"Dude, I really have this if you want to leave. Cheri can help me box up the supplies when it's over."

Lex wanted to go home, but at the same time didn't know what he'd do in an apartment that was annoyingly silent. He'd gotten used to having Tally around. He *wanted* Tally around. *This is ridiculous. Why am I torturing myself? Again.*

"It's okay, Trav. I'm going to stay and finish this out with you." *Not like I have anything better to do.*

Lex couldn't help feeling like his feet were stuck to the ground, sinking into the cement and holding him in place. He hadn't known it would hurt so much. Okay. Not true. He did. But there was always the hope that it wouldn't. Lex leaned over to box up some of the extra drink cups to take back to the shop. When he had his back to the counter he heard a quiet voice call his name.

"Lex?"

He turned to see his friend standing there fiddling with a straw. "Hey, Drew."

"Have you seen Tally?"

Lex gave him an odd look. "Of course not. Shouldn't I be asking you that? I haven't seen him since the store opened yesterday. I've been out here the whole time."

Drew cringed.

"What?"

"Let's just say he looks worse than you did last Sunday."

Lex froze. Then he slowly put his box down and looked at Drew.

"What happened?"

"I'm sure you can guess. He found out that Brock got off practically scot-free and kinda lost it."

Lex was half-horrified and half in love with the idea of Tally championing him. "Please tell me he's not in jail… or the hospital. I think we've all had enough of both."

"He's not—and neither is Brock. God, Lex. You should've seen him."

Lex did let himself smile at that one. "I think I'll be happy imagining it. Did he at least get a few good ones in?"

"A few?" Drew laughed. "Brock's eye looks like an eggplant!"

Lex laughed too. The moment was pleasant, oddly, until they both stopped laughing and Drew looked at him calculatingly.

"Lex…."

"What?" He caught the gleam in Drew's eye. "Don't, Drew. I don't want to talk about it."

Drew sighed. "You have to. You guys still love each other. What the hell's going on?"

"This doesn't sound like not talking about it." Lex tried to give Drew the stare down, but Drew wasn't having it. "Listen, I don't know what happened. Things just got… weird."

"Then un-weird them! You're both fucking miserable, and you're making me miserable too."

"No one's forcing you to stand here." Lex couldn't help but be annoyed at Drew's meddling.

"He's right, you know." The voice was quiet and behind him, but he couldn't miss it.

"Travis!" he hissed.

"What? It's not like we're in a huge room. I could hear you, and he's right. You and Tally have both been all fucked up for days. You're not happy unless you're together, and none of us are happy with you guys moping around like you have been."

Fuck. They're both right, and you know it. He squeezed his eyes shut.

Lex was silent for a long time. "Maybe."

"Maybe?" Both Drew and Travis looked incredulous.

"Maybe I'm ready to talk to him about it. Maybe I'm over being mad at him about Brock." *Maybe I'm full of shit, and I'd like nothing more than to spend the rest of my life in his arms. Damn.*

Drew shrugged and turned to walk away. "That's better than no."

"Where are you going?"

"Walk around, whatever."

Lex felt something shift in his gut. "Tally's here, isn't he."

"Wouldn't you be?" Drew shrugged again and walked away.

Lex went back to his stacking. He didn't know if he could talk to Tally, but he wanted to. So bad. He wished everything was back to the way it had been back before the return of Brock The Rock and his assholes. Why'd it ever have to happen?

The music started, and people filled the cordoned off area of the street. Children, parents, people of all sorts danced to the mix of classic party favorites. They all looked so happy. Like he had been. Lex wished the night would be over. Sort of. He didn't want to be there any more than he wanted to be alone in his oh-so-empty apartment. He wished he knew what he was supposed to do. He kept cleaning, putting his booth together so it would be easy to transport when the night was over.

"Lex."

It was the third time in less than an hour someone had called his name, but it wasn't Drew, and it sure as hell wasn't Travis. His heart went kerthunk at the sound of that sexy, mellow voice. He'd missed it. It hadn't even been twenty-four hours since they'd talked, but it felt like forever. Lex looked up. Oh, God, Tally's face! It was bruised and cut and more gorgeous than anything else in the world. Lex felt another momentary thrill at the thought that Tally had done it for him. He tried to school the excitement out of his features.

"What are you doing here, Tally?" Even Lex was surprised by the lack of emotion in his voice. Maybe there was just too much inside of him and it was bottlenecking somewhere painful.

"Hoping you'll forgive me for being the biggest asshole in the universe. I'm dying."

Lex shrugged, trying to pretend Tally wasn't the most important thing in his world. "Tally, it's no biggie. People change. We never said we were forever." *Why the hell did I say that? Moron!* Lex wanted to touch him, wanted to reach his arms out, grab on to Tally and never let go. He ground his nails into his palms. Tally came closer and cupped his face in those amazing, warm, calloused hands. He looked uncertain, like he thought maybe Lex would pull away.

"But that's just it," he finally muttered, voice hoarse. "You *are* forever for me."

Lex's heart stopped, and all of a sudden the weirdness didn't matter. Nothing did but the look on Tally's face.

"I want to wake up kissing you every morning, go to sleep holding you in my arms, make love, make amazing coffee together." Lex couldn't help smiling. "Babe, I've never wanted to spend my life with anyone but you. I can't imagine it any other way. I'm not going to cop out and blame these last few weeks on getting scared, but Jesus, the way I feel about you scares the hell out of me."

"Why, because you're still afraid of what people will think?"

"No. Hell no. I'm scared because you might not feel the way that I do: like you weren't really breathing before you saw my face. I know

I was only half-alive until I saw yours. This past week has been fucking torture."

"What are you trying to tell me, Tal?"

"That I want us back. Any way I can have it. However you want it to be. I mean, we were happy, weren't we?"

Lex's stomach did a flip, then a long shivery back dive from his mouth all the way down into his shoes. "Yeah, I thought so."

"So, will you try it again? Let me make everything up to you?"

"And you'll stay with me. Out in the open and for real?"

"Yes to all of it. *Yes*. I was acting like an idiot. I *love* you."

"Are you sure?" Lex's heart was between his teeth. He didn't know what he'd do if the answer was "I don't know." Tally's slow grin made it beat even faster.

Tally pressed their foreheads together. "Yes, I'm sure. Lex Barry, I want to stay here, with you. Love you out in the open, for real and forever." He glanced around at the crowd. "Come dance with me. In front of all these people. I want everyone to know how I feel about you."

Lex felt the flutter of fear in his stomach. It was one thing for the whole town to know he was gay, but for them to *see* it, to see him being intimate with a man, with *Tally*, in public. It wasn't the same thing.

"Go dance with your boyfriend, Lex. I've got the stand." Travis, his apparently nosy employee, grinned and pushed on his shoulder gently. Of course he did.

Lex allowed himself to be pulled onto the dance floor. It was crowded, but nowhere near crowded enough that their presence couldn't be easily seen. He tried not to notice his heart pounding as he called himself a hypocrite. Here was Tally, ready to tell the world who he loved, and *Lex* was scared?

"Um, people are staring."

Tally raised his eyebrows as if in challenge, and he drew Lex closer, threading his hands through Lex's hair and cupping his head. "I don't care. Do you?"

And that's the question of the day. He decided the answer was no. Fuck it. Let them stare. No more hesitating. He pulled on Tally's hair, drawing him closer, and in front of a grinning Drew, who was poking and pinching at Amy, and the rest of the staring townspeople, Lex kissed the man he loved, slow and soft and binding. They were smiling at each other like fools, laughing softly at nothing, and Lex had never been more scared or more damn *happy* in his entire life.

"Love you, Tal."

"I love you too, baby. I'm so sorry about the past few weeks."

"It's okay. I forgive you." Lex smiled slyly. "I suppose if you eventually decide to go back to Brock again I can always start dating Drew."

Tally attacked his sides with tickles, and Lex threw his head back, laughing and realizing he didn't give a shit who saw. He was so in love, nothing else mattered but that.

"Don't even think about it." Tally swooped down and took Lex's lips for another long kiss that left him breathless and wishing they were home and in bed.

"I won't." Lex kissed him back.

"It's not going to happen, you know. I'd never have anything to do with him after what he did to you." Tally's voice was serious and soft.

Lex nodded. "I know you won't. I trust you."

"You sure?" Tally looked nervous still. Lex kissed him again to get rid of that look. He hated that it was there in the first place.

"I'm sure."

"And you really want me back?"

Lex nodded and tightened his arms around Tally's neck. "You're not the only one who's been miserable. I've missed you so much."

"Really?"

Lex grinned, glad to finally be feeling happy again. Like himself. "Of course."

"Can we go home, then?"

Home. With Tally. He liked the sound of it and everything it implied. Lex smiled and looked at Travis, who smiled and waved for him to take off.

"Yeah, home sounds good."

M.J. O'SHEA grew up, and still lives, in sunny Washington state and while she loves to visit other places, she can't imagine calling anywhere else home. M.J. spent her childhood writing stories. Sometime in her early teens, the stories turned to romance. Most of those stories were about her, her friends, and their favorite cute TV stars. She hopes she's come a long way since then…

When M.J.'s not writing, she loves to play the piano and cook and paint pictures, and of course read. She likes sparkly girly-girl things, owns at least twenty different-colored headbands, and she has a little white dog with a ginger eye spot who sits with her when she writes. Sometimes her dog comes up with the best ideas for stories… when she's not busy napping. She's a relatively new author, but the great folks over at Jessewave.com named her as one of the new M/M authors who rock in 2010.

Visit M.J. at http://www.mjoshearomance.com or at her blogs, http://mjoshea.com/ and http://mjandpiper.blogspot.com. E-mail her at mjosheaseattle@gmail.com or follow her at Twitter.

Read more by M.J. O'SHEA in

http://www.dreamspinnerpress.com

Also from DREAMSPINNER PRESS

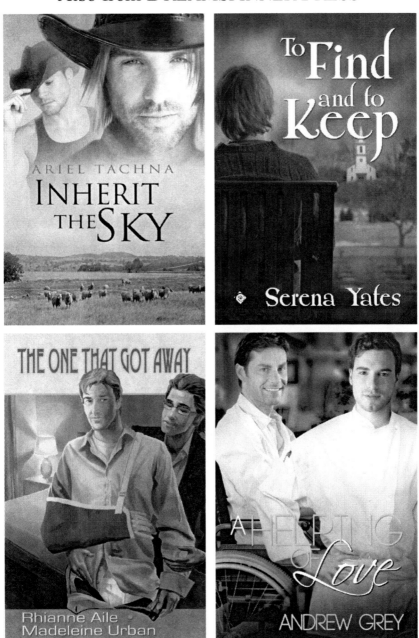

http://www.dreamspinnerpress.com

CPSIA information can be obtained at www.ICGtesting.com
Printed in the USA
BVOW040106280912

301596BV00005B/128/P